A DAY'S PLEASURE & OTHER TALES

T0158518

PARTHIAN

LIBRARY OF WALES

Nigel Heseltine (3 July 1916 – 1995) was an author of travel books, short stories, plays, and poetry, as well as an agronomist for the Food and Agriculture Organization of the United Nations. Born in London in 1916, Heseltine was the son of composer Philip Heseltine, better known as Peter Warlock, and Minnie Lucy Channing, an occasional model for Augustus John, nicknamed "Puma". He spent most of his childhood in Wales with Warlock's mother and Welsh stepfather (Edith and Walter Buckley-Jones) at Cefnbryntalch, Montgomeryshire, and attended Shrewsbury School.

From 1937 through 1949, Heseltine's poetry, stories and essays were published in a number of literary magazines and anthologies, including *Wales, English Story, The Penguin New Writing, Modern Welsh Poetry,* and *The New British Poets.* In 1938 Heseltine published *Scarred Background,* an account of his journey on foot through Albania the previous year, as well as a poetry pamphlet, *Violent Rain.* He married Natalia Borisovna Galitzine or Galitzina, an aristocrat in Budapest in 1938 and married four more times over the course of his life. During World War II he was in Dublin, working as a playwright and actor for the Olympia Theatre company. A collection of poems, *The Four-walled Dream,* was published in 1941 by the Fortune Press and was followed in 1944 by some translations of Dafydd ap Gwilym's poetry (*Dafydd ap Gwilym: Selected Poems*). Thirteen of his short stories were published by the Druid Press in 1946 as *Tales of the Squirearchy,* but a second planned collection, *Tales of the Landless Gentry,* was rejected by printers in 1947 on the grounds of obscenity and consequently never appeared. In the early 1950s, Heseltine was based in Rome and, in 1953, he published the novel *The Mysterious Pregnancy.*

After this, Heseltine largely reinvented himself as an agronomist and post-colonial development specialist, working in as many as thirty countries across Africa, South-East Asia, and the Indian and Pacific Oceans. In 1959 he published an account of crossing the Sahara on foot, *From Libyan Sands to Chad,* and was elected a fellow of the Royal Geographical Society. A series of lectures Heseltine gave in the United States on African development were published in 1961 as *Remaking Africa*. Heseltine enjoyed a long relationship with Madagascar, and published a wide-ranging study of the island nation in 1971 (*Madagascar*). Heseltine fled the island during a coup in 1972. From 1974-77 Heseltine served as Governor of the Rodrigues Islands, before moving to Perth, Western Australia, in 1982. *Capriol for Mother,* a memoir of his father Peter Warlock, was published in 1992. Heseltine died in Perth on October 21st, 1995, aged 79.

A DAY'S PLEASURE & OTHER TALES

NIGEL HESELTINE

Edited and with an introduction by
Daniel Hughes

LIBRARY OF WALES

Parthian, Cardigan SA43 1ED
www.parthianbooks.com
The Library of Wales is a Welsh Government initiative which highlights and celebrates
Wales' literary heritage in the English language.
Published with the financial support of the Books Council of Wales.
© Author's Estate 2020
This edition published 2023
Series Editor Kirsti Bohata
All Rights Reserved
ISBN 978-1-913640-17-0
eISBN 978-1-913640-33-0
Cover design by theundercard.co.uk
Typeset by Elaine Sharples
Printed by 4Edge Limited

Contents

Introduction

Nigel Heseltine crossed the Sahara Desert on foot (three times), trod the boards of Irish theatres such as the Abbey in Dublin, fled a coup in Madagascar and was at the heart of Welsh literary circles in the 1930s. He was hated by Dylan Thomas, employed by Idi Amin, and once used the office of the then Senator John F. Kennedy. Along with a number of short stories set in a fictive rendering of the Montgomeryshire countryside in which Heseltine grew up, he published a novel, two volumes of poetry, memoirs of travels in Albania and Africa, a study of Madagascar, and texts on post-colonial development and administration. In its globe-spanning extremity, Heseltine's life was larger than fiction.

Heseltine's short fiction is also fascinating. This is the first time that the stories in *Tales of the Squirearchy* (1946) have been republished and the first time that these have been published alongside Heseltine's uncollected stories. Cariad County, the imagined, exaggerated setting of Heseltine's short fiction, features such surreal episodes as soldiers and medieval Welsh poets returning from the dead, a countryside hunt interrupted by the camel-riding Thwaite – a recurring character, who, in another story, takes pot-shots at competing sides of a different hunt – and fictive characters coming to life before their author's eyes. Cariad is the site of comedy and farce, tragedy and violence; it is a Wales rendered both in realist and surrealist ways. The stories both lampoon and lament the anglicised, rural Welsh gentry from which Heseltine himself hailed, the so-called 'Squirearchy'. Heseltine's squires inhabit a declining and disintegrating world, the gentry class clinging desperately to their estates and titles, to their codes of behaviour and ways of life. Heseltine captures all the subtleties and oddities of this world in its dying throes. Yet, today, the globe-trotting Nigel Heseltine remains virtually unknown. Who was Nigel Heseltine?

Even the circumstances of his birth are mysterious. Heseltine was the son of the composer Peter Warlock (real name Philip Heseltine), and Heseltine's birth certificate states he was born in Middlesex Hospital, London, on 3 July 1916, though Warlock only officially registered his son's birth in January of 1930.[1] Initially, baby Nigel was boarded with an Irish family (the Hallidays) in Surrey, but was then retrieved, at the age of around 15 months, by his grandparents: Walter and Edith Buckley-Jones, of Cefnbryntalch Hall, near Llandyssil, Montgomeryshire. Heseltine inherited his surname from Arnold Heseltine, Edith's first husband, who had passed away in 1897. Edith then married Walter Buckley-Jones in 1903. The Buckley-Joneses were members of the anglicised land-owning gentry class in Wales and the magnificent surroundings, esoteric individuals, and eclectic events of this rural Welsh upbringing would go on to inform Nigel Heseltine's anarchically comedic and often surrealist short fiction.

Heseltine was treated as 'the Heir' to the estate by his grandmother, who had given up on her son, Warlock, as a hopeless eccentric. Letters from Heseltine to his grandmother indicate the esteem and affection in which he held her throughout his childhood and early adulthood.[2] Peter Warlock died in a gas-filled Chelsea basement in December 1930, probably by his own hand; the jury reached an open verdict, unable to decide whether the death was suicide or a tragic accident. Nigel Heseltine was just 14 years old when his father died. In his

---

1   Rhian Davies, "Scarred Background: Nigel Heseltine (1916-1995), A Biographical Introduction and a Bibliography", *Welsh Writing in English: A Yearbook of Critical Essays* 11 (2006-2007).

2   Letters from Nigel Heseltine to Edith Buckley-Jones are held in the British Library: see *HESELTINE PAPERS. Correspondence and papers of Philip Arnold Heseltine (the composer 'Peter Warlock', b.1894, d.1930) and related papers of his mother, Edith Buckley-Jones née Covernton, widow of Arnold Heseltine; A. Correspondence: 57958-57964.*

1992 biography of Warlock, *Capriol for Mother*, Heseltine alleged that Bernard van Dieran, a composer and sole beneficiary of Warlock's will, had in fact poisoned him. Despite the loss of his father at a young age, Heseltine enjoyed a luxurious upbringing of yacht holidays off the coast of Scotland, as well as private schooling, and hunting on the estate. In 1935, Heseltine was awarded a scholarship to Sandhurst, but left before being commissioned. Fearing he would turn into a version of his dissolute father, Edith Buckley-Jones managed to plant Heseltine in a 'safe' office job in London in 1936.

In 1938, Heseltine's first poetry collection, the pamphlet *Violent Rain*, was published by the small letterpress and printers, the Latin Press. The previous year, he had travelled to Albania, toured the country on foot, contracted dysentery, and travelled through northern Italy before returning to Wales briefly to allow his grandparents to nurse him back to health. A travel memoir based on his Albanian adventures, *Scarred Background: a journey through Albania*, was published by the Lovat Dickson Press shortly after *Violent Rain* in 1938, and by August of that year, Heseltine was in Budapest, Hungary, where he married Princess Natalia Galitzine. Heseltine was not quite his debauched father, but a settled life in an office job was not what the young writer seemed to have in mind. By June 1939 he had returned to Wales, bringing his wife and baby daughter (Elizabeth) to be looked after by his grandmother. He sequestered himself in a separate part of the manor house and focused on his literary work.

In Wales, Heseltine enjoyed social and literary connections with other major Welsh writers of the time, including Lynette Roberts and Dylan Thomas. For his part, Dylan Thomas "intensely" disliked Heseltine, as he admitted to Keidrych Rhys in a June 1937 letter.[3] In a letter sent to Vernon Watkins in July 1937, Thomas promised that he would "rid" *Wales* of Heseltine.[4] Thomas wrote the letter assuming he would take over

---

3   Dylan Thomas to Keidrych Rhys, June 1937, *The Collected Letters of Dylan Thomas Volume 1: 1931-1939* edited by Paul Ferris (London: Weidenfield & Nicholson, 2017), pp. 289-290.

4   Dylan Thomas to Vernon Watkins, 15 July 1937, *Collected Letters,* p. 294.

editorship of *Wales* in 1938; somewhat ironically, Thomas never did, but Heseltine edited a number of issues of the magazine in late 1939 – even after Thomas had demanded that Rhys cease publishing Heseltine. For his part, Heseltine included a limerick which pilloried Thomas in a November 1937 letter to Rhys, and seemed to enjoy mocking and antagonising the far more widely established writer:

> A young fellow of Swansea called Tummas
> creates a disturbance among us,
> with a purgative pill
> he produces at will
> effects that are published by some ass.[5]

It seems that Thomas's dislike of Heseltine was not just artistic but also personal; Thomas referred to Heseltine as "Nasty Heseltine" in a September 1938 letter to Vernon Watkins.[6]

Indeed, some of Thomas's dislike seems to stem from a short story Heseltine submitted to *Wales* in 1937, 'The Drunk'. Thomas was virulent in his criticism of the story, describing it as

> so worthless from every aspect, so transparently an adolescent fake without either the excuse of adolescence or the intelligence to be even moderately, accomplished charlatanism, that it doesn't matter at all. It can't matter, because it isn't there; there's nothing there except the knock-kneed and bilious shadow of weak bad-taste indifferently cultivated.[7]

No story titled 'The Drunk' ever appeared in *Wales* and no story of that name appears among the tales Heseltine completed for his two

5   Nigel Heseltine to Keidrych Rhys, 12 November 1937, NLW MSS 22744D – '*Wales* Papers', National Library of Wales, Aberystwyth.

6   Dylan Thomas to Vernon Watkins, 1 September 1939, *Collected Letters*, pp. 456-457.

7   Dylan Thomas to Keidrych Rhys, June 1937, *Collected Letters*, p. 289.

intended collections. By way of contrast with Thomas, Glyn Jones, another key figure in *Wales*'s success and an accomplished short story writer himself, told Rhys (twice) he would "certainly" print 'The Drunk'.[8] 'The Drunk' may be an early version of a Heseltine story published in *Tales of the Squirearchy* and included in this edition, 'Constable's Ruin'. In it, a drunken poet with "swollen lips", who is "acclaimed in the USA and abuses his own kind", roams Cariad County's "Port Harlot" on a night out with the recurring character Thwaite and a policeman. The poet frequently slurs his speech, admits to having "a pot-belly" which is "full o' beer", and is dressed "like a Bangor student". Quite what Heseltine thought Thomas's connection with Bangor was is unclear, but, if this is a portrait of Thomas – and it seems likely, given Heseltine's limerick about a young fellow called "Tummas" – then it is not a flattering one. It may well have been the root of Thomas's intense hatred of Heseltine, yet Keidrych Rhys – and other Welsh writers, like Glyn Jones – clearly saw some promise in the young writer. As noted, Rhys entrusted *Wales*'s editorial duties to Heseltine for a brief period and Rhys's independent press, the Druid Press, would publish Heseltine's *Tales of the Squirearchy* in 1946, the same year in which they also published the debut poetry collection of another young Welsh writer charting the decline and difficulties of the Welsh countryside (albeit the decline of the working class), R.S. Thomas's *The Stones of the Field*.

Following the outbreak of the Second World War in September 1939, Heseltine signed up with the RAF. However, after a final visit to Keidrych Rhys and Lynette Roberts in their Carmarthenshire home in December 1939, Heseltine next appeared in Dublin, in the 1940s. Here, Heseltine studied medicine (supposedly) at Trinity College, published translations of Dafydd ap Gwilym's poems with the help of the noted Irish writer Frank O'Connor's Cuala Press, contributed articles and reviews to major Irish journals of the day, such as *Envoy*

---

8   Glyn Jones to Keidrych Rhys, September 1937, NLW MSS 22744D – '*Wales* Papers', National Library of Wales, Aberystwyth. In a second letter later the same month, Glyn Jones reiterates that he would publish 'The Drunk', telling Rhys "I don't think I'm wrong about the story."

and *The Bell*, and adopted the name 'Michael Walsh'. Under that pseudonym, Heseltine co-founded a theatre company with Shelagh Richards, called Richards-Walsh Productions, and wrote, produced and performed in productions across the Olympia, Gate, and Abbey Theatres. Heseltine enjoyed social and cultural connections with major figures in Dublin; including major playwrights such as Sean O'Casey and even the well-known novelist Erskine Childers, who would one day become the fourth President of Ireland. Considerable mystery surrounds Heseltine's time in Dublin, though he may have worked as a British spy and, at some point, he married for the second time. In 1946, following the deaths of his grandparents, he returned to Wales to sell the estate of Cefnbryntalch. In the same year Keidrych Rhys's Druid Press published his short story collection *Tales of the Squirearchy*, but his second collection, 'Tales of the Landless Gentry', was rejected by the printers (*The Cambrian News*) on the grounds of obscenity. Following this, Heseltine left Wales. With the exception of his 1953 novel *The Mysterious Pregnancy*, Heseltine would not publish any further creative writing. He wrote several unpublished novels over the course of his life and revised the tales that comprised 'Landless Gentry' shortly before his death in Perth, Australia, in 1995.

Following his departure from Wales Heseltine travelled extensively throughout Europe, before joining the Food and Agriculture Organization at the United Nations in 1951. He was subsequently involved in development projects in at least thirty different countries across Africa and South-East Asia. In 1959, Heseltine published his second travel memoir, *From Libyan Sands to Chad*, an account of his *third* crossing of the Sahara Desert, and in April of that year, was elected as a Fellow of the Royal Geographical Society. In the following year, 1960, Heseltine delivered lectures on African development under the auspices of the African American Institute in universities across the United States, apparently at the invitation of then Senator John F. Kennedy, whose office in Congress Heseltine was allowed to use. Throughout the 1960s and 70s, Heseltine continued working across Africa, including a brief stint as a technical adviser to Idi

Amin, though Heseltine was mostly based in Madagascar (where he married for the third time, this time the daughter of a Madagascan chieftain). Heseltine published a far-ranging study of Madagascar (*Madagascar*, 1971), the dust-jacket of which describes him as an Irish citizen (contributing to his reputation as an international man of mystery), a graduate of both Dublin University and the London School of Economics, advisor to the Madagascar Plan Commission, "occasional adviser to the Mauritius Government", a former "Under-Secretary in charge of Development Planning in Zambia" and, from 1968 onwards, "economic adviser to the President of Madagascar". Even this brief summary is testament to Heseltine's impressive array of occupations and accomplishments.

In the midst of a Communist coup in 1972, Heseltine barely escaped Madagascar with his life. He did rescue his personal poetry collection, and the majority of his father's notebooks and papers, which he donated to the British Library in 1973. They form the most important Peter Warlock collection in the world. Heseltine later moved to Australia, where he spent the remainder of his life and married for (apparently, at least) the fifth time. Heseltine never really retired, working for the Department of Aboriginal Affairs, delivering lectures, dipping into local politics, revising his 1940s short fiction, and publishing a memoir of his father's life, *Capriol for Mother*, in 1992. Heseltine delivered a lecture on his father in Wales in 1994, and professed a desire to return to Wales and keep working, though he died in Perth in 1995 at the age of 79.

It is perhaps unsurprising, given the nature of his life and his professed desire to return to Wales, that exile and return are prominent themes in Heseltine's writing. The final story in *Tales of the Squirearchy* and the shortest in the collection, 'The Soldier's Return', is also the most realist of the collection, and is directly concerned with the idea of the return home. Elizabeth, a young woman, sits with Mrs Vaughan-Thomas, waiting to meet Rhys, a young man who has been away at war. Hal, the older brother of Rhys and, it is implied, Elizabeth's husband, has died. In "some other room" in the house, a third, youngest son, Owen, who "has pictures of Communist Russia all over his walls", is playing "dreadful revolutionary songs" on the piano; these are later mocked by Mrs Vaughan-Thomas as being an expression of "bim bam bim bam, workers unite!", situating the story in the turbulent politics of the 1930s. While Owen plays the piano, the family's maids "tread on their tired servants' feet" in the carpeted passages; Heseltine ironically juxtaposes the privileged young squire playing communist anthems with the laborious "to and fro" of the lower-class servants. Despite this clear class imbalance, the servants are "so glad" that Rhys is returning home; the servants are "devoted to him", suggests Mrs Vaughan-Thomas, while they dislike Owen's "familiar manners". Heseltine allows his readers to view the complex class dynamics of this gentry household with an insider's eye.

As well as establishing the privilege of this household, Heseltine also situates the story within the traumatised inter-war years, specifically, the late nineteen-thirties. Elizabeth suggests to Mrs Vaughan-Thomas that Owen will "grow out of" toying with revolutionary music and communist politics, yet "the old woman" (as Mrs Vaughan-Thomas is repeatedly called) responds "Rhys didn't grow out of it... Going off to fight in someone else's war. That had nothing to do with him: (What has Spain to do with us?)". It is never clear how Hal died, but it seems that Rhys is returning to Wales having volunteered to fight in the Spanish Civil War. Hal's absence and Rhys's return point to a decidedly feminine household, as does the description of servants as "maids". There are no husbands or fathers in this household, only maids, young sons, wounded veterans and widows. What masculinity exists is damaged or immature.

Rhys's return is a violent interruption rather than a heart-warming reunion and his first words set the tone: "Stop that bloody row!" he shouts, presumably at Owen's piano-playing. Rhys is described immediately by the narrator as "lame"; he looks at the floor as he walks, and is "not like he was before". His family are horrified when they see he has lost a leg:

"Yes!" he shouted, "My bloody wooden leg! Thirty pounds of real wood," and he slapped it so that they all looked in horror at his leg and the wooden sound that came out of it. [...]

His leg creaked as he sat down and he looked from one to another of them.
"Stare at the bloody thing! Go on, look!" he pulled up his trouser and showed an inch of it.
Owen looked away.

In his anger, Rhys flaunts his missing leg at his family. The revelation is phrased in almost obscene terms, with Rhys's physical trauma a source of shock for the assembled household. There is an unsettling focus on not only the physical cost of war, but also on the psychological burdens faced by the returning soldier:

His mother began to talk quickly about the people she knew, and local happenings; anything so long as it was to talk, to fill in, to cover up [...] Rhys didn't hear a word, no one expected him to.

In this story, exile is not enforced, but voluntary: Rhys chooses to fight in a war which his mother believes has nothing to do with them.
This soldier's return is traumatic not just for the physically and psychologically scarred soldier, it is also traumatic for Elizabeth, who seeks a replacement for Hal; for Owen, whose implied romanticism of the Spanish left's struggle against Franco is shattered by the reality of his returning brother; and for Rhys's mother, who desperately attempts "to fill in, to cover up" the physical and mental wounds Rhys returns with. The essentially feminine household struggles to contain Rhys and Rhys is ill at ease with domesticity. He refuses his mother's offer of tea and briskly demands whisky; she pours out "a finger holding the bottle and the glass high, like medicine", as if the alcohol may cure Rhys. Rhys pours himself "half a glass" and drinks it neat, before

Mrs Vaughan-Thomas attempts to elide this trauma by discussing the events in the local area; but Rhys "didn't hear a word, no one expected him to." The soldier's return is left unsettlingly incomplete, with Rhys physically present but mentally and emotionally absent.

This very brief story achieves its dispiriting and discomfiting tone by creating an abrupt turn. By beginning with Owen's anarchic, almost comedic "bim-bam" of leftist anthems and the anxious, yet joyous anticipation of Rhys's return, the story suggests a romanticisation of conflict. The title, the soldier's return, is, on the surface, seemingly unproblematic in its promise of a return to domesticity. Elizabeth, who has never met Rhys, implicitly views Rhys as a replacement for her lost husband, Hal: "Elizabeth said he [Rhys] would probably find some girl, and marry her". Again, there is the subtle suggestion of a settled future for Rhys and Elizabeth. Yet, the combination of anger, frustration and silence that comprise the returned Rhys suggest not just an ambivalence towards war, but an uncompromising disgust – embodied in the heavily disaffected Rhys – towards the glorification of conflict suggested by Owen's music at the start.

The brief story also hints towards the decline of the anglicised gentry. They only have maids left to serve in the household; the oldest son, Hal, is dead; the next eldest traumatised and wounded, and Owen is both young and perhaps improper (his "familiar manners" with the servants imply as much). In this short, subtle story, Heseltine captures the intricacies of his landed background. Indeed, elements of Heseltine's life bubble beneath the surface of this tale. The repeated descriptions of the "old woman" as the mother of the household bring to mind Heseltine's formidable grandmother, the only motherly figure in his life. Heseltine, like his father, did not actively serve in any conflicts. In his editorial to issue 10 of *Wales* (published in October 1939) Heseltine describes war as "the catastrophe which has been our nightmare since we first heard from our fathers and elder brothers of what war is"; war, in Heseltine's lifetime, was handed from one generation to the next, the past an inescapable reality in the present. As the Second World War breaks out, Heseltine uses the editorial to reinforce this sense of collective responsibility, concluding that fascism (at home and abroad) "is what we shall have to fight if we are to live". And yet, Heseltine spent the war years in the Irish Free State, a neutral nation. As 'The Soldier's Return' testifies, war and its after-effects seemed unavoidable – even in the fading opulence of Cefnbryntalch – but the scepticism and disgust expressed in this story are, perhaps, indicative of a man who wished to escape the seemingly inescapable.

Heseltine's Cariad County is repeatedly marked by the memory of war. In 'Data on the Squirearchy', for example, a war memorial is the most significant landmark of the village. It is situated in the centre of the village, is home to the village clock and is mentioned several times in the story. With "carved names representing bones and unlived lives", next to which "young men meet, and whistle and talk about girls", it is also seemingly the place around which the village's masculinity is centred: the girls, we are told, "have their conversations too, elsewhere". In the same story, an "ex-soldier" who lost his hand at Gallipoli and who "would never have any children" looks after a young boy, Thwaite (a recurring character in Heseltine's stories). Mr Thwaite, the young Thwaite's father, has "a hole in his head and he limps", both disfigurements a result of the Great War. This same soldier appears in 'The Life and the Burial', in the shape of "a lame man trepanned from the war of '14." During the course of a drinks party, this 'lame man' is continually referred to in disfigured, alienating terms: "no man is normal with a hole in his head", the 'lame man' has a "battered spine" and a "plate under" his "black velvet cap". As in 'Data on the Squirearchy', this old soldier is Thwaite's father, though by the time of 'The Life and the Burial' Thwaite is now a young man.

For Thwaite, the gentry garden-party that forms the initial setting of the latter story is a matter of "endurance"; by extension, so too is the upper-middle-class lifestyle Thwaite and the gentry experience. If the codes of behaviour that underpinned the Welsh gentry are subtly explored in 'The Soldier's Return', then in 'The Life and the Burial' they are more openly mocked. Indeed, the mixture of the surreal, mockery, humour, social and sexual tensions are recurring tropes throughout Heseltine's fiction. The seemingly dim-witted Miss Menzies, subject to Thwaite's near-predatory attraction, "thought as she should think". She thinks as a good gentry girl should and, given her description as "bone-faced", Miss Menzies is seemingly not capable of much thought at all. Thwaite's pursuit of Miss Menzies is couched in surreal, grotesque terms, another favoured technique of Heseltine's: Thwaite (imaginatively) "slipped the skin from her and looked at her organs". The fading glory of the gentry is more prominent, with the unnamed hostess and her cousin, Cam-Vaughan, bickering over the mortgage. The "long unpaid" mortgage demonstrates the financially precarious nature of this gentry household, while the fact it is a "family matter" – with Cam-Vaughan chasing payments his cousin cannot afford – suggests the gentry's decline is also cannibalistic. Cam-Vaughan's covetous nature is present time and again across the stories and is effectively a universal condition of the squirearchy. Cam-Vaughan's dismissal of the Welsh-speaking Mr Bach ("It is rot", Cam-Vaughan says of the Welsh language) also indicates the superficiality of the anglicised gentry, who care not for the language and culture of the declining world they rule. Ironically, the Welsh-speaking Mr Bach is a parson for the Anglican Church in Wales, pointing to the reach of anglicised institutions.

Typical of these stories, in 'The Life and the Burial' the relationship between the past and the present is unsettled, with the past impinging on the present in numerous ways. One elderly guest, Mrs Golos-Williams, reminisces about the Edwardian era of "dragoons" and "frilly parasols". Set against this nostalgia is the lame man, a haunting and destabilising presence who brings the trauma of the trenches into the comfortable garden-party. Both characters create the sense that the gentry are of another world; one which has entered an irrevocable decline but which still lingers on, attempting to defy or ignore the violence, crises and passage of time which have afflicted the wider world. As with Rhys Vaughan-Thomas, it is the figure of the returned soldier that disassembles the gentry's pretences.

The lame man dies in the seat of his car as he attempts to leave the party, and there is, in the narrative voice, an element of scepticism towards conventional, Christian attitudes to death:

> The lame man is in Church and is prayed for, he will make journeys on the shoulders of other men before he is committed to what Mr Bach will call 'rest' in the trench in the earth which will bring about the collapse of his wooden coffin and the decay and the absorption of the flesh of his body.

The tone in which Mr Bach's notion of Christian 'rest' is described implies disbelief, and the narrator is in no way uncertain about the grotesque fate of the corpse. The funeral congregation is comprised of the gentry establishment: the "Lord Lieutenant, Chief Constable, High Sheriff and Sheriff, the Archdeacon, a baronet, two knights, many gentlemen entitled to bear coat armour, and their wives" are in attendance (note the gender imbalance in this hierarchy). Among these are Mrs Golos-Williams, who remarks "how dreadful" it is for the unnamed hostess that the lame man died at her party, and thinks chiefly that the death is punishment for Thwaite's immoral behaviour. Cam-Vaughan, busies himself scrawling "figures" in his prayer-book, presumably tabulating the debts owed by his cousin. Thwaite himself is drunk on brandy, and attempts to flirt with a "pretty cousin" despite the occasion. The superficial, amoral nature of the gentry is paralleled by "the empty box" and the "hollow sound" of the coffin, as well as the nihilistic language of the funeral service, as Mr Bach says: "That which is empty shall remain empty." The grief of the good and great is meaningless and their presence at the funeral is for appearances' sake only.

The grave is referred to as "the trench in the earth", this physical rupture in the landscape a deliberate reminder of the lame man's war-time past, as well as the ways in which that past remains present. The lame man returns from beyond the grave, interrupting and haunting the establishment mourners. This return is not some kind of hallucination on the part of Thwaite, but rather a supernatural event which the entire funeral audience witnesses:

> The lame man came to the edge of the grave and threw in a wreath of grass bearing on the label: "An empty box," in his own handwriting. And many people saw him, and they went very white and said nothing.

Eventually the lame man leaves, "away up the hill and disappeared as the dead should". Stylistically distinct from 'The Soldier's Return', yet still exploring conditions of return and exile, the ending of 'The Life and the Burial' is a surreal episode which, along with other stories collected in this volume, marks Heseltine as a contemporary of other experimental Welsh writers, such as Dylan Thomas and Glyn Jones. Such visions of death and resurrection recur across Welsh modernist writing, as M. Wynn Thomas has suggested.[9] The revenant is a figure with roots in anxiety, as Thomas argues, and I would suggest that Heseltine's lame man is a literary embodiment of the psychologically and physically scarred soldiers that returned from wars throughout Heseltine's lifetime. In this sense, it is the surreal manifestation of the tensions and anxieties embodied in the similarly "lame" Rhys Vaughan-Thomas: not just the recurring trauma of war, but the increasingly fraught and uncertain circumstances of the squirearchy, as well as their own moral failings.

Return, exile and home are not just present in Heseltine's war-stories. Heseltine's sole published novel, *The Mysterious Pregnancy*, revolves around a cast of émigré English, Welsh, Irish and American characters in mid-20th century Paris. The primary protagonist of the novel, Lu Rienzi, is pregnant as the result of an affair, and has fled to Paris to escape her husband and to search for the father of her child. Over the course of her time in Paris, Rienzi meets other exiled figures, like Sara Blake, a young Irishwoman engaged in a pre-marital love

9   M. Wynn Thomas, *In the Shadow of the Pulpit: Literature and Nonconformist Wales* (Cardiff: University of Wales Press, 2010).

affair; Sara in turn meets Owen Blayney, an older man who grew up, like Heseltine, in rural Wales. Blayney describes his childhood home as "an old red brick house on a hill near a river, with an oak wood on three sides of it, and rookery. You can hear the rooks cawing home in the evening". Even this description plays with the idea of the return home, "cawing home" a pun on 'coming home'. Blayney's red brick childhood home is certainly a fictional rendering of Cefnbryntalch Hall, the opulent, though declining, rural Welsh estate in which Heseltine grew up. By 1953, the year in which *The Mysterious Pregnancy* was published, Heseltine had been away from Wales for over a decade, and had sold his childhood home in 1946. The pain of Blayney's exile may reflect some of Heseltine's feelings at this time: "What did rooks cawing home mean, when they covered a whole lost country of love and promise; what the red house, but a betrayed face, a childhood, manhood betrayed". While Blayney's painful past is firmly located, he now lives in a "rootless present", the condition of aged emigrant bestowing upon him a sense of exile. Wales, or the Montgomeryshire estate of Heseltine's childhood at least, are a "whole lost country of love and promise". Heseltine's single published novel may, on the surface, appear to have little to do with the short fiction collected in this volume, yet Owen Blayney's moving tribute to rural Wales seems redolent of a man who, for all the distance of space and time, has never moved on from that "old red brick house on a hill".

The sense of a declining, disintegrating rural Welsh past is most strongly captured in 'Homecoming'. The story reads as a longer, more detailed exploration of the regrets and longing articulated by Owen Blayney, as Idris Brain returns from America to a Welsh countryside where "everything is small and falling to bits". Like Heseltine's and Blayney's childhood homes, Idris Brains' home is surrounded by rooks: "The rooks stayed. They cawed round the house, built their nests, did a shillingsworth of damage and eighteenpennorth of good, as ever". The 'squirearchy' at the heart of Heseltine's short fiction are now all dead or dying, as Brain notes: "And Lord Jones, too, another loss for Wales: another madman the less for poor old Wales". The setting is the same Cariad County as many of Heseltine's stories; the narrator another prodigal son, returning to a crumbling estate his family have since sold, to a Wales which is now empty: "No one seems to live here at all [...] No one in the fields moved about the fields. No dogs barked, no hens crowed nor crows cawed." As with Blayney, painful but endearing childhood memories mark Brain's line of thought: "on my heart lay the ache of dear childhood lost". 'Homecoming' is the imagined version of the return to Wales Heseltine desired throughout his life, with his "inheritance fastened to [him] like a chain, pulling [him] back from across the world".

Letters in the National Library of Wales suggest that 'Homecoming' was potentially one of Heseltine's earliest stories and that Keidrych Rhys considered some version of the story for publication in his independent magazine *Wales* in 1937.[10] From his early adulthood, as he first began to rove the world – first London, then Albania, then beyond – it seems Heseltine was attuned to conditions of exile and return. Beyond this, though, Heseltine was particularly attuned to the codes-of-conduct and failings of his gentry world, as well as the wider traumas of the modern era. Heseltine depicts and constructs his squirearchy with an insider's eye and from first-hand experience of its dying days. The results are stories that are both playful and precise, which range from anarchically humorous to starkly surreal to subtle and fine-drawn, even mournful, in the world they capture and construct.

At the heart of this work is Cefnbryntalch, Heseltine's Welsh home; the home he grew up in among dogs and hunts; the home he returned to in times of trouble; the home in which he edited a radical, independent Welsh magazine; the home he brilliantly rendered, time and again, as Cariad County. It's fitting, then, that it's an independent Welsh publisher, Parthian, who, much like Druid Press before them, are giving Heseltine an outlet; a return; a homecoming.

10 Keidrych Rhys to Glyn Jones, 14 March 1936, Glyn Jones Papers A12/16, National Library of Wales, Aberystwyth.

BIBLIOGRAPHY

Stories
Nigel Heseltine, *Tales of the Squirearchy* (Carmarthen: Druid Press, 1946) [includes 'Cam-Vaughan's Shoot', 'The Life and the Burial', 'Eve of Something Will Be Done In A Week', 'Milk of Human Kindness', 'Data on the Squirearchy', 'Gothic Halls', 'Boring Story', 'Skirt in Long Strips', 'The Word Burning', 'Lords A-Leaping', 'Rich Relations', 'Constable's Ruin', 'The Soldier's Return]

'The Lay Reader', *Wales* No. 8/9, August 1939.

'Flaming Tortoises', *Wales* vol 24, Winter 1946.

'Break Away If You Can', *The Penguin New Writing* 28, Summer 1946.

'Homecoming', *Celtic Story* 1, ed. Aled Vaughan (Pendulum Publications, 1946).

'A Day's Pleasure', *The Penguin New Writing* 32, 1947.

'A Young Night of Love' in *English Stories Eighth Series* ed Woodrow Wyatt, 1948.

'Generous Patrons' in *English Stories Ninth Series* ed Woodrow Wyatt, 1949.

Other works by Nigel Heseltine
Violent Rain (London: The Latin Press, 1938).

Scarred Background: a journey through Albania (London: Dickson & Lowell, 1938).

The Four-walled Dream (London: Fortune Press, 1941).

Dafydd ap Gwilym: Selected Poems (Dublin: Cuala Press, 1944).

The Mysterious Pregnancy (London: Gollancz, 1953).

From Libyan Sands to Chad: an account of the author's third journey across the Sahara Desert (London: Museum Press, 1959).

Remaking Africa (London: Museum Press, 1961).

Madagascar (London: Pall Mall Press, 1971).

Capriol for Mother: A memoir of Philip Heseltine (Peter Warlock) (London: Thames, 1992).

THANKS & ACKNOWLEDGEMENTS

I would like to thank Rhian Davies, Tony Brown, Tomos Owen, and M. Wynn Thomas for their support and guidance on all things Heseltine over several years.

Excerpts from Glyn Jones' letter to Keidrych Rhys (September 1937, NLW MSS 22744D) are reproduced with permission from Literature Wales and the National Library of Wales.

The epigraph on the following page is taken from a letter Heseltine wrote to John Cowper Powys, which is held in the National Library of Wales, Aberystwyth (Nigel Heseltine to John Cowper Powys, 7 August 1947, NLW MS 21873C). This is reproduced with permission from the National Library of Wales.

A DAY'S PLEASURE
& OTHER TALES

"I believe that somewhere there is always the link by which one may be drawn into living communication with readers. I think that if a work has true and sincere power, it will come out, even as these qualities come out in people."

– Nigel Heseltine

A Day's Pleasure

Tempers cooled suddenly, but rose again and burst like the pomegranates on the wallpaper, scattering the seeds of dispute about the house. We were going on a day's pleasure, the house was too full, my mother was bilious, the car would not start for my father but roared for a moment in the yard, then spluttered and stopped.

There were already in the house, my uncle by marriage, ex-Governor of Bintang, and all his family who had returned from that island to find houses were not to be got for the mere clapping of hands and calling "boy". Yet still letters came in at every breakfast from those others who wanted to come to our house. Uncle Percy wanted to come, being home from Burma, to do some fishing, and Uncle Brit. Therefore, when the cousins were down late to breakfast in our cold climate, the letters were handed round and my mother said:

"Percy can't come, Watkin, and certainly not Brit!"

"The old fellow wants to see about his fishing at Glanavon," my father said.

"He can stay at the public there!" Though we were miles from Glanavon.

A camp bed had been put where there was never a camp bed before, in an attic full of chests of drawers, burst screens and a knitting-machine, for the nurse, who, I was told in the kitchen, did not like her room at all.

I knew from the closeness of my mother's eyes together (they had moved a good half-inch in the night) that she had a bilious attack, but she ran harder than ever up and down the stairs, clattering her keys and calling out to the maids to see that they were running too. As my father would often tell us, she never spared herself.

"Oh bother!" I heard her say as she turned a corner. My two cousins and I were stationed in the hall, having been got ready well before anyone else, since my mother had said we would start on our pleasure at eleven sharp and it was now half-past.

From the front hall you could hear the uproar of us all getting ready to enjoy ourselves; feet galloped on the landing, angry voices cried out, and some shot suddenly into the lavatory to take a last chance before we started. I organized my cousins and we went up and down with very long strides saying all together: "Oh bother! Oh bother!" Nobody was pleased. The maid came through a door carrying three rugs and a lunch-basket out of which a thermos was falling. The nurse caught it while we ran round the pillars in the inner hall, shouting loudly: "Oh bother!"

All at once the nurse ran at Anne who was the eldest. Both girls began to cry, and I wondered if she would hit me. I thought, it is the old room with the burst screens and the knitting-machine, and I turned aside to gaze into the dog's bowl where my mother had scattered tobacco on the water, against worms. Outside, the sun shone, and it was a quarter to twelve.

My mother came down the stairs so bilious that not a pin could have been put between her eyes, and sped into the front hall where my uncle the ex-governor was looking at the glass.

"Falling," he said.

"Look at the time!" my mother cried.

"I meant the glass."

Being a dog, I moved on all fours from the dog's bowl and peered round the corner, as my uncle, yellow in the face and in long thin tweeds, said:

"I meant the weather..."

"It's Watkin!" my mother said shrilly, ran past me, almost treading on my hand with her sharp shoe, careered up to the half-landing and shrieked his name out into the yard. I heard the car start, roar, splutter and stop as it had done this last half-hour.

I peered at the grandfather clock in the front hall but the hands told me nothing as I could not tell the time. Looking nearly as high as the clock was the back of my uncle, the ex-governor, looking at the weather-glass.

"Blow your nose!" the nurse ordered, and pushed Anne and Clara into the front hall. "Get up off the floor, you!" I got up, though I did not take orders from her. Anne looked at her father's back. All of us had long faces.

The maid had propped open the front door, and as we looked out at the fine sunshine, the heat haze in the valley and the cousin's car, we moved slowly towards the open door. The nurse called: "I told you three to stay in." And the ex-governor, turning, said: "Anne, do what nurse tells you."

I looked at the sunshine on the drive, and could not move towards it. As I went up to Anne to whisper, I heard the nurse say: "She's crotchety to-day, sir."

"Tebence," I whispered. We turned our backs and gently bumped our bottoms together, murmuring "Tebence!" This game was not allowed, we went at it gently while nurse was combing Clara's hair. From the yard another roar came from the car, spluttering into silence, and my uncle went through the door, I suppose to help. As the door closed Clara saw us, and being only two shouted out loud: "Tebence!"

Nurse turned, rage sitting on her face.

"I told you two what would happen if you played that dirty game."

Thinking of hairbrushes, we knew there was nothing for it but to run. We let out a kind of cheer and shot at last out of the front hall into the morning sun. We heard Clara hooting after us, then our car had started and was coming round. My mother had her head out of the window and was shouting at my father who couldn't hear because he was racing the engine, the ex-governor was riding on the running-board smiling out of his yellow face at my aunt who had appeared on the steps.

Although we were hiding behind a bush in a tub, we saw nurse speaking to my aunt who shook her head, but went down to her own car. Nurse made a face at us through the bush, meaning, "You wait," and was going down too, when the maid signalled and between them they carried another lunch-basket, the nurse looking crosser than ever.

"What'll she do?" I asked.

"Smack me in the bath," Anne said.

"I won't let her," I said, giving her a sideways bump and murmuring "Tebence." Nurse dragged Clara so fast down the steps that her feet left the ground, and as Clara tried to hit nurse, she was pushed into her mother.

My father was in his shirt-sleeves, and my mother on the doorstep said:

"It's twelve o'clock already, Watkin."

"There was a beetle in the jet."

"There shouldn't have been. Why can't we start?"

I saw my father go past her into the washplace and my mother went back into the house. Keeping the far side of the car from nurse, we went round to look at the lunch-basket which was strapped behind. Then over the back of the car, Clara shouted: "Tebence!"

"Shut up, you ape!" we hissed.

My aunt said: "Your aunt thinks we've forgotten the cups, Anne, I wonder if we could give her a helping hand with them?"

I knew where all the cups in the house were.

"I know!" I shouted.

"Be very careful, and don't fool about."

We took a basket and went the far side of the nurse who murmured, "Just wait till I catch you, Miss," although we were within reach then.

"She'll go for me in the bath to-night," Anne said.

"I won't feel it," I said.

We went into the pantry where all the cups in the house were behind wooden doors. I turned a tap, put my thumb under it and squirted. Anne shrieked, and we laughed so much we had to lie on the floor. I always wondered what went on when Anne and Clara

4

were bathed by the nurse, and once I looked through the keyhole, but saw only a towel wrapped round the nurse's waist.

We had to get the cups out before the maid came or we'd never be allowed to do it. I stood on a chair, then Anne pushed me off, then we both stood on it. I opened the door and we saw hundreds of cups.

"The blue," I said.

"No, the pink!"

"Pink's silly."

We took some of each. We counted the aunt, the uncle, my father and mother, elderly Miss Wall who never got up for breakfast, Mr Cobb, who'd tried also to help my father in the yard.

"And three of us."

"And nurse," Anne said, putting out her tongue. We put the cups in the basket and went back. In the hall my father was standing with his coat on, and from somewhere above I heard her mocking, "Too-too!"

"What have you got there?"

"Cups," I said.

"Confound it," he said, and went through the door to the washplace saying: "And don't drop them." We carefully carried down the cups to my aunt.

"Are they nice cups?"

My mother was now shouting in the house for my father.

"Why can't we start?" my uncle asked.

"Because we don't know the way," my aunt said.

Hats on, facing front, Mr Cobb and Miss Wall were seated in our car, and my father ran down the steps and began blow the horn. Shortly afterwards my mother stuck her head through the bedroom window and said she was not coming. I had been thinking of rocking the car for fun, but my father cried out, "Confound it!" like a boiler, and leaped off the running-board, nearly knocking me down as I tried to get up beside him, and ran into the house.

Anne and I got in with Mr Cobb in the back, and Miss Wall sat in front. There was a silence while Mr Cobb brought out his pipe, looked at the back of Miss Wall's head, and put it away again.

"Looking forward to a nice picnic?" he asked us. Anne and I looked at him and said nothing. Then I saw that Miss Wall had on a fur collar and a dustcoat over her fur coat, and dark glasses and a veil. I whispered to Anne:

"She's delicate."

"What's the secret?" Mr Cobb asked.

We looked at him and said nothing. Clara, who was two, made faces at us from the other car, but suddenly disappeared, pulled in by nurse. I heard a howl.

"I hate her," Anne said.

I said: "She's a damn fool." My father damned the dog when he trod on it, and Charlie Pugh damned his sister when he came to shoot the rooks and she wouldn't pick them up. Anne gave me a pinch.

"You wouldn't dare call her," she said.

"Yes I would," but not so loud that Mr Cobb could hear. We giggled, and wriggled on the seat.

"Must be a good joke."

"Curiosity killed the cat," I said to Mr Cobb, before I had even thought it. Mr Cobb's face became stiff, but Miss Wall turned and through the veil and dark glasses said:

"If you said what I thought I heard, you are a very..."

Anne exploded and I saw a piece of spit go over the side of the car. I had to hold my nose not to laugh. All I had to do was even think Miss Wall was a damn fool, and I would blow up.

My father ran out of the house and down the steps, and because there was only one door in the front of our car, he had to climb over Miss Wall who'd settled herself well in with rugs, and Miss Wall tried to get out and let him in, so that they rolled on the front seat together till my father fell into his own seat apologizing.

"I am so sorry," said Miss Wall.

"Poor old dear has a bilious attack," my father said. He got into gear, and as we moved there was a shriek from the house.

"Damnation!" cried my father, jamming on the brakes.

"Whatever you do don't forget the fish!"

He grunted and the car moved.

"Watkin!"

"Oh, what is it?"

"Did you hear?"

The car shot away, and I saw my uncle following, with no one sitting in front beside him.

"Poor old dear felt seedy ever since she got up," and both together they said: "She never spares herself."

We came to the drive gate which was shut against sheep, and my father shouted to me:

"Did it never occur to you to go on down and open the gate?"

"I thought we were going to start," I was saying, but seeing his face, I jumped for it. Going down the hill the speedometer already showed 40 m.p.h. Mr Cobb was failing to light his pipe in the slipstream, and my uncle had fallen some way behind.

"Tell me about the naked natives in Bintang," I whispered to Anne.

"Not here."

"Were they naked?"

"No."

"You said they were."

"Well why ask?"

"Liar!" I hissed, and pinched her; we wriggled and Mr Cobb's face showed dislike. My mother said he had had such a painful operation for his stones.

We shot round a corner, and there from hedge to hedge was a flock of sheep. The brakes shrieked. Anne and I were thrown in the bottom of the car, Mr Cobb clutched the side, my father cried:

"Damnation!"

The sheep flowed slowly round the car. As I was still a dog since the morning, I got up and barked at them. My father whirled round.

"Do you want to get out and walk home?"

My mouth went dry with terror. Mr Cobb looked and Miss Wall turned round.

"I only barked," I heard my small voice saying. Then the man came up, and my father could say nothing since it was Jones the Bryn with fields both sides of the road.

"Good morning, sir."

"Good morning, Mr Jones, you damn fool," I said under my breath, not moving and not barking, though there was another dog with Jones, that had a silver eye. Under my breath I growled.

We crossed the curved railway bridge which my father took like a roundabout and on the far side was a van which my father passed, leaning out and shouting:

"On the confounded wrong side of the road, idiotic lunacy, take your number."

Then we were out on the tarmac where my father could really go fast, furiously hooting to pass a steam lorry in the middle of the road, at which he shook his fist as we passed. Fifty, fifty-five. The sign 'Go Slowly Through the Village,' shot by, and one or two people seemed to draw back into their doorways and touch their hats.

A train was ahead of us, so my father put on speed and we passed it at sixty, Anne and I waving. I was going to whistle when I remembered. My father was driving with one hand and pointing out to Miss Wall with the other where the fatal railway accident had been in 1921, but Miss Wall had sunk a foot lower in her seat. I looked at Mr Cobb, his hat was jammed over his eyes, and sparks flew out of his pipe.

At the end of this long length, we rounded a corner and a man on a bicycle dived into the hedge as if he had hit a turnip. "Wrong side!" my father shouted. We slowed to fifty-five.

Round every corner there was something, and round the next a steam-roller and fifteen men tarring the road. Brakes screamed, and we crackled over the new tar smelling the smell. Anne and I made silent faces at the dirty men, and put out our tongue but they did not seem pleased.

We went through the small town of Trallwm, forgetting the fish, I knew, but I said nothing, not wishing that day to be helpful; so we groaned without stopping in heavy low gear up out of the valley among the salty-smelling grasses and the purple heather. We stopped

8

in the silence of the moor and the faint hiss of the breeze in the grass, while Mr Cobb and Miss Wall got out and stretched their legs and made exclamations and my father walked up and down, as if he didn't know what to do after the drive.

My uncle's car arrived, boiling from his efforts to keep up with us. Cautiously, Anne and I began to walk along the side of the ditch away from them, but we had not gone far before the harsh voice of the nurse called Anne back, which also meant me. We were to sit still and enjoy lunch.

We were not allowed to take off our coats since clouds were blowing up, and nurse was anxious that we should sit by her in a hollow near the road, and several yards from the food, which my aunt was now unpacking. My father had walked up the road with the two men to show them the moor, and Clara was trying to stand on her head.

In a low voice Miss Wall said to my aunt: "That was a dreadful drive."

"Just bad tempers all round," my aunt said, then seeing my eye on her smiled.

"Why didn't..." Miss Wall began, but my aunt shook her head at us saying loudly that food generally tasted better in the open air.

I began to push Anne off the rug towards some thistles, while nurse with a very long face carried the other lunch-basket out of our car. My aunt said: "Anne, come and sit by me, dear." But nurse forbade it, saying she was in disgrace, and Clara was put there instead, being told to stay right way up. Miss Wall was whispering to my aunt and I could not hear.

"Lunch!" my aunt called in a shrill voice, and the men came slowly back, Mr Cobb from a clump of trees where he had been by himself. My aunt did some of the things my mother did on a picnic, laughed loudly and waved the thermos. The cups were missing, and like good children we were sent for them to the car.

"Good heavens, they're the old dear's best blue ones, and the pink!" my father cried, picking up one in his heavy finger and thumb and dropping it. The handle broke off and a large piece out of the side.

"How could you be such a young fool!" he shouted at me. My aunt murmured and hissed, and the nurse glared at me with steely delight.

The pieces were put into a paper bag and lunch began. I was hungry and Anne and I began to bounce up and down on our rug, two yards from the food. I saw the tin go to my aunt who laughed and handed it to Miss Wall, who handed it back. Then Mr Cobb pressed a leg of chicken on to my uncle, and finally my father had a pick and gave the tin to the nurse. This took some time, and the spittle swam in my mouth as I thought of the chicken in it.

Nurse gave us the tin and before we had anything in our hands I heard: "Don't be greedy, Anne!"; cries of "Anne!" from her parents and a shout from my father at myself. There was little left. We had wanted a wishbone, so that we could wish, but we had a drumstick and another small scrap at the bottom of the tin. I wanted the drumstick, but the nurse pulled even this to bits with her hateful fingers and put the scraps on thick slices of bread so that, according to her, it was a fair deal. The grown-ups laughed and handed food, but the nurse sat a little way apart, being unable to laugh with them, and kept her sour eye on us.

Clara was kept away from us, and sandwiched between her mother and Miss Wall, did what she could to shout against them all, but in spite of this had better bits than we. There was a cup of milky tea between us, and a medicine-bottle of milk for Clara, which she knocked out of her mother's hand on to the rug.

"Let me!" said the nurse, trying to take over from my aunt, but Clara shouted:

"You're a damn fool, nanny!"

In the silence, only Mr Cobb tittered.

"Where... where...?" my aunt asked.

"Him!" Clara shrieked, pointing at me.

My father was staring, my uncle had a face of stone, Anne pinched me quietly, and fear came suddenly on me that it was not Anne who would be smacked to-night, and not nurse who would do it.

"I never..." I began, but seeing they did not believe, I stopped. Clara was boiling over with laughter, pointing at everyone and calling them damn fools, but the nurse reached over past her mother and caught one of her waving hands a hard slap which put a stop to anything but yelling. A hot blush came up from my waist to my head, so that my whole scalp prickled.

Gradually they began speaking among themselves again. Time passed slowly, and there was nothing more to eat. To go away from what I had done, I looked out at Cwm-y-rhiwdre, at the swelling line of the hill coming up from the pine wood where the road dived down, the hill that travelled against the sky to... where? Bintang where the naked natives walked? How naked, and what showed? No one would tell me, and I saw a naked black with a blur about his middle.

While I looked, they broke in, and with a start I was running about as told, but Clara was held fast by the nurse because of what she had heard. The clouds came sailing up and went away into the distance, and a salty wind blew among the moorland grasses. I shivered.

"As far as those trees and no farther," we heard after us, but we walked in the opposite direction, because we had come up that way, along the road that ran over the mountains into the grey clouds.

I pulled Anne by the arm, and we had gone some way before I turned and saw nurse waving us back. We waved with our hands and handkerchiefs to say good-bye, and stamped in puddles and splashed.

"Tell me," I said. "I mean really tell."

"I told you."

"Did they wear loin-clothes?"

"Yes."

"All the time?"

"All the time."

"But you said..." Anne laughed and ran on. I thought, we have bushes with a secret tunnel leading to a secret cavern under the laurels under the oak-trees by the kitchen garden. But I wanted to see a naked native, and see everything as big and strong as a tree.

The grown-ups had moved off the road up the hill, as small as twigs or little cows far away. The nurse was on the road with Clara.

All their eyes were on us, there was nowhere on the huge hillside to hide.

Anne said: "Look at the clouds, they're giants."

"They're no such thing," I said.

A mist swept up around us, warm and wet and drizzling, but we turned back, because if we were wet they would be angry. The mist ran ahead, blotted out the hill, the little figures of our relations, and we were alone on the mountain. I began to push Anne off the road, over the grass, towards the ditch full of water and weeds at the side, but I wouldn't dare push her in. She shrieked. I jumped in a puddle to splash her, but most of it shot up my trouser-leg.

"Why are you so beastly to me?" I thought she was going to cry, and if she came back crying, there would be more trouble. What had I done to her? What had I been thinking?

"What've I done? The water's gone up my trousers." When I said "trousers" we burst out laughing, and because we were alone in the mist, we ran into the road bending and banging our bottoms and shouting "tebence" louder than we'd done since the first day we discovered it and it was forbidden.

The mist lifted and we were nearer than we knew. There were the cars and the grown-ups large as gateposts hurrying down the hill towards them. Suddenly the sun came out, and everyone stood still where they were and looked up at the sky.

"I want to go somewhere," Anne said. The nurse, whom we had not seen, rose up from a hollow where the lunch had been, and seized her. I moved away across the road and looked at the mountain. There was my father on a rise, standing like the statue of an explorer, one foot ahead, and my uncle the ex-governor below him like a follower and Mr Cobb.

I looked behind me at Anne and the nurse who were close together holding up Anne's skirts so that I saw the big white curve of flesh like a huge white face against the moor, while Clara stood close behind and watched. I must look, and the nurse looked at me and I must look away. Then back I looked to that white curve, but it was over and clothes were being pulled up, and I looked up at my father standing like an African explorer on a mountain, to see if he had seen me looking.

The sun lasted only for a fraction, and Miss Wall, careful of her health, was wrapped in rugs in the car as the next rain began to fall. All ran to the cars, and my father and others struggled with the hood that rose and fell and caught my father's fingers.

"Damnation!" I heard, and the hood rose like a black flapping rook, and was fixed. As I climbed in after Anne I lowered my head lest my father see me and remember.

"Have you got the broken cup?" he asked my aunt. The pieces were packed. Would my mother be as cross as when I broke the window in the disused hen-house, deliberately, by firing a stone? We were in, and the rain spattered on the hood and dripped down beside us in the back.

My father asked if Miss Wall would like the side-curtains.

"Oh, no, thank you."

"It's no trouble, they're in the back under the seat."

"Oh, certainly not."

Mr Cobb leaned back and began to light his pipe.

"A sad end to a nice picnic," he said to us. We looked at his pipe and said nothing, but Miss Wall turned:

"What did you say?"

The car started, we hissed along the wet road down the steep hill into the valley full of rain and mist. My father, being as my mother said such a careful driver, said:

"Have to go carefully on these skiddy roads."

"Yes," said Miss Wall.

The smell of the exhaust came up through the floorboards. I began to feel sad, because I might be sick and nobody would care. What would be said about the cup? Would they forget me, and saying damn? As I looked into the mist and thought sad thoughts, I saw a van ahead, then it was a caravan with gypsies with dark faces and red handkerchiefs sitting up in the doorway; then several horses and another caravan, and a lot of gypsies walking along under old sacks.

As we passed the last gypsies they cheered the car with my father looking so stiff and dignified in front, with Miss Wall under her rugs and dark glasses, and Mr Cobb puffing at his pipe.

"Hooray!" Anne and I shrieked, and "Hooray!" again. My father gave a violent swerve and nearly went into the ditch.

"How dare you?" Then, seeing that Anne had cheered too, he said to me: "If I were in your shoes I'd keep as quiet as possible." I shivered and became very sad, and smelt the exhaust fumes. Perhaps if I could make myself sick over the side they would be sorry for me and forgive. But my only hope was in another car. A great shining car of golden brass and red paint, waiting at the door when we got home.

A tall, lovely woman in furs and lilac-scented veils would be there and a bronzed man, a General from the East, long and smiling, beside her, and they would be my true parents who had been in the East all these years, now come to take me to my real home, among kind loving faces and long-lost brothers and sisters.

What did these other two care for me here with their cars and their visitors and servants? When they hated me, trod on me, and were angry about the cup. But I hadn't broken the cup. Had Anne told them about our cavern in the bushes? Did they hate me because they had found out?

We hissed past the station and again I knew that we had forgotten the fish but did not say so. Past the tree where the white owls nested and the young ones snored, straight through the village where the people had all gone into their homes.

At the drive gate I hopped out quickly so that my sins might be forgotten if I appeared willing. Miss Wall gave me a smile.

"Walk up!" my father shouted, roaring in bottom gear through the gate and leaving me standing. My uncle's car came and I was kindly allowed to stand on the running-board in the rain, splashed by the bushes on the side of the drive, although there was a seat inside by him. I went round to the yard and planned to remain in the stables or climb into the loft and hide; perhaps hide all night and in the morning run away to sea.

Old Carlo the brown spaniel passed me. "Good Carlo," I said, he being my friend, one with me, who lived in a kennel and was called and fed, and sometimes beaten. Carlo wagged his tail. As I walked past the loose-boxes, an upper window went up and my father yelled my name.

"Your mother wants you. She's lying down."

Slowly I walked towards the house; slowly dragging my feet I went up the back stairs, meeting no cheerful maids, hearing no screeches from the kitchen. Anne and Clara and the nurse had disappeared.

Slowly I went along the passage, up the steps, out on to the landing. My mother called my name, my heart beat; in a few seconds now, only a few seconds, I would not be the same any more. I would be punished, crying.

My mother called again. They had found out much more besides. Anne had told all. I pushed open the door.

My mother was lying without her glasses on, under the counterpane. Half the blinds were drawn. By her was a tumbler with some nasty salts.

"This awful word," she said in a low voice. "When Mumsie feels so bilious. And now you see what an evil, wicked thing it is, I mean… you are, when little Clara… little Clara calls her nanny a… damned fool. Don't you know that no little gentleman ever, ever uses such a word before a lady? Can't you think how it hurts Mumsie to see her little boy growing up into a little cad? A regular cad. Using language a guttersnipe might use, but never a little gentleman."

She took another sip of the nasty salts. I waited, my throat throbbing, the tears near.

"I want you to promise me faithfully never to use that word again. Never. Say: 'I promise.'"

"I promise," I gulped.

"We try to love you, we do love you, and why, why do you insist on doing these horrid things? Now go and get straight into bed. No, it's no use being sorry. Go on, and be quick."

I turned and went slowly from the room.

"Shut the door," I heard. I shut my mother into her room by

herself. I turned to my bed in my father's dressing-room, now shut off from the day, from Anne, from the servants, dogs, stable and the woods beyond. Slowly I opened the door, surveyed my bed covered with the counterpane of the day, not even turned down, jammed in among my father's monstrous chests of drawers and tallboys in that narrow room.

I would not sob yet, standing in that cold, narrow room. Slowly I undressed and put on my cold pyjamas and climbed on to the bed. I squatted, looking at my father's football groups from Cambridge, where the players had tasselled caps and white trousers tucked into their stockings, and long moustaches. My mother moved in the next room, calling my name to ask was I in bed.

I pushed my feet down into the cold sheets. My mother's clock chimed four. My throat trembled, sobs came, I turned on the pillow and bit it. I saw those tall people in their car, come out of the East to rescue me, and love me and take me away for ever. With all my might I wished, but when the wish went, here was I in a cold bed, and four hours to go before my bedtime.

My father's feet climbed the stairs, and into my mother's room. Through the closed-up door behind my father's washstand I heard their voices. It was me then. My mother, too bilious to beat me, would send in my father to do it. I lay very still, hardly breathing. I must run away; but my clothes were off and my legs would not move. I must plead; but I knew they took no heed of excuses. I must be sorry; but I was sorry.

"One of my good pink cups!" I heard. "My good set that Mother gave us for a wedding present," her voice rose. "Oh, I do think it was unpardonable of you!"

My father's voice murmured.

"To deliberately take one of my best pink cups up to Cwm-y-rhiwdre for a picnic. And then break it. No, it's no good talking, Watkin. It's unpardonable, unpardonable. How can it be riveted? And is that the same thing? One of my good pink cups."

I could imagine her standing, opposite my father's red, angry face, he not able to answer her. Then I remembered that Anne and I had fetched the cups and Anne had chosen the pink when I wanted to bring the blue. Therefore it was Anne's fault, and she should be punished. But why was my father taking the blame?

"And the fish, Watkin. Couldn't you remember just that one little thing I asked you?"

"My dearie!" my father cried, then giving a kind of strangled cough, ran out of the room banging the door. Soon my mother went downstairs also, to her guests, not sparing herself no matter how bilious she felt, as I had been often told. I lay and heard nothing. They were having tea.

I reached to the hanging-cupboard over my head, feeling among the bottles of pills and patent medicines with which my father crammed every shelf in the room. I would read a book and hide it when I heard them coming. I saw: *Manual of Railway Engineering, English-Spanish Conversation Dictionary, Handy Tables for Brewers,* then—*Beautiful Thoughts.*

At the title I felt a sudden happiness at the lovely words, like the pictures of our Loving Saviour which hung over my mother's bed, watching over her, as she said, like a tender shepherd over his little lamb. I liked best the beautiful thoughts in Greek where I could pore over the strange alphabet wondering should I ever penetrate the mystery and read these words clearly.

But the clock chimed, and I wandered from the book to the hours that had to pass, and myself lying forgotten in bed while life went on, and people laughed and talked. Then I suddenly thought of the girls having their bath together, and remembered that the nurse would smack Anne. And I remembered the white bottom I had seen on the moor and thought of it being smacked. But they would forget to do it, I should be forgotten in bed and could not be near the door and listen for sounds, nor go near the keyhole as I had planned. Then I wished that we all slept in one room together and could laugh and talk and keep away the heavy hours that weighed on me in the narrow room.

I heard them cross the hall, laughing and talking, all in good tempers after the nice run up to our grouse-moor and the jolly picnic.

And perhaps my mother now felt less bilious and would come smiling into my room and tell me to get up. I heard the little clock strike five next door, the voices ceased, a door shut, and I lay listening to the singing of my ears in the silence after a day's pleasure.

A Young Night of Love

Like a gross purple fuchsia Mrs McCraw greeted me, but her smile told me nothing I wanted to know and I looked round for her daughter, Daisy. I didn't even worry (like my parents worried later) whether the McCraws thought me a catch for their little Daisy; only it seemed strange that all this swollen purple meat contained in a powdered lilac skin was Daisy's mother, because little Daisy had a gorgeous face like a ravishing little monkey with a seductive *retroussé* nose, and her hair hung lovely in soft permanent ringlets down her neck.

I left home in my normal febrile ill-temper, since I was going to spend a night and maybe two under Daisy's electrifying and unknown roof; and what did my parents contribute to this enthusiasm? They refused to let me drive the car there, refused to lend me a solid leather suitcase which had belonged to my travelling grandfather, advised me hatefully against my favourite check shirt, and practically demanded a haircut when I had arranged my hair over my ears in a becoming swirl.

However, Mrs McCraw was smiling and my mouth was opening and shutting on the right small talk, while my brain was alive with electric thoughts and my eyes and ears were all for Daisy. I talked to her mother about the hunt, and I managed to mention the man I'd sent back with the car, as if not liking to have him hanging around for a couple of days: in fact he'd been a decent man and let me take over the wheel when we were out of sight of the house, but it'd have been nice to have the car standing out there under the monkey-puzzle and say "my car". The Duke of Wellington who, like me, knew how to carry on under fire, said he had no small talk and Peel had no manners, but I at this moment had both, and the polished flow which I sent at Mrs McCraw obviously entranced her with my breeding, though I listened to little of it myself.

While I thus oiled the wheels and Mrs McCraw smiled her purple agreeable smile, I took a look at the room as I jabbered. It was not a room like our rooms at home. For one thing it was fairly new. Nor was Plas Parrott like our house, being near the road and of modern construction and having a monkey-puzzle in front of it. In fact the house might have been a largish villa, and the road was tarmac, not like our rocky pot-holed causeway built by my great-grandfather in an effort to ruin us. Also the room in which we conversed was "the lounge," whereas none of our rooms were lounges. I suspected I'd seen slick furniture like this in some deep shop window.

Daisy came in in jodhpurs, and birds sang in my stomach and bells rang in my head: altogether I felt astonishing. I looked at the floor and muttered "how d'ye do". I hadn't recovered from her determined effort to shake my hand, when Mrs McCraw advised Daisy to kiss such a handsome young man coming into the house on New Year's Eve. This was a joke only but I was struck by lightning in the belly, I was galvanised and could not move. Also it was in bad taste. I looked at Daisy and felt waves of heat pouring over my cheeks. She didn't kiss me. She put a record on the gramophone, "Forty-seven ginger-headed sailors," but other guests arrived and it was turned off.

We might have danced alone in the lounge and melted dreamily together, but not with Mrs McCraw there. Several people arrived now on time, that is, two girls I knew and two men I didn't know. We began all the rites and ceremonies of being shown our rooms, switching on lights, falling down sudden steps, having baths, undressing and dressing and wrestling with incredible shirts. I was reeling and alone in a strange spare room, and had to deal with everything in a staggering daze knowing Daisy was marvellously near in an unknown other room.

Just before dinner I met Mr McCraw so I turned all my energies on him although he was a little man. I couldn't stop talking, and it was magnificent to hear my polished voice going on in this polite worldly way. I had a glass of sherry and I beamed round the lounge, which was lit with orange-pink shades; I smiled an eternal grin like a jolly skull because all around me were two girls in shining sheer silk smelling of bath-salts and powder, and Daisy was late. Even the men looked tolerably less like waiters than many people do in their black ties. I was wonderfully groomed because my hair was wet and lay flat, and I'd got my grandfather's white silk handkerchief showing a neat triangle out of my pocket; I'd a gold watch-chain, a bit heavy but real gold, ear-rings of my mother's called New Zealand greenstone, which I'd screwed into my shirt for studs.

Mr McCraw was astonishing. He had opinions about everything and till this evening I never knew he existed. The other men were plainly clever and made a noise. I had another glass of sherry and Daisy flowed into the dining-room like a meteor, I believe she was rude to her mother over being late. I didn't hear.

Let me say that I was crowing on a strange dung-hill, and even trying out in a way, the *bas-fonds* of our local society. My parents' noses hadn't quite smelt this out, though there was hell when they did; but when you see a house separated only by a monkey-puzzle from the road, and are shown into a "lounge" it is a pointer; and when there was new furniture in our county and not burst chairs that smelt of dog, it was a sure sign of social novelty; the McCraws might have lain fallow in the county for twenty years, but you could lie among us in that county for thirty years and still swim your own aquarium. Mr McCraw, whom I now knew existed, was, of course, very small, and I'd say scarcely a gentleman from certain signs; but being Daisy's father he *was* a little angel, and I excused all. We talked about the hunt. I was amazed how he knew all those connected with it after only twenty years among us. Looking soberly back I suspect that Mr McCraw first insinuated himself among us after some world war, having made quantities of profitable towels for soldiers, or dry batteries or whetstones, in Oldham, Rochdale, or even Nelson.

Barring the two dumb Tudor sisters whom I knew well enough, though to-night they smelt of enticing soap and whispering silk dresses, there were two clever men there, blasted rivals to me, when Daisy smiled at them: called Laurence Powell with glasses, and, I gathered, a famous footballer from Oxford called Griff, like a heraldic beast. Griff I learned was another of those natives of our county whom surprisingly I didn't know, though as a parson's son he'd not be too conspicuous among us. It was a meal with elaborate baddish food, that is a little of everything one after the other, and a sweetish white wine. Over the table hung a celestial collection of blue glass eggs nine inches in diameter by way of chandelier. If it had fallen, God knows what might have hatched.

I didn't sneeze, but in my dazed confusion often blew my nose on my napkin as I peppered the weak soup. Coming in *boulversé* by Daisy and gusts of love, I was bemused by the McCraws' incredible table, heavily laden as if for the Lord Mayor's Show. That is, there was a regiment of knives and forks in shapes and sizes unknown to me, and on the wall were water-colours of Old Morocco and Archibald Thorburn's of grouse, widgeon, and partridge. Divided completely, reeling with emotion, and my eye searching that extraordinary juxtaposition of pictures, I sat down like a drunk, saw my hostess hadn't sat, stood up, sat down, seized my unlucky napkin folded like an artichoke, then when I shook it free of its shape a roll flew up and hit the ceiling and bounded under the table. I after it, cracked my head against Juno, the youngest Tudor sister, and we laughed so much, under the table, that our faces were as purple as Mrs McCraw's.

Coming slowly to the surface to let the blood drain back, I must have been sitting in the wrong place, because it had certainly been arranged for me to sit next to Daisy. But Daisy came in late and Griff, that footballer, was next to her, so that though my heart was pounding I must sit as if not caring where. Daisy pouted since I giggled and didn't care, and turned a heavenly smile on Griff, and by that time I'd offended Juno through not wanting a seat by her, so she pouted too. "You tank!" I hissed, and kicked her on the ankle; she kicked me back on mine.

Thus dinner was going on in no sort of order at all, and held there by forcible good manners between little McCraw and Juno the Tank, I'd have buttered my soup or peppered the sherry. Mrs McCraw, knowing Griff too well to let him lord it over me with footballs, called down the table:

"'Asn't... that's 'aven't Mr Vaughan-Thomas 'ad a blue for running, isn't that the case?"

So delighted was I, that the missed aitch floated away like a silver star, because Daisy looked at me with lovely admiring eyes.

"Not exactly a blue," I simpered.

"A half-blue then?" Griff asked generously and I almost loved him too.

I noticed Laurence Powell paying some attention to Ida Tudor, the other sister I'd made mud-pies with as a child, but I supposed this was in order.

"The great thing about sports is you can't keep them up after thirty!" McCraw said, and began to laugh so loudly that I bared all my teeth to show my goodwill, and would have slapped my thigh too, only that was under the table with the dog. Dear little Daisy's dog! A *little* dog, not the stinking wet sporting monsters our friends annoyed their guests with.

"Dogs," I said, "go in a great profusion of breeds. They spoil the old breeds by giving them too square jaws. Now give me a Dandie Dinmont," I said with an eye under the table.

"'E's not a Dandie." said McCraw, "'E's a border terrier."

"Sorry," I said, thinking them to be one and the same.

"Used to fancy a nice little pup myself, too old now," McCraw said.

The pup bit my foot under the table, I yelped like a dog.

"'E's 'armless, only a bit playful," McCraw said.

Laurence Powell and Ida began to titter carefully together; about themselves I could see, not about my foot. I turned my shoulder on Juno and poured out my regard to McCraw in waves of informed talk about dogs. On every point he contradicted me: I laughed melodiously and had some white wine.

It didn't matter that I couldn't engross Daisy, sniff her perfumed hair, and touch by accident her little arm; so long as she saw my profile, my gay brilliant jaw talking to her father, agreeable, entertaining, enough to draw any girl's admiration on me. There was no mistaking that her mother saw, and every time I caught her eye, she smiled a purple smile and nodded. As if dazzled by my brilliance, McCraw blinked, shovelled food into his mouth, and everything I said he contradicted. Now we were on bending-races at the gymkhana, which I must say I knew about though I never cared to take part; and I mentioned the incredible clumsiness of the competitors who knocked down all the obstacles.

"Do it yourself then and see!" McCraw quite snarled, and poured out such a flood of technicalities about horses and so on, that he must have been groom, stable-boy, and even jockey, before he came to own those polished mounts I saw Daisy out on. I never went to gymkhanas myself, I said. I turned to Juno and we abused one another in undertones.

I won't say that we were aiming for any shimmering gilded function in spite of our clothes. The dance was called truly enough the Mochyn Hunt, but owing to the crucial social texture of our hunt, where some would not be at ease with 25/- tickets and boiled shirts and others were undetermined people like the McCraws, it was in fact a farmer's dance, for which we'd been good enough to dress, in the Parrott Memorial Hall nearby where we dined. The admission was 2/6. Where was I? I asked in a depressed moment, looking up at those blue glass eggs on the chandelier. Daisy giggled now and grinned at Griff. They'd been children together. Where was I then when I counted only four meetings with Daisy: three at small dances and that heroic day I rode my hairy hunter Lobster nine miles to a meet of the Mochyn, galloped all day nowhere near Daisy's gleaming oat-fed chaser, and jogged nineteen miserable miles home in the dark and drizzling rain. As a rule I hunted with the United. I couldn't dance properly. Daisy was the type that scorns. I'd be left with the wretched Tudors and Ida had even found her way to giggling and smiling with Laurence Powell. A night with Juno! I kicked her again on the ankle and she kicked me back. McCraw belched, into his napkin I will say.

"I've ordered the limousine," said Mrs McCraw, smiling genial and purple on us; and I'll sit next to Daisy, I thought, if I can hold her hand. McCraw vanished through some door as though he had never existed, and at once Mrs McCraw took her easy place among us, knowing so well the ways of our world. There was a cursed bunch of mistletoe in the lounge outside the dining-room. I knew here what sort of damned horseplay Mrs McCraw would insist on: that jeering, joking manner of demanding the young kiss in public. It'd end with my kissing Juno.

It did; but I kissed Daisy first and she was quite shameless and kissed me slowly full on the lips in front of them all; so that they shouted and jeered, and without thinking I kissed her twice which brought the house down. Ida was keen to kiss me, I could see: too keen in fact, and our noses banged together. I dug my chin into Juno's cheek and the thing was done, since no one was expected to kiss Mrs McCraw's heliotropic face.

But Daisy's kisses! They weren't the first, since at each of the three dances I'd managed a kiss on the stairs. None on the unlucky day's hunting, though I'd dreamed of an embrace under a tree while the hounds cried distant music. Her warm lips on mine, as the magazines said, and all at once choirs sang in my stomach, the fire flamed like a conflagrating holocaust, and thrilling birds could well have hatched out of those blue eggs in the dining-room. I was struck as if by lightning.

Ida, if you please, dragged me down a passage as if we were looking for coats, because coats had to be got and all were occupied getting them.

"Don't you see, you silly idiot..." (Ida you have a round face like an ugly little furry animal, and what are you talking about?) "Daisy's making a *direct* set at you like she does at every man, and *look* at her and Griff. *Laurence* says the same. She's all smiles and *simpering* and she doesn't care *who* she kisses in *public* under the mistletoe."

"Why?" I asked.

"I only want to save you making a fool of yourself."

"You're just jealous," I said, as any man would have done.

"Jealous! Me jealous!" She'd have gone on indefinitely with her "me jealous" and a shrill laugh.

"They'll hear," I said.

"I hope they do," she said. "Me jealous!" We went back and got our coats which weren't in the passage.

"You've a face like the backside of a cow," I said in a low, rather dignified voice. This wasn't a true comparison, but she pinched my arm so hard I nearly yelled.

Daisy was there in a gorgeous thing of white fur floating round her throat, so that her little dark head was like a piece of coal on the hearthrug. She came to me and took my stinging arm as we moved towards the night.

"You aren't jealous?" she murmured.

"Me jealous? Who of?" I asked.

"Griff," she said, pouted for a second and then smiled again.

"Oh, no!" I said with a little loving laugh, and gazing at each other's face we went out of the front door, past Mrs McCraw who stood like a swollen purple plant in a pot, smiling as if she'd arranged it all.

In the rolling limousine I sat pressed against Daisy. I held her hand. That wonderful moment when a man first feels the hand of the woman he loves returning the pressure of his hand, as the magazines said, occurred. I struggled and freed my left hand under the rug and got it round her shoulders, and grabbed her hand with my right. But by the time I did this we were at the Parrott Memorial Hall. God knows who else was in the car with us: the others I suppose. There was a patch of light, blazing dance music, stark locals in the shadows, hoots and cat-calls in the darkness, warm thick air composed of smoke, heat, and local bodies. We were in the Mochyn Hunt Ball on a floor ridged like a ploughed field cultivated by the hob-nails of farmers and their assistants, and round us milled landworkers of all sorts in blue suits, and thick-faced girls bulging out of printed dresses; shouting, laughing, grinning, sweating, while the incredible band fought with their instruments and hurled a gigantic liquid blare out through the hall far into the night.

Like a fool I didn't get the first dance with Daisy. I counted on her taking off her white fur, but Griff seized her in it and waltzed her away among the farmers. I wouldn't dance with Juno. But she grabbed me and we floundered on the furrowed floorboards.

"This isn't a show for carthorses," I said as she waddled ahead of me thinking she was dancing, but the trumpet bellowed like a sick ram and I was drowned.

"Not much is it?" Juno said odiously close to my ear. "But then the McCraws aren't much either."

Why was she here then?

"Daisy's quite nice if she didn't think so much of herself, but Mrs McCraw she's an awful snob and Mr McCraw's so common. You're their latest catch you see."

Why were the Tudors here then?

"Daisy's all right," I said.

"Oh, any one can see you think so, and doesn't she think so herself? Of course, the McCraws are rolling in money, though you'd hardly think so from the house. Rather common."

The dance ended. I left Juno in the middle of the floor and ran at Daisy. We moved off gloriously together, and I thumped and tripped over the nails and splinters in the floor, and trod on her little satin toe. I couldn't believe it. I babbled like a man with laughing-gas, all about myself. We were alone, at least I was alone with her, pillowed and cushioned on a billowy satin solitude of what must be love.

All around us the farmers cavorted, but I didn't see them, nor the sweat nor the smoke, nor the howls and horrible throbbing of somebody's Roisterers or Rhythm Merchants. At these dances incredible tales conceive themselves, where men go out into the night with a girl and begin a pulsating human cycle. I thought of it. When I was alone, extraordinary desires did a tarantella in my head. So now I crushed Daisy tighter, still talking about myself. Where there's a will there's a way out into the night. I'd whisper in Daisy's little ear, and she made it easy because her sweet head she laid against my shoulder as I stumbled on those harrowed floorboards. But was there a will? Oh, not with Daisy, I said. Or with Daisy where we walked under the flowing moon and I leaned in long shadows among the trees.

In my eye I saw the racing clouds across the moon. I murmured in her ear, and was amazed again: she squeezed my hand. "Later on," she whispered, and I did a cavatina to improvise my joy and stumbled on those cursed splinters.

She smiled and melted away from me in Griff's arms. And where was I? Standing by the rows of chairs which lined the walls under the crossed flags of all nations. In my head I threw down Daisy on a grassy bank: it wasn't possible. Some nightmare took place under a septic moon. Among the sly, sweating, smiling, odiously tanned-faced farmers I could see no trace of her.

Laurence Morgan, I found, was my companion against the wall. "Let's sit," he said, "not stand facing the firing squad." We lowered our faces to the level of the farmers' bottoms, and tried to save our feet.

"A quick one would be nice," Laurence Morgan said.

"Where are the Tudor two?" I asked politely.

"Dancing with farmers out of politeness."

"Very suitable," I said, and Laurence made motions of pulling corks and drinking. I was expecting the next dance with Daisy.

Like a sleepwalker I beamed over the floor and swayed gracefully toward her because I loved her and she loved me. She was lying in Griff's arms, upright under an extended paper bell. I asked, and she simpered up at Griff, that fabulous dancer. I couldn't believe it.

"Ask me again," she said.

I asked.

"Not now," she said.

They danced away and the farmers jostled me where I stood and gaped and couldn't believe it.

I stumbled on Laurence lost in a cavernous yawn.

"That was a good idea I had," he said.

I was lost in this appalling mystery.

"Griff cut you out?" he asked. "I wouldn't worry."

"I'm not worrying," I said. "A drop of something'd be better than this miserable miasma."

"Miasma?"

"Rises out of stinking ponds," I said: Laurence dug me in the ribs and furtively we insinuated ourselves into the night. I was lost in the damned thing Daisy had done to me, and had no idea we were in the pub till I was asked.

"I always drink mine neat," I said, which wasn't true, and to show Laurence, tipped up my three fingers of Scotch. It crucified me. I saw the barman smile, and I ordered more.

There we were, all set about with farmers playing darts till the barman or owner took us out of his bar that smelt of piss and cider into his back room which smelt of funerals and varnish. My stomach was desperate so I tipped down another neat Scotch.

"That'll burn you out before you're thirty," Laurence said.

"I'm not thirty," I said obstinately.

We got talking, about women, of course, and the damned dull evening: and about this bloody hop in a stinking village hall.

"I've to be back at the works on Monday; what a Saturday, I ask you!" Laurence said.

We had more whisky. We began to talk very loudly about Wales as a nation, Wales as a republic. We were the Welsh Ministers to Dublin and Washington respectively.

"When I am a dictator," Laurence cried, "every man shall be compulsorily ordained in Wales: every man his own *parch*!"

"And every woman, too!" I called, seeing them all in their black gowns and circular collars.

"Women are sluttish sluts!" he shouted and we sang as many hymns as we could remember, and "The Ash Grove," or "Llwyn Oh". Over the velvet-tasselled mantelpiece bored into my eye a white girl in a white dress and some fool with her in whiskers, called "The First Kiss".

"Hell!" I screamed and threw my glass at it. The man put his head through the hatch, so remembering I had on a white tie and therefore things were expected of me, I bowed low and kissed my hand.

"Look at you," said Laurence, "and the way she handled you. I like you, I like you Vaughan-Thomas, and I don't like you ill-treated: ill-treated."

That was damn nice; I took his hand. "You're a man," I said, and was going to say more, but Laurence said:

"When you've two girls it's bad enough to carry on with two, but look at her! Doesn't she encourage you? Doesn't she go off with Griff? Doesn't every one know she's been Griff's girl since she was eleven in a manner of speaking?"

I shrieked and broke another glass; always I missed "The First Kiss". The head came and went.

"Hell holds no fury like a scornful woman," I said. "I mean I..."

"She's led you up the tree, the little monkey!" said Laurence; he tittered into his drink. I swallowed back my stuff.

"They can't chase us here, let Griff waste his time with her if he wants to," I said, thinking what a safe place from a woman a pub is.

"There's many better than her at the works."

"The works!" I cried in joy, "I'll be down at the works with you on Monday," and do a man's job I meant.

And Laurence shrieked, "And we'll all be Queen of the May!"

The head appeared. "Two more!" Laurence cooed. "You've had enough," the head said, "you gents."

"*Cymru am byth!*" Laurence bellowed, "Heel it Swansea! Wales for ever! They don't understand Welsh the bastards," meaning the bastards in this pub.

The head came into the room and the owner after it saying, "We're as good bloody Welshmen as you Mr Whatever you are, and we can behave ourselves like when we have a drink; this is a quiet house whatever!"

I was up against it. The room reeled and I was going to be sick. I went out and was, and with Laurence's help I fell into the parked limousine.

"Wales for ever!" I muttered, and fell asleep.

It seemed they could hardly get themselves in after the dance because I was wedged across the back seat. I woke feeling very ill. There was Daisy; but I didn't want to smite her; I wanted to sleep and forget. All I heard was, "You're a nice one," from Juno and in a quiet astonished voice as if I'd climbed Mont Blanc. I laid my head on someone's shoulder, probably Griff's.

Ida said, "My cousin in the Camel Corps says it's hot even in winter."

The limousine kept me awake. We arrived at Plas Parrott, and furtively I wiped my mouth that tasted of vomit. Horrible sandwiches were left out and cake and something in a thermos. I was shivering. Griff gave me hot coffee. No one seemed to like Laurence and he went away to bed giggling to himself. I wanted sleep, and my legs ached and wobbled under me like flies.

As the dreary boards creaked under my feet and everywhere the sickly pink-shaded lights of the McCraw's oppressed my eyes, I became by slow degrees on my way to sleep and forget, alone with Daisy in a passage and she took my arm.

"It's not your fault," she murmured. "It's all Laurence's fault." She drew me by the arm. "Come in here," she said. "It's my room."

Oh, the sweet scented purity of her little satin room, her hand, the permanent ringlets of her hair!

"Laurence's old enough to know better," she said, meaning I suppose that I wasn't old enough. "It's his fault, not yours."

Rather feebly I said, "He's a Welsh Nationalist, I think."

Her dear firm voice pronounced, "Welsh nonsense! And he's no business teaching you to drink. This is my room. Isn't it nice?"

Oh, paradise! More vile and pinker fringes to those lights, a sea-green bedspread, a lilac satin nightdress spread out. Where were we sitting? On a couch, there was the bed ahead. I tasted vomit in my throat. I must have forgiveness.

"Forgive me, I've been such a..." I searched for a word.

"A swine!"

She forgave me but my spirits sank. I wanted sleep, my eyes ached, the pink was awful, the green bedspread gastric; the walls were yellow now at last I saw and I began to despair.

"I forgive you, but you must promise me"— anything, oh, anything! — "never, never to get drunk again, mind?" Side by side we were sitting as in a bus, our hands resting one on top of the other.

"I promise," I said.

"And now," said Daisy, "I'm going to give you a kiss." Oh, Lord, the dried vomit on my mouth! Was this the first? Who had I kissed on those dark stairways? The light was cruel. Holding my doubtless stinking breath I kissed back as she lunged and leaned on me, with tight closed lips and folded eyes.

"Daisy, what about Griff?" I murmured when it was safe to draw apart.

Firmly she arranged this matter too. "I'm very fond of Griff," she said. "Griff and I are old friends. And I'm very fond of you, too."

That was it. She leaned for another kiss, but the other one had started my stomach downwards like a lift, down through the green couch, and the carpet which I now saw was beige and yellow. She got my cheek this time, and together we sat side by side, our cheeks pressed thus. I am in love, I thought.

Shortly afterwards I went to my room and saw my disgusting face in the glass, with my tie under one ear and spots of something on my shirt, and my greasy hair hanging down my loathsome face. I'd no muscles that a woman could admire. I'd only arms like tripe, and the hair had fallen off my chest. I slid between the McCraw's cold expensive sheets and slept.

I woke knowing I was finished. I was certain of it. There was nothing left for me. I'd had a hopeless love affair and I must go away, only my blasted parents hadn't let me keep the car and I could never go by the ignominious train. The car would come only to-morrow. I must endure. I began by arranging my face stoically for Daisy, for all to see. In this horrible house they didn't have breakfast till 10.30. I was parched for a cup of tea and the tooth-water tasted of tin. I was thin and old and bent, and flaccid, and past the pleasures of young heroic love. I'd failed, and I would never smile again.

Boring Story

Colonel Blinding was a jaunty man with his painted tower in the garden, his elaborate doves, his invalid mother. In his tall house he listened to the four winds, and to see him and Mrs Blinding you could not imagine that they had ever been unmarried: the idea of one without the other was like an egg without its yoke. If they had been sprightly and slender that was in King Edward's reign and there were only photographs to prove it.

In his tall home Colonel Blinding listened to the four winds when the curtains were drawn, and in the daytime he watched the preening of his elaborate doves. The painted tower in the garden supplied water to the house for washing, for drinking, for flushing the closets.

Pamela Blinding lived at home with her parents at the age of twenty-four. Though not unattractive, her diversions were bounded on the one side by the tennis-parties, the County Balls, the hockey-matches in which her neighbours took part, on the other by visits with her parents to the hotel in Queen's Gate, when her mother took her to a matinee and bought her a hat and her father came in so late from his old acquaintances.

A man in her bed was unknown to Pamela, and though, in the backs of cars, 'intimacy,' as the papers say, had almost taken place, Pamela (known as 'Pam' to her friends) had resisted and been sober enough to shame the man with his lust.

These experiences had not been so unpleasant, but 'Pam' was not on the look-out for love: at twenty-four she lived at home with her parents, played hockey, and went to the County dances.

Ignorance and upbringing in ignorance managed in a mysterious way to keep down her natural passions amongst the savage surging reproductions of the herbs and the beasts of the land. She never wondered what her father did so late in London, nor what he did with the large body of Mrs Blinding in their brass marriage bed, nor did she wonder about the past instincts of Colonel Blinding's invalid mother, whose feeble voice could be heard complaining at all hours by those who stopped near her door, and whose attempts at managing interference often upset Mrs Blinding and offended the servants.

"I know I'm an old woman and nobody cares what I think, but if I were you, I wouldn't go out without your coat, and why do you wear that jumper with that skirt, why don't you wear the other? But don't think I want to interfere, you must please yourself, run along now, and change."

And as 'Pam' was leaving the room, "Just run down and see if your father's got the paper and bring it up. He never sends it up. I could sit here all day and nobody ever comes near me."

'Pam' looked into her father's room and could not find him because he was in his chair behind the door, reading the paper, so she went out. She had been walking out of the drive gate for some years now, with the dogs, but only now was she beginning to notice that Charles Frame, of Brag's Hotel in Faldwyn nearby, passed the gate on a bicycle every morning as she came out.

The young man must be going somewhere. Every morning he said good-morning, she said good-morning; then he turned to look at her and nearly fell off his bicycle. This morning he seemed to have broken down, he was fiddling with his tyre when she passed.

"Bit of trouble," he said after the good-mornings.

'Pam' paused.

"Chain's loose," he said: it looked all right though.

"Where d'you go to every morning?" 'Pam' asked.

"Oh, you've noticed me?" Charles Frame asked. "I thought you never did."

"Well, of course I noticed you! You go by every morning; where d'you go to?"

"Just for a spin," said Charles, and grinned.

It was peculiar that he should go for a spin, and peculiar that he should grin.

Mrs Blinding 'ran' the house until the floors and the walls vibrated with her energy. After she had ordered the dinner, given out the stores to the cook, told the house-maid about coming in, reprimanded the scullery-maid for grease in the sink, told the man about bringing in more logs, mowing the lawn, and about the rake she had found left in the rhododendrons, gone into Colonel Blinding's room, said, "Oh, there you are," and disturbed him by that unnecessary remark, she told the footman that the silver was not clean enough.

The footman's brown eyes deceived with their look of innocence: even Mrs Blinding in her violent careering through the morning could not savage such a dove-look. The impression which should be left by Mrs Blinding's extraordinary activity is how well she runs that house and how she never spares herself. The servants took cups of strong tea and prepared to recover.

Colonel Blinding in the garden watched the movements of the fans and ruffs of his elaborate doves, with his stick he rapped the structure of the painted tower and it rang true. He bellowed jauntily at his gardener and the man jumped.

This was Colonel Blinding's morning, and after it he would tell his daughter that there was no one kinder than Mrs Blinding, no one who did more for them. But he had come out into the garden because he dared not lock his study door.

Charles Frame had grinned, 'Pam' held the bike for him while he fixed the chain. This action gives him an opportunity to talk, and he may even penetrate her reserves.

At last, when no reasonable man can continue fumbling with the chain, Charles stands up and asks 'Pam' which way she is going.

"Why, with the dogs somewhere."

Not yet thrilling to his penetrating glance, nor strangely stirred by an unaccustomed conversation, she thought his question peculiar.

Colonel Blinding's invalid mother calling him to her, told him to repaint the painted tower: "I can distinctly see bare patches where the paint has fallen."

"It's moss!" cried Colonel Blinding, "Or eggshell! Or the droppings of birds."

"Oh, shout at your poor old mother, at your poor old mother who loves you, at your poor old mother who has done so much for you, at your poor broken old mother when you owe—don't you love your mother, don't you love her a——."

The door is shut, Colonel Blinding's hands twitch, the roof of his mouth is dry: from his dear old mother there is no escape. From the voices of dear old mothers there is no escape but death.

When Mrs Blinding comes into the room, the old woman tells her how to run her house, how to bring up her child. When the Colonel is there, she tells him to paint his tower. So she lives, with her demands and her grievances, her sticky chains of sentiment, her maudlin conceptions: so she lives with the papers and the photos and the fetishes, the blue ribbon that belonged to some departed dear one: for all her dears are gone, and she is left without love—and she cannot live without love.

The Colonel grinds an empty match-box in his palm and leaves the room, and is called back to be asked to fetch the paper.

Mrs Blinding searches for her husband; she is conscious of the need for her husband. She cannot find him. She needs him, she needs to say something to him that she cannot say: the highest poetry of their joint life has been expressed in grunts and gasps.

The house runs, the days are lived through, 'Pam' was twenty-one, twenty-two, twenty-three, and is now twenty-four, she needs her husband to speak to; if not her husband, why not her husband?

The days are lived through, Monday, Tuesday, Wednesday. She looks in his room, the newspaper lies by the chair on which he sat; his pipe is there and his glasses.

The footman comes silently in and disturbs her.

"What day of the month is it, Albert?"

"The 29th..." he answered.

"29th, 30th, 1st, 2nd, 3rd."

"The Colonel's on the lawn, Madam."

"Thank you!"

One must say thank you, to him who guesses one's thoughts. On the lawn there is nothing to say to the Colonel; here the footman has brown eyes and a kind heart. His voice is soft. And she talked to him as you can imagine.

Soon they were shy because they were talking, and the footman went out. But she had talked to him before.

Frame and 'Pam' are in the lane walking slowly. Is it boredom with her own lot, latent revolt, or simplicity, which helps her to talk to him? To him she is stiff with strange iron view-points; to her it is all a little peculiar, but no possibility has appeared in her mind.

Frame feels he can do nothing in the daylight against this breeding.

"Will you meet me here this evening here by this gate at six o'clock?" he asks, having thought out the sentence and jerked it out five minutes later.

'Pam' produced a whistle and blew upon it to get the dogs back.

"No," she said; "Well," not to be rude and abrupt.

Then it was difficult to refuse.

"All right"; but she need not turn up. But later she knew she would meet him on her walk if she did not turn up.

At six-five she was there.

It was dark. Soon he kissed her.

For those who do not know, these matters are decided by violence on one side and by surprise and instinct on the other. 'Silent pressures' and 'liquid glances' may be ruled out. But he did no more than kiss her this time—he hardly dared.

It would be interesting to number the barriers overcome on succeeding days; to say how 'Pam's' class-prejudices were worn down by love, though they did not exist after the attractive Frame touched her; how her well-bred modesty revolted against coupling in woods, though she was willing as another woman when properly worked up; to reproduce as realistically as possible the conversations which led her into a train with Charles Frame, ('Will you?' 'Oh, I couldn't' 'Why not?' 'I just couldn't,' etc.) with splashes of artistic colour—('When I used to see you I thought the sun, moon and stars, etc.')

But it was done by acquiescence.

They exclaimed that they were happy; they kissed, they coupled, they exclaimed that they were happy: they were happy.

They got into a train and went away together.

Charles Frame was heir to Bragg's Hotel and money in the bank, so he was a better catch than a young lieutenant in the Gunners with £200 a year and no conversation.

"I wish I had a son." Mrs Blinding said to Albert.

He thought she felt her daughter's departure and the disgrace that she had departed with a publican's son. She was not old enough to be his mother.

In the servants' hall Albert bragged: "I know when I'm well off: and not for my sweet conversation only. Something'll surprise you."

"You look out for the old man," they said.

"Old man'd never notice if the house fell down; all he wants is peace, probably be only too glad."

"You weren't quick enough," they said. "You should have took the daughter, not the mother."

"I know when I'm well off," he said, "Who has the most cash now? Who has the most cash?"

And they admired him for his luck and hated him for his luck. One day Mrs Blinding kissed him on the cheek during one of their conversations, after telling him she wished she had a son. Albert, being a son to her, kissed her the next day, but warmly, since she was not old enough to be his mother.

Mrs Blinding convinced that it was affection only did not trouble to be shocked.

"Kissing and cuddling, that's it now," Albert bragged in the servants' hall, "Something'll surprise you soon!"

And one day as the Colonel inspected the paint in his tower, and watched the movements of his elaborate doves, Mrs Blinding and Albert the footman, went to different stations by different routes, and boarded the same train, sat in the same compartment on the same seat. Now they live in the South of France and Albert wears white flannel trousers to walk upon the beach.

When the news was broken with the speed of news after their departure, when the servants grinned behind their hands at the victory of their class, and Colonel Blinding thought it peculiar, but did not believe it had happened, his invalid mother was unable to hide her delight.

Having put off the inevitable interview for three days, Colonel Blinding is called to her room as he passes the door propped specially open.

"You haven't been to see me for four days, how do you suppose I feel with all these terrible happenings. I am so cast down. Of course nobody came to me with their troubles, nobody confided in me, if they had asked me—but they never think, nobody thinks. Now," she said, "*Now*, we can have dinner at eight o'clock like we used to before you were," (she was going to say 'married') "And not half-past seven. Of course I'm only an old..." but Colonel Blinding struck her on the head with a hatchet, and killed her, and at the sound of her dying the elaborate doves flew about and banged against the painted tower.

And with many expressions of horror on both sides, Colonel Blinding was tried for the murder of his poor old mother and sent to a Criminal Lunatic Asylum where he founded Colonel Blinding's Band of Hope.

Break Away If You Can

I am going out to the lettuces, and my Mother called after me something vague in words about weeding the little ones and not picking them, or not picking the little ones and letting the big ones grow. What could I do to let or make things grow in that sour winter soil? The wonder was that they were up at all: but I called yes. Mums' head I saw over the wall, and it glided like a bird and swerved at the drive gate like a gull. She dashes on her bike like she can't dash in life.

Our life is the speed of… its own speed. Here where you see us live, here are no tumbling valleys or hills where the wind roars like a trumpet, but low hills, and worn hills, and choked drains in the fields where the Haran runs like the rain returns to the sea.

I trod through torn puddles, through the bronze muck standing down the yard, and I hummed under the arch: but the echo was the drip among the ferns and mosses was the music of the day. In Trallwm Mums is to buy rice and candles so that we don't sit in darkness to-night; so the days follow smaller days, smaller outings for smaller things we buy; till the days are low and in a piece like the piece since I was eighteen.

Over the low hills that day, of course, hung the mist that hangs in the shallow Haran valley. There was tree where nectarines had grown last summer, and round the nails plaster fell away where the last frost broke into the wall. Every year Mums said to me, Beth the nectarine's dead now; and then it lived through another winter. Another winter.

There were those small lettuces under the straw shelter. I plodded up the garden in my gumboots, and the split had let in water in the yard cold on my foot. Look, you see my stained old skirt, old greasy raincoat, that battered sodden hat.

As I walked the wet earth path I was walking up the wood one morning. A young man came out of the wood to me, he had a fine smile but he was like Colley; only finer. I hummed but my throat caught the thin sound, caught against my cough, and I stopped at the thin sound. Then there was the beginning, as I called it between us, by the lake as we sat looking at the lake between the tennis; and that young ass Thwaite who knocked the ball into the lake, knocked the lemonade out of Colley's mouth and down his neck. I could have kicked him. Then Thwaite pulled a hair out of my leg and Colley kicked him. When we were looking for the ball in the bushes, he grabbed me and I beat at him and turned my ear to him because I wanted... I wanted his kisses.

I pulled some lettuce, pale and full of grit, older than it looked too, hearing down in the ruinous yard we have, the cow bellowing after her calf we had had taken away. I am little and father takes my little hand to look at the pigeons: up into the loft we come at the pigeons from behind through their smell: and father opened little doors to look at them sitting so quiet on their eggs. Father! Cold leaves cold lettuce damp round my fingers: I never clean my hands out of the dirty cracks in them. Because I've not time? They say how men like soft woman's hands, a gentle mother's hands. Why did I not look in the glass this morning? There was no light: I'd no time.

If a man came down out of the wood, what sort of a sight should I be for him? In the dark mornings there's the little green light rising over the hills beyond the river: then I'm creeping out of bed with the dirty sheets dropping on the floor, creeping down on the cold boards, smelling my own smell off my nightdress, I reach to get on my stockings and my knickers before I'm properly awake before the cold strikes. Because Mums does so much and Mums cannot do so much and feed the hens and milk that cow. Mums is getting old, tired, thin.

I staggered with sleep this morning across the yard, my clothes stuck to me because I didn't wash with my hair hanging down my face. What sort of a slut would he find if he came down, smiling down?

The lettuce are like little cold fingers; pull and they should cry. These are the lettuce we were to sell for sixpence in Trallwm, but we do not. They're like hands. In my ears the waters whispered, trickled in the wall, sucked in the soil at my feet. The cow cried like a distant trumpet. After her baby. Her baby soft as little hands. I set down the lettuce where they could wait and I took a step through the door into the wood in the wall.

That door must be pushed because of the weight of rotting leaves against it, a door that was made for to step out into the pleasure of the wood! It's like a meal sack. I walked in the wood up the steep slope, and at each step I was so tired, and I'd have sunk in a chair with my mind wandering sadly from a faded magazine. But there is so much to do.

In the morning in the house I couldn't sit down, if Mums was there doing so much. Mums is out. There's no fire in the drawing-room, but twigs dropped by jackdaws down behind the painted screen where a blonde woman floats down a painted stream in summer.

Here at this spot the boys caught a jackdaw in their hidden trap, here at my feet: and the horrible bird hopped round the stairs and pecked my legs. The boys. I climbed the wire down into the slanting lane. Where am I going? At each step the fatigue mounted up my back. I looked into a bush seeing nothing.

Behind the bush there was a man squatting, there was his head and the smoke going up from his pipe. I couldn't go by and have him see me: nor go back and let him see me walking away. With my back to him I turned to the bank and pulled at orange fungi on a twig. The man made no sound. In my mind I saw the man's head and the smoke of his pipe, but on the rest of him squatting there was a mist. I stared at the orange cups of the fungi and did not think of what he was doing. He stood and I turned, but I saw him pull up his trousers and tuck in a grey shirt. He walked away, and I bent down and my heart beat because he might turn and see me see him.

He went through the gap and now I saw horses steaming and standing there all the time. He shouted, they moved. At the jingle of the harness I came out into the field.

I moved on the edge, but the man stopped his horses. Now he was another old man, and the man squatting in the bush was only a head and a pipe. He had an old tin cap on his pipe and a sack over his shoulders against the damp.

What is she doing walking the fields?

I wish he was the far side and I'd not have to speak.

He said about the gulls pecking behind the harrow: "Stormy weather at sea," he said.

And I looked at Evans who had stoked his way to Buenos Aires, charged with a bayonet in France like my brother. And came back to his wife. Had he killed a man? Killed? At sea. There was a noise in the distance.

"Hounds," said Evans and grinned.

I said: "They met at Glan-haran."

He grinned and said: "You never saw them kill in this country, not this side."

They cried over the hills, no nearer, rising and falling.

"I was in the Feggy," Evans said, "in Cae Issa."

"I was fifteen and they come. Those was hounds, Miss."

"Old Mr Johns hunting," I said. "The old things were better I suppose, Evans."

He went on: "They come right down the gap: I hitch old Brown out... flying over the hedges like a bird!"

I didn't believe a carthorse could do that, but these people exaggerate.

"And when I come back, there's my Dad waiting with a thick stick!" His voice went up in a screech, broke in a laugh.

My Dad... Father is coming at me across the hall with the riding-whip: there's the broken tobacco-jar on the floor and I near it: he's so tall and terribly angry: I'm crying and crying, then there is a blank.

"No horses round about now," Evans said. "And I remember the Colonel, and you couldn't hold him as a lad."

I thought no one held Father now as far as I knew.

"You hop on a bike now," Evans said. "Cut across by the Madoc; you'll catch them down the Dingle they're coming."

Mums has the bike: or there's the old one, would it carry me down past the Madoc: up the Dingle: beyond the Sarn: by the Bwlch: left, and up the grassy drive to Colley's? But that's fifteen miles, woman. And is Colley there? Where was he last? Driving through Trallwm top speed. Where is he now?

I stood back on my heels to move away from Evans and the field and the horse and the mist. I walked off and the gulls flew up off the earth and lighted, to be further from me. Evans's back moved away from me under the sack, with his horses into the mist, and continuously the bellowing of the wretched cow came up to me.

When Evans was young he galloped on one of those steaming horses and nothing could stop him. Not his Father. I saw the sort of young man Evans was, with all his teeth and black hair: like in a mist I saw the sort of muscles that kind of man has under a thin skin where the weather doesn't reach it. But this youth was on a horse without a bridle or saddle, with a sort of sheet round him and bare legs clinging to the side of the horse. At the end was a beating from Father. There are no such young men now.

Sixteen years ago I was young, so young that I panted in a white dress when a boy took my arm to dance, and the touch of his hand pierced my stomach. I never jumped on a horse and galloped after the hounds, because there wasn't a horse and the boys were there and Father.

"We'll throw you off the roof," they said. "Or down the lavatory."

Colley was such a fool, then he kissed me. He made up jokes and shouted and tripped up people for fun.

My father, snarling over the cold meat and potatoes, snarled: "Why doesn't he join the Territorials?"

I knew that it was because he was quite different from Father and the boys, but I said nothing.

Father went off and must shoot grouse and pheasants with Lord this and General that, and play the gallant Colonel. I think it was better he stayed away, though so quiet; but Mums was sad though she said nothing.

He plays this sort of make-believe wherever is, but Mums and I get up at seven. We said we must keep the place decent for when the boys came home: but they stay where they are and don't come.

At twenty I looked east across those same hills to everything in the world and it was all open to me: all the love and the riches and the joy I read about, was for me. But I never crossed over. Then the Haran was a stream I'd leap over: now it's a river and the hills are the same hills. I'm here to keep things going with Mums, because she does so much. Where did I read about those other things? I suppose in some magazine. There are girls of sixteen who were born when I went to my first dance; and I cried afterwards because it was over, because I was so happy, or because I was a failure and said nothing like a fool to my partners.

I came down into the yard and that cow was knocking against the stable door, but I pumped that wretched bike while the music of the hounds died away. I'd hurry after them because they were running towards Colley's: I will ride up the drive and there he comes down the steps and takes my hands. I'll go. Mums must eat by herself. The chintzes can wait. I was on the bike, rattling down under the dripping trees. How can I get back those years? Where is the I in that white dress, and my beating heart?

I went down past the Madoc, left up the Dingle, up the hill. Yes, they'd checked. I heard the horn. Is this a golden day then? I began to run down to the Sarn where the road joined the Trallwm road, and I saw the horsemen in file against the skyline. I'd found them! Hounds were moving up over the Rallt, and I could turn off the main road over the Rallt; beyond was so few miles, and my heart would beat again. I'd be panting in my white dress.

There was a little person slowly pushing a bike up the hill to me, but I had my eye on the Rallt skyline. It was Mums coming back. I couldn't fly past her when she had all the groceries piled on her bike. I told her I was following the hounds.

"You must have got finished very quickly."

I said nothing because nothing was finished, beds, kitchen, dinner started: nothing. Mums didn't stop, so I turned my bike and wheeled after her, and at every step the weariness climbed up my back, and my stomach hung like lead.

"Did you scald the pans, Beth?" Mums asked without looking round.

"No."

"Everything'll go sour, Beth."

"When I got up I was so tired all morning."

"Not if you went flying after hounds on your bike, in that dirty old mac, and your hair."

I must stop at every step, I must stop because the hounds were going away: I must hurry over those miles: or it would be too late.

But I knew what my hair was like, like dirty string: what sort of a smile would he smile at me in a filthy coat and wispy grey hair: and my face? Oh why hadn't I done the thing properly? Put on another coat, washed my face, gone slowly over to Colley's. But you know there must be a reason to go over there or I'd never dare pass the drive gate. Suppose he asked me: "Well Beth, what brings you over?"

"Beth, I've got all these parcels."

"Give them to me."

"We can't stop now as you're so behind. And the chintzes must be done to-day too."

I asked couldn't they wait. Mums said Mrs Price was coming on Friday and the drawing-room was so awful: and perhaps the chintzes wouldn't stand another wash. I knew those chintzes, they tore if you laid a finger on them, so we'd be all day mending them. Of course I would be glad to help Mrs Price with her sale of work next week. How long since Colley kissed me that first time? Nine years last August. Then he was abroad: then he had the big party for the Balls, and I couldn't go because Mums fell and hurt her back.

We came down the Dingle, up under the dripping trees. Evans was taking a shortcut home down the drive.

He said: "You didn't get far."

"No," I said, and tried to smile. "Not far."

When we were past, Mums said: "Mrs Evans owes me for pullets since last August."

August, for me nine years last August.

The cow had broken down the door and was ranging round the yard bellowing misery: we got her back into the old loose-box. I had meant to clean the dairy while Mums was out, but there the churn was in pieces since yesterday, unscalded, all the lids off the crocks. As we went in, a yellow cat flew out past our feet.

"Whose cat is that?"

"Mrs Evans's I think," I said.

"I do think you could have not shut a cat in here last night."

"I'd no light, I couldn't see."

Mums said: "Unless I see to everything myself... Beth, these crocks..." She clicked her tongue as if it was my fault things went sour. "Where did you put the lettuce?"

"On the path. I left them."

Mums sighed and said nothing.

Taking the chintzes off they tore and must be stitched: I hung over the tub till the blood beat in my head and I could have cried because of my back. Mums went away for some time, and came back to say she'd been mopping up where the water came through the missing slates. I could have helped, but she only told me when she'd done it. "We're behind enough as it is," she said. "It's not like you to go after the hounds when we're so far behind." I said nothing, and then Mums said there was the Straight wedding on Saturday.

"I've nothing to wear," I said.

"Nonsense," Mums said. "We can both go in our black."

"There's the badminton to-night," I said, half hoping she wouldn't hear.

"In Trallwm? Beth you could have saved me a journey."

"Everything would be shut by now."

"You could have waited for your badminton."

"Where?" I asked. "In the Lion?"

"I thought you were feeling tired," Mums said.

Father used to go and drink in the Lion, so perhaps I could have gone and waited and had five whiskys in the Lion like Father: on the slate, I suppose. It would feel good. The local paper tells us this is the country where old men are found in their cottages with their heads split by an axe; I read it, and girls have their babies alone in the fields and drown them.

Mums said: "Ella Williams is in trouble again: I don't know why they don't send the girl to the asylum, the men should be ashamed."

The men took Ella Williams at her idiot grin. "Oh well..." I said.

Mums straightened up and almost shouted: "Well, what's the use of bringing wretched deformed idiot children into the world one after another?" I was surprised at Mums shouting.

If I really wanted to help, because of the badminton to-night, I'd go down to Mrs Llewellyn about those slates. But I saw Mrs Llewellyn's old withered white face with the black eyes staring out of it, and a sponge-bag on her bald head. And Mrs Llewellyn's cat staring up and rattling the door-handle with its paw. I couldn't stand that cat. Mums used to say Mrs Llewellyn could put the rent up if she liked and turn us out if she liked, so we never asked for anything.

We got the chintzes out of the tub: "Pull," Mums said, and "Twist."

We swayed and staggered and twisted at the sodden chintzes.

My back hurt: "Oh," I said.

Mums said: "You're not a young thing any more to be going to the badminton."

The distances we all drove and bicycled to badminton showed you did not need to be young. I was going up now to wash and brush my hair for the first time to-day. Suddenly I shouted at Mums: "You had Father even if he was no good you had him and you had the boys... and you had me..." I ran quickly upstairs and I heard Mums call out

"Beth," not very loud. When I shouted she looked so surprised and little and old.

If we started a row, the work only piled up under our hands. How long had we been without a row? I saw Mums' little old frail face with a smudge on her forehead.

As I got the bike out I was crying because Mums would be sitting by herself while I was out. I'd shouted at her and left her. I moved quickly across the yard with the tears going down my cheeks; and there was the little light at the scullery window where she was mixing the hen-food. On the road the trees towered up in the dark and the wet road hissed under my tyres towards Trallwm.

Cam-Vaughan's Shoot

In a moment of rage Cam-Vaughan called on them. In a moment of rage he stuffed the mouthpiece of the receiver with burning fragments of his address-book and his listeners heard sounds like gunfire in Wales. He cried out. He stammered and swayed in his boots. In his passion he miscalled the names of the days of the week.

It was Thursday. From the lodge, from the cottage, from the butler's pantry, shivering and stamping, the assembling servants, rattling their feet on the concrete, on the gravel, on the brick staircases, strapping the bags on their backs and whistling to the dogs, advanced on the doorway in irregular fours and some of them entered and some stayed outside rattling the nails in their feet and whistling the dogs.

There was the General from Darkest America, veteran of forty, defeated in the race for promotion. His boots were from Poxy's, his belt from Moxy's, his trousers from Coxy's (Bond St.) and his hat from Roxy's.

"My half-pay's not enough," he used to say.

He came through the beaters like a wind through the bamboos and his host clutched his hand, they were two long men together among Welshmen.

The ranks of the beaters parted and Owen the headkeeper grinned like an evil ghost at his masters. The other guests came; three of them with round heads and moustaches like unbending reeds, the fourth, Thwaite, (his moustache was like a little bird on his twitching lips) stood in his quiet tweeds padded with leather at the shoulders, his father's hat on his head, his grandfather's dog on a leash at his feet.

"Thwaite's brought his damned dog again," said the General.

Owen, grinning up obliquely like a dark and evil man (he's Welsh), limped on his twisted legs among the men, and the leaders advanced and handed the guns their weapons and stood behind them, and the bodies of the leashed dogs shifted and whined. The guns handed back their weapons to the leaders and climbed in the throbbing brakes.

They're off! Three brakes roared down the four-mile drive of Parc Gweledigaethau-Sais scattering the stones and the mud and the few villagers who were not among the beaters, and who stood in a gaping group at the gates of the park. The park was like a rolling kingdom of oaks and deer; the walls around it were forty feet high. Cam-Vaughan saluted at the gate and the few villagers there acknowledged his salute.

The van with the beaters went by a different road from the brake, Thwaite thought, that's sinister; and Owen grinned out of the narrow window at the back of the van as it vanished in the deep lane.

"Ugly face that damn Welshman's got," the General exclaimed.

"He is good for the work," said Cam-Vaughan. "The poachers will not kill him this winter, he never goes out. The poachers think he is behind them (with a gun) so there is no poaching this winter."

The General and the three guests threw up their moustaches (stiff like reeds) and roared; Thwaite smiled and his moustache twitched on his fluttering lip. He thought of the evil Owen going by another road with the massed beaters; by a deep and twisted Welsh road, while the brake with the guns glided on the broad smooth road of the Parc Gweledigaethau-Sais estate.

"Sit up Thwaite!" cried the General. "And keep your damned dog from licking my feet."

"He is in the other car, sir;" said Thwaite. "It is a convulsive movement of my own feet against yours."

"Twitcher!" exclaimed the General who hated young men.

"Where do you get your boots?" Cam-Vaughan asked him.

"Poxy's of course," cried the General.

"He meant mine," said Thwaite; "They are home-made."

The brake stopped in a farmyard, far from the park, among steep woods and precipitous dingles of the farthest corner of the estate. Owen and the beaters and the loaders were already there; grinning and standing close like a crowd at an accident. The loaders advanced and handed the guns their weapons. Thwaite's dog strained at his leash to bite the General's boots. Owen shouted and the beaters departed by another gate. The guns moved away and their voices fell until they were no lower than whispers; they moved and separated until they stood each with his loader by a stick bearing a name on a piece of card. They stood, and the steep woods in the farthest corner of the estate were silent.

The General was below Thwaite; he lit his pipe and waited. He could shoot Thwaite and ease his hatred of young men, when Thwaite would be dead and he still standing on two white shining legs; but it was too late to help his damned promotion. He could shoot Thwaite's dog which sat looking into the wood, but that would be ill-mannered; he looked at his boots from Poxy's. The guests felt their moustaches, and there was a sound of crackling fire around them. The General hissed past his pipe, and hated them; but he was not so young as Thwaite.

Cam-Vaughan felt his loader look at his shoulder-blades. But everything was in order. The gate was in good condition in the hedges before him; the hedge was well-laid; there were birds in the wood, beaters to shift them, guns to shoot them. He did not turn to look at the man. The beaters knew their way in the wood, they were all poachers; the man behind him was a poacher, he held the second gun as if to shoot at close range. His feet sank in the soft ground and he thought a little; of Owen's face, of the beaters, of the General's hatred of Thwaite; he stopped thinking—Thwaite's dog looked into the wood and his nose twitched.

There was a distant tapping like the beaks of birds hitting stone. As it came nearer there were shouts. Pheasants scuffled in the dead leaves. They broke from the cover rocketing and screeching into the air, the beaters yelling and waving their sticks among the trees, breaking small branches. The veteran General shot, not at Thwaite but in the air; many birds came over. Thwaite shot, Cam-Vaughan shot. The three guests lowered their moustaches on their guns and brought down each other's birds. The beaters came nearer the edge of the wood. Cam-Vaughan grudging his expensive birds, angry that as host he must stand in the worst place, killed birds on the wing at impossible distances. Thwaite was firing, not in fear of the General, but waiting, looking for Owen's face among the tree-trunks. The General, forgetting honour, shot dangerously at low-flying birds. As they fired and the birds fell, and the loaders handed the hot guns as the excitement of the dogs mounted and the beaters approached the final flushing, Thwaite thought of the loyalty of servants (disturbed by Owen's face) of the butler's pantries and emblazoned houses.

Cam-Vaughan shooting the bird of the man next to him had no time for regret.

Out among the crowded pheasants floated little balloons. The General shot and one exploded; Thwaite heard the beaters laughing in the wood. More balloons came out from among the trees, yellow balloons and green. The General shot another (he was short-sighted it seemed) and his own loader laughed. The General turned and exclaimed. Thwaite heard Owen calling in his high Welsh voice. When the beaters appeared on the edge of the wood, guns and beaters stood still; they stood still and regarded one another. Thwaite's dog walked away from him and whined. Then the General raised his gun and fired; there was nothing else to do. Quickly the loaders ran into the wood and joined the beaters; some of these produced guns from down their trousers.

"They're armed, the swine!" cried Cam-Vaughan, and he too fired.

The three guests fell on their faces and began shooting into the wood. The General lay on the ground bellowing orders at the air from habit; Thwaite went up an oak tree and fired at both sides impartially; a shot-gun wound at ten yards is a nasty thing.

There could be but one result. The beaters came out and beat the wounded with their sticks till they died. Thwaite sat up in his tree like a capercailzie and grinned when he saw Owen slit Cam-Vaughan's throat. Then as the beaters and loaders went noisily away, as the dead turned on their faces in their own blood he came down from the tree. He collected his dog and watched them get into the abandoned brake.

There was a car left and he followed them.

At the brass gates of Parc Gweledigaethau-Sais Owen saluted the few villagers and they acknowledged his salute. Along the drive of the rolling park they drove singing *Swspan fach* and Thwaite followed three hundred yards behind. The villagers walked into the park after his car and closed the gate. The brake drove on, up to the distant house, and the butler took Owen's victorious arm to lead him through the leaden entrance-doors. The beaters stood around the brake stamping their cold feet on the gravel and on the brick stairway; then they followed Owen in and shut the door. Thwaite stopped his car by a thicket in the great rolling park, and urging his dog into it began to shoot the rabbits which ran out.

Constable's Ruin

Sipping his beer in the Saloon Bar, (they say he's a poet, though he dressed then like a Bangor student), his burning tongue is plain in his head.

The mirror opposite is clustered with gold and letters; they spell whiskey. In the poet's head is his tongue like a flame in a tube of brass. He says, "Crish! Crish!" and his tongue traces in the puddles of spilled beer before him.

"Crish an' Golflake, there's conflagration!"

He opens his mouth, his tongue is a little flame between the swollen lips; the constable watches fascinated the little flame.

"In Tiger Bay," he says, "Must be from Tiger Bay; flaming tongues and whores with three legs, anything you like in Tiger Bay."

Thwaite leaned forward in his mackintosh, put his elbow in the puddle of beer.

"Is there no bloody bore of a retired sailor here?" he said. "Is there no bloody bore of a sailor here to tell us of Tiger Bay?"

"I can tell you," said the constable. "Were you never in Tiger Bay?"

"We want a shailor," said the poet.

The little men at the bar with their big hats and the big men with their feet squarely on the ground, the young men with their scarves looking at themselves in the mirrors, and the spruce smart bottles in their military rows, all are immovable in drinking-hours; never moving they stand in drinking-hours like the spruce smart bottles in their military rows.

Talk is on the air, already Thwaite is brave, powerful, witty, lascivious.

"Too far inland for a sailor," said the constable. "Let me tell you about Tiger Bay."

"I was at Shea," says the poet, "Shea two years. When I was sixteen."

"You're always sixteen," said Thwaite. "Prodigy of sixteen publishes poems. New poet of sixteen publishes second book. Always sixteen, always new."

"Crish," said the poet, "Crish you bloody Welshman!"

"This is the man," said Thwaite, "acclaimed in U.S.A. and abuses his own kind. Welsh poet of sixteen staggers with Cymric thunderbolts. He staggers, we applaud. O bitter benighted bloody Welshman! Your own kind doesn't know you."

"Shorry," said the poet.

He was shorry, the constable told Thwaite;

"Take it back about bloody."

"He takes it back about bloody."

"Welsh as you are."

"Welsh as you are," said the constable, "And me, too!"

"If you make your living out of being Welsh," said Thwaite the moralist, "You can't bloody us in our own pubs."

"You don't make your living at all," said the poet.

"I think you gentlemen are looking for a sailor;" this was a young man with a scarf tearing himself from the mirror.

"Doesn't he make his living?" asked the constable.

"No gentlemen here," the poet said, "All bloody bums;" and he banged his square hand in the puddle of beer, splashing them.

"If you gentlemen are looking for a sailor," said the young man with the scarf, the tweed overcoat, and the oiled wavy hair, "I'm a sailor."

Thwaite pulled a silk handkerchief from his sleeve and wiped beer from his face: he intoned

"You're looking for a sailor
and the sailors are looking for you."

"Make a note of that, my good poet. For your twenty-sixth poem."

The poet mumbled, "Given it up, sh'all bloody good," into his beer glass with a hollow sound; he was trying to lift the glass between his teeth and drink from it.

"Is he writing his twenty-sixth poem?" asked the constable.

"Wait till he opens his mouth," Thwaite said to the sailor, "And you see his little tongue."

He opened his mouth and the glass and the beer fell on the constable's coat.

"I see little flames like that in Tiger Bay," said the sailor, "And whores with three legs."

"Nice man," Thwaite said, "He helps us out."

"He was listening behind my chair. He'sh not a shailor."

"Quiet!" Thwaite cried. "Now sailor, have a drink, yes, have a drink on me!"

"Can't you fraternize with me?" the constable asked.

"We've fraternized with you," the poet said, "We fraternize with you, then we go home and we know all about conshtables."

"Very useful for a writer."

"Thanks, I'll have a grapefruit," said the sailor.

"Of course, I don't always know what you gentlemen mean," the constable said, "Like now. A bit uncomfortable. Though when I'm with you, gentlemen..."

"In Tiger Bay," the sailor said, "Boys are brought into the world on the run. Not belly first, like here. And the docks jammed up with constables jumping in the docks after the people drowning."

"They all say the same thing," the constable said, "'Just going for a swim, officer!' But we don't believe that... I got a life-saving medal."

"Quite right," said the sailor, "Boys running come into the world up the hill and the unemployed dive out of it into the docks; that's where the law steps in to restore the balance."

He was making an excellent impression on the constable who put a large ruddy hand on his thigh: "You see it in the right way," he said.

"Crish! You've got bloody evening-dress on," exclaimed the poet.

"I am going to a function," Thwaite said.

"An' he'sh told us nothing about Tiger Bay: he ishn't a shailor... I know a shailor."

"You ought to have a girl," the constable said, "A nice girl for a nice sailor."

"I don't like girls. Girls are vulgar," said the sailor.

"Girl'sh a' bloody vulgar! raucous voices and fat arshesh, piping voishesh an' thin arshesh, fat breast thin breash. All bloody vulgar!"

The constable ordered another round of drinks and the three men took their elbows from the puddle of beer, checking the level of beer in the glasses as it was drawn. It was the thin Welsh bitter, the worst beer in the world. The pub is new: the town, Port Harlot, port of the county of Cariad.

"Girls are a wire stretched across the road, Trip, and you fall on them," Thwaite said.

"Knock all the wind out of them," said the constable, "Then you can do what you like. They never tell on a policeman."

"Sounds a bit rough to me," the sailor said.

"And that bloody bore of a shailor," cried the poet, "Who tells us no shailor's stories."

"Fraternity is sterile," Thwaite said. "A melancholy duty."

"You're in bloody evening-dress."

"I am going to a function."

"It's great to hear you gentlemen talk," said the constable. "Like a play: you ought to be a footballer with shoulders like yours."

"It's my overcoat," said Thwaite, "all padded out."

"I've got a pot-belly," said the poet, "And isht full o' beer."

They rose together, the door drifted toward them and let them out into the night. The sailor straightened his scarf before the mirror and went back to the motionless figures at the bar.

"Won't see him again," the constable said. "Wonder what he came up to us for."

"He wanted to tell shailor stories, but I wouldn't lishen," the poet said.

"Well constable, going home?" Thwaite asked.

"Oh, no, I'll stick along with you gentlemen for a while."

"I am going to a function, of course," Thwaite said.

"What a pity," the constable laughed, "If I was in my uniform, I could come too, couldn't I?"

"No," Thwaite said.

All the straight way lay before them where they could go down among the dark houses, look into the black water of the sea under the wharves; which they could follow out into the dark lanes and hedges of the country.

The poet fell over a woman, a woman lying on her face in the road and the poet fell over her.

"Sh'drunk," he said, and put his finger to his nose.

"Oh pick her up," Thwaite cried, "If she has been run over..."

"No blood on her at all," said the constable. "But pick her up."

"Sh'drunk," said the poet.

The constable looked down at the girl and at her legs under her skirt and at the edge of her thighs where the skirt had gone up above her knees:

"Nice bit of fun we could have up a back street," he said.

"Sh'drunk," said the poet, "No fun if sh'drunk."

The constable nudged Thwaite. "That's the way," he said, "Have them and push them: nice opportunity too."

"What about your great wife?" the poet asked him. "Haven't you a great wife at home?"

The constable's honest face grinned under his honest trilby hat.

"Well what an honest fellow he is!" Thwaite cried. "Good old constable off-duty, takes his honest pint, smokes his honest pipe, doesn't mind a bit of honest slap up the lane, perhaps; but then back to the old woman that's served twenty years!" and he slapped the constable on his broad honest back.

"No good picking her up if sh' drunk," said the poet.

Thwaite stooped and picked up the girl's face, with the trickle of mascara coursing out of her eyes on to her cheek.

"Why can't you be an honest fellow like the constable?" Thwaite asked the poet.

"I've got friends in Cardiff," the poet answered, "Cardiff toughs too: contacsh with the people."

Thwaite got the girl sitting up, and she put her arms round his neck.

"Been beastly drunk," she murmured.

"Gin, I wouldn't be surprised," the constable said. "You gentlemen are fine gentlemen, lots of fellows might take advantage of a girl in her condition, but not you gentlemen."

"Who shaid?" cried the poet: "She wouldn't tell on a policeman?"

Thwaite got the girl on her feet, and she put an arm round the poet's neck.

"Take her off! Take her off!" the poet yelled. And the three of them swayed, the drunk woman swaying between them like a lay figure, and the constable laughing respectfully at the gentlemen out of his honest red face.

Already they are at the door of the Bear; the gentlemen put the girl on the sill of the window of a fruit-shop and she was sick again.

"Missed a good opportunity there," said the constable.

In the bar of the Bear are uniforms, men pleased with their uniforms who look with contempt at the civilians that come in. They do not take off their hats, for without a hat no man can be a soldier.

"Th'eternal sholdier," said the poet.

Now one of them came over in his uniform and asked what the little man with the beer-belly said about a soldier; there is his ham-fist to shake under the small man's nose, and his four pals there to help.

"Thousands of years," Thwaite began, "We have cheered the soldier going out, have listened to the weary tales of the returned soldier. There are no bores like soldiers, no stories as old as soldiers' stories."

Now comes the one with the ham-fist to see what is being said about soldiers. Those with hats on and pleased with the uniform colour of their coats, are there to back him up.

The constable rises from his seat:

"I am a police-officer."

"Well what did he say about soldiers?"

"I am a police-officer," showing his police-card.

Two limbs of the State face each other; slowly, as is the habit of officials, one obeys the other. The soldier glares at the poet and goes back to the other soldiers.

"Bloody sholdier," said the poet, "Wanted to tell sholdier shtories. Like the sailor."

But there is a mirror on the wall and the letters on it spell whisky, and the sailor is combing his hair before it and looking at the people reflected in the mirror.

The pride of the soldiers was hurt, so they said: "Well you watch your step," loudly, so that they could be heard.

The sailor turned from his reflection in the mirror and smiled at the poet, but the poet snorted and gulped his drink; he wanted no admiration from sailors.

"Change to whisky," Thwaite said, and they had the warming melancholy fluid going down their throats and lying warm in their stomachs.

The sailor is dreaming of the beauty of scarves and pointed shining shoes. There is a dreaming man in the conversation, the one who listens to the words and who thinks of scarves and pointed shoes. And the poet and Thwaite and the constable sit in the bar semi-silent with cold feet and the dregs of beer dry on their lips and the whisky warm in them. The sailor is looking at them; the soldiers go out into the night with their hats on. Nobody speaks.

The drunk girl came in with her hair over her forehead and fell into a chair beside the poet and was asleep again.

"If I had my choice," the constable said, "I'd have a little bit like that. Not as she is now, of course, all plastered up, but long legs and fluffy hair though."

"I like 'em dark," Thwaite said, "Big breasts."

"Conshable talksh about women in shexshternal," said the poet. "I want a dark hormonic relation with a woman, deep whorled and twished."

"When you talk about women, your face is red and your eyes leer," Thwaite said to the constable.

"That's the man in me," the constable answered, "I'm still as good as my blood-pressure!"

Now they were all a little drunk and the sailor at the mirror could be drawn into talk. But the constable smiled on his two companions and patted their shoulders, and Thwaite could talk politics to the constable, or sex, or life itself. When you meet a policeman out of his uniform you are safe.

But the poet's speech became thicker, and his eyes watered, and his lips sagged and were covered with spit. He waved his hands with the scabs of disease on them. Thwaite thought of his function, and glowing with power and delight he stood up.

"Sh'in bloody evening-dress," screamed the poet, "I hate bloody Welsh snobs!"

"But I like to see a gentleman dressed as a gentleman," said the constable, and he stood up.

The sailor laughed and stood picking his teeth before the mirror.

"And what might you be laughing at?" said the large constable with his fists.

"Outside!" cried the proprietor, a bigger man again than the constable, "Don't care if you're a cop or what."

And they were hustled out while the sailor smiled.

Outside the door are three police; the poet opened his mouth and the flame of his tongue shone on their buttons.

"Shut that mouth," they said, "Bit of trouble in there."

"*Symbols of tongues and of crowns*, (cried the poet),
Staring sailors and girls we shape with our eyes,"

"There's a drunk in there, you'd better look."

When they had gone in eager, the constable said, "Narrow that; bit of a fool with my own boys."

"They didn't see you," Thwaite said.

From the bar came shouts and sound of blows as police throw

themselves on civilians. The three made swiftly down Neerdowell Street, towards the bad clubs.

"A scarlet lot we are," said Thwaite, and licked his lips as they came near to the bad clubs.

Delicious to be in Johnny's bad club in evening-dress! but with a policeman even out of his uniform, you are safe.

"Ah! I will foul my shoulders," Thwaite is thinking, "In the bad clubs of Port Harlot with the tarts and thieves and waiters off-duty, and then I will go to my function and my hand will sit on the backs of well-born young girls as I dance with them." But he turned up his coat-collar to hide his white tie.

In the poet's stomach mixed liquors turn. The constable links his two honest arms with the two gentlemen, and his honest face blushes with coursing liquor. I can take my pint with my pals, he thinks, but now I am with two gentlemen down the bad clubs: but I do not understand them and they might laugh at me: his right fist clenched as he thought of this.

The poet saw the ground rising and heaving under his feet.

From the arch of a shadow came the rags and the bones of a woman: "Buy a rose, buy a rose, gentlemen," even the constable is a gentleman to-night.

"Ex-tart, of course," said Thwaite.

"Red roses are class shymbols," the poet muttered, "No class here."

"Red blood is brown," said the woman, "When it is run out damn you. You may think you're bad now, but wait."

"We are a scarlet lot in our head," Thwaite cried; this will confound the woman, and such a good remark will awe the poet.

But the liquor in the poet's stomach jumps with a life of its own.

Down Neerdowell Street is long and the houses are of paper with torn doors and windows: here are disasters, monstrous tumours on the neck, burned children, screaming and shouting quarrels in the night; here all their nerves hang out like rags and great feet of police and doctor pass monotonously harking from house to house. Scarred houses of paper. In the sweetshop window was a bowl of goldfish as well. Oh, fish in your lonely bowl, who has scarred houses of paper? In the poet's brain is an ache and a sickness, lamp-posts crowd about him like shooting stars; and still the honest constable has the arms of the two gentlemen.

* * *

The travelling-circus is shut and the performers soak near-beer in the bad clubs. You open the door of Johnny's and they are sitting there, with tea-cups before them. Two youths with hats and shapely overcoats to play the penny-game: click! bang! and the balls run away down into the machine.

Johnny sits with a tough customer. The walls are pale green. Before a haggard mirror the sailor is picking his teeth.

Johnny came over to them... "Near-beer for you..." and they got the stuff from the still under the stairs in their tea-cups. Thwaite paid five shillings.

"You know," Johnny told them, spotting Thwaite's white tie, "Police have a great Easter ceremony. They all get drunk and play tambourines; pale-blue uniforms at Easter!" He laughed loudly and slapped the poet (who was the smallest) on the back so that he fell under the table.

The constable stood up and Thwaite thrust a chair between them so that Johnny fell down.

The circus performers came around them and one of them had roses round his throat like a cut windpipe.

"He'sh dead," said the poet from under the table, "And his cut throat showsh roseeesh."

Johnny is up and his shoulder clocks in, he does not fall but the constable.

Thwaite dragged the poet quickly out into the street, and soon the constable was thrown out after them; he was full of fight, but the door of Johnny's bad club was shut against him, and when he beat against it with great fists, Thwaite whispered how his own boys in blue were by the Town Hall, and how they would come and break the doors of Johnny's bad club in Neerdowell Street.

Police are blue syllables in his ear.

"Split damn and split you, but they will break you in soon!"

The boys at the penny-game groan together and mock him through the barred doors; click! bang! and the balls run away down into the machine.

The poet can hardly stand and he will be sick soon.

*   *   *

"I know a short cut here," said the constable. "By damn I was here often and we will get those boys and break him in, we will. Near broke the gentlemen's back ribs off, the great slob, he near broke them. And the gentleman looks ill now, he does look." The poet will be sick soon.

They scale a wall and fall, twined with rose-briars and the smashed remains of climbing plants. Thwaite climbs quickly back so that his ceremonial clothes will not suffer; he listens to the crashing tearing sound as the poet and the constable break a way through someone's garden, and then he steals off on tip-toe, hoping to escape them both. He bounces on oiled feet along the bland streets that lead from the Neerdowell Street to the rich centre of Port Harlot. To the rich centre where the merchant gentry of Co. Cariad have their fine offices and emblazoned windows.

He came up to the Town Hall entrance and it was thronged with respectful attendants; the red carpet was down, and in the corners of the hall palms wagged. The attendants bowed and took his coat, his silk muffler, his embroidered hat. With the distant music he advanced among the pots and the palms, the carpets, the ephemeral splendour.

But the constable, festooned with briars and roses, was beckoning to him from among the palms, and there was a rushing noise with detonations of the poet being sick, with him is the drunken girl, her arm around his neck; she is being sick too, and their vomits mingle among the roots of the palm.

Thwaite glanced at them and would have passed on, but the constable came heavily behind him and put a hand on his shoulder.

"Why did you not take the short cut? I arrest you," he said. "Let me arrest you for your own good. Gentlemen should be arrested for their own good; look at that poor gentleman and the young person with him."

The vomit flows in a violent stream from the poet's mouth, and it has extinguished the little flame of his tongue; the girl leans beside him but she has no more vomit and the spasms of her retching shake the roots of the palm.

"My good man," said Thwaite, "I am perfectly capable of avoiding my own friends; let go my shoulder. Oh my God!" for there at the end of the gilded passage was the sailor combing his hair and humming at himself in a mirror.

"Long legs and fluffy hair, though," said the constable. "All plastered up with the gentlemen. If you will not go quietly with me, I must come quietly with you."

And they go gently forward, Thwaite's shoulder twitching under the constable's hand.

They came near the sailor and heard his humming louder and the poet's retching fainter. His smiling reflection grew in the mirror, his hand moved smoothly with the comb over his hair. His humming blends with the throbbing dance music. Thwaite shrank back with twitching mouth but the constable propelled him on.

When they were abreast of the sailor, he smiled at Thwaite in the mirror; then, at once they were among the soft rustling dresses of the women, the bare powdered flesh, their tumbling sweet-smelling hair, the perfumes they have sprayed between their breasts.

Groomed, perfect bodies of women float in rich stuffs around them. The constable gasps like Moses and sees every imaginable gentleman in the county of Cariad; in black coats, in hunt coats, sober and intoxicated.

Thwaite got a creature by the downy waist whose chin fell away among the jewels on her throat, the dark fringe of whose eyes leaped among fluttering eyebrows, whose artificial mouth promised nothing, told nothing, withheld nothing.

"This is Lady Olga Fayre," said Thwaite, and the constable soothing the latticed wrinkles of his suit and wrenching the briars from the crook of his sleeves, took her in his arms and careered among the dancers.

Thwaite danced by himself in that glittering scented company; clasping an imaginary partner with great respect he gyrated among the family jewels and the hunt-club facings. The constable is charging with Lady Olga among the dancers; they cannot stop: her eyes are closed with the pleasure of this burly man: his breath comes in short gasps and he is near apoplexy.

Thwaite shrugged his shoulders and his friends fell away from him. A girl came to him but he passed her by, another and he trod on her foot, another and he slapped her (familiarly) on the bottom and took her round the waist and into the bar. Among the glittering bottles and the happy drunks, he would sit in sweet companionship with the listening woman. He has not seen her face, she need not speak: he need only tickle her thigh, and talk, and be happy.

He stretched out his legs, "Constable's ruined, I'm afraid," he began:—

*"Oh the police shall keep their places
And the favoured shall go free..."*

but his feet kick the poet who is lying under the table with the drunken girl, and he howls as the poet's teeth sink into his lower shin. Thickly the poet speaks through his mouthful of Thwaite's leg:—

*"Gray roses in chalk and sky
Poet bites snob
So in the headlines."*

Data on the Squirearchy

Now Thwaite at five years old seated on the pony by the ex-soldier, and the string from the small beast's muzzle to the ex-soldier's hand, which was at Gallipoli. Now the mother who sees her small son, and smiles through the glass window to see him on the pony. She smiles through the glass window and the pony and the ex-soldier walk down the drive and disappear behind the laurel bushes.

At fifteen there are no girls for Thwaite to see in the wide country round, except those he has seen at young folks' dances, (which are rare), and this is important when he thinks of them. He imagined that he would find a girl under a small tree in the wood, (and that is the same tree under which, uncomfortably on a slope, he lost his virginity at sixteen); that some dark-haired girl would have come to stay, to live, at a house near, and wander through the same wood as he, towards him. He made love by letter to a girl named Endurance, whom he saw once at a tennis-party: they were long letters with little love in them, but some was meant.

At five Thwaite had a nurse whom he kissed and who kissed him: the nurse had much rounded hair in buns and masses; when she kissed him, her hair had a smell and a feel like hair. Sometimes the ex-soldier kissed him, for he loved him: it happened that the ex-soldier would never have any children. Once the house-maid came and sat by Thwaite's bed and told him how slaves were flogged in the old days and how their backs bled.

Now Thwaite's mother looked through the glass window at the laurels and thought of him as her little boy on the pony. The ex-soldier is reliable: the pony trots, the ex-soldier runs, Thwaite bumps in the saddle and is afraid.

2

Raskolnikov-Jones is his neighbour and is still rich and wicked, yet Thwaite's father has now thirty acres out of the four thousand. Cam-Vaughan is another neighbour with huge resources. So Mr Thwaite's estate is a large house, a large yard, large stables, a large garden: two small fields, a small wood, some scrub. He walked with his second unnecessary servant to the broken fence. There were bottles and rabbit holes at his feet.

"It's down," he said, and the servant mumbled. There was no wire in the stables, no posts were cut, only twenty staples were in the box.

They remember him because the war has left a hole in his head and he limps: they remember Gallipoli and the Great War. Now Thwaite was fifteen and on holiday from school.

"I don't think much of Allsop," his father said, "You should keep off her."

("Why is my son with a girl at fifteen?")

"What did my father do before forty when he married?" Thwaite asks those whom he can ask.

Cam-Vaughan had a son, now in the Guards; at home this young man gave orders to the keeper (Owen) and they walked to the edge of the estate and looked at small holdings cut out of the farms Thwaite's father sold.

"In the Great War," one says of Mr Thwaite. "Piece out of his head. Very sad."

In Mr Thwaite's study there were rows of estate books and an estate map, but it is thirty acres now.

There is bone in that horse. Father Owen, of the Society of Jesus, says there is a wife in all ports. Neighbours eyed Owen and thought, a Roman Catholic, as if that were strange, which it was. Mrs Bound was furthest west in the discussion; has she not the first place in the small bourgeoisie of Llanpumpsaint?

Thwaite now had gone outside the tin shed where the Women's Institute were meeting, he strolled in the April evening as if he should meet the horse-coper's daughter. When one addresses the W.I. on My Travels On The Continent one sees Father Owen in the front row listening, and one sees the farmers' wives and the small bourgeoisie of Llanpumpsaint parish.

The young men are standing by the clock which is the War Memorial in the middle of the village; some have gone off into the lanes with girls, but they will pay for that.

In this northern village there were two lots longing, the one for the other. Under the memorial to Our Glorious Dead, carved names representing bones and unlived lives, the young men meet, and whistle and talk about girls.

The girls have their conversations too, but elsewhere. Thwaite met the horse-coper's daughter where she knelt picking a plant at the turn of the moon. Thwaite stood, she knelt, she leaped up with the plant in her hand and the division of her face was half a moon, part black, part shining. She panted and stood before Thwaite and they said nothing.

Father Owen has not taken the chair nor the stage, but Mrs Bound's daughter who gives them Lycidas; the Members are all broad and well-seated, not a sigh is heard to show that any of them comprehend the words. And Mrs Bound's daughter sat down by Father Owen with the round of applause and Father Owen congratulated her.

By-the-river is a forbidden place and a little boy (that is Thwaite at five-and-a-half to six) is there to paddle and catch minnows; approaching is an ex-officer on the farther bank, and Thwaite hides because this is a forbidden place. But the man had seen him and called: Thwaite answered that he was paddling, but he felt fear in his stomach and in his throat.

The minnows were in a muslin net, skipping on their silver bellies. It was half-past one and they were calling for him in the woods by the house. When women call it is like distant trains, and Thwaite, picking a minnow to bits with his nails and smelling the smell of dried river-mud on the pebbles, heard only distant trains. It was ten past two when he came home and they were waiting with long faces, as if they thought him a great sinner. (Do they *really* think one hour and ten minutes a great sin?) He feels fear in his throat and in his stomach. He is told how worried was his mother. He has been in the Garden. Not to the River. In the Garden. That is a lie. How long are their faces? How high up?

It is a lie. Now he is sorry. Lies make him sorry. They punish him for lies and their faces are long. He is in bed and hungry and the curtains keep out the bright sun. When they came in their faces were long as if they thought him a great sinner. He cried and was sad. Because of the lie? The faces?

He must not go to the River; if he goes he is punished. If he lies because he will be punished, he is punished. Meanwhile the ex-officer has rung up to say that Thwaite is by the river in a forbidden place. But he is in bed.

5

Mr Thwaite bent towards bottles at his feet and bills fell from his pocket and covered them. The servant set fire to them, for he was loyal: this is the loyalty of servants to burn the bills on the bottles.

When Mr Thwaite straightened he had a red face, but when he put his hand on the post of the fence this fell, for the wood was rotten. Now there are nettles in the paddock: if these are cut three times in one year they are rooted out, but these nettles grow again after the fourth cutting.

There was paint wanted for the stable doors; stables with grindstones, lime, wire, implements, and planks there, stabling for sixteen, without horses now. Cam-Vaughan's son was here for a call yesterday, and wore a Guard's tie. Thwaite talked up to him, and his father was silent as if his wound hurt him. This is the Army, Thwaite thought, Red-and-Blue tie, and big moustache.

Thwaite had a girl called Allsop to whom he telephoned, and Cam-Vaughan's son spoke kindly to him about polo and point-to-point; Mr Thwaite was silent and knew that he was poor. Now the fare has collapsed, but the servants' wages are paid: they went down to the woodshed, and there was nothing there but logs.

6

Father Owen talked to them of China and the missions; tea was had, tea brought by each, and bread-and-butter. The ladies of the *plasau* had paid for the cakes. A lady (that might be Mrs Vaughan-Thomas) rises and tells them: it is a good thing: there is exchange between the gentry (Mrs V.-T. and others) the farmers' wives and the small bourgeoisie of Llanpumpsaint.

Father Owen had Mrs Jerman to talk to, and she was confused, for she was never in conversation with a Roman Catholic priest. Father Owen is easy, and easy to talk with.

"There is bone in that horse," he talks to her of horses but she knows more of poultry and the subject is changed to poultry.

The horse-coper's daughter had the plant crushed against her throat, but Thwaite could not take her in his arms; the moon has turned, there is a full moon in each of her breasts, under her skirt... they are ready, she is ready, but Thwaite cannot embrace her. If they had stood gazing at each other in such silence, he would have embraced her after another minute but she spoke in a high voice, quiet, but nervous and high.

"Now this is undenominational," Mrs Bound said, "strictly."

"This," looking at Father Owen and the Non-Conformist ladies in the farthest corner from him.

It was an interesting lecture indeed, that Thwaite gives. The road from Darmstadt to Karlsruhe we found broad and wide. And Thwaite the only man with so many women, quite handsome he has grown up: Father Owen was there but he is a priest and counts as either. In Darmstadt there are houses and schloss, there is a pond in the park.

Thwaite thought that the precious minutes of spell would return, but those two stood near and talked quietly in high nervous voices. For Father Owen there was a tea-cup in his hand, smooth as the pond at Darmstadt, smooth as his own chin; for Mrs Vaughan-Thomas, Mrs Golos-Williams, Mrs Cam-Vaughan, Mrs Raskolnikov-Jones, there are farmers' wives' babies, children of the small bourgeoisie of Llanpumpsaint. These must be regulated.

Thwaite's hand was so near the horse-coper's daughter's hand that he could feel its warmth. Yes, a draught for the horses, several herbs. Why is so much resolution needed to move your arms round a girl? They have different accents, they have nothing to say. This is a northern town with a War Memorial where they are taught not to lust.

7

One Sunday the sun shines in his nursery where Thwaite (five and a half still) sat on his pot. A wooden train was near and the Just-So stories where the cat walks by itself down fore-shortened forest paths in the wood-cut. The ex-soldier lay in bed on Sunday morning looking at the ceiling in the cottage where he lodged, and a bell rang in a little church across the valley.

Thwaite's mother came and beamed at him on his pot for all was well. Later, when Thwaite put on his yellow jersey, the ex-soldier met his nurse in the lane to court her, and Thwaite went with his mother to the river to the forbidden place.

When the old dog fell in, when the old dog slipped in the water, his mother knelt, his mother was among the summer grasses to get him out. They saw a great pike in the still water below the willows. There were rats, moorhens, minnow, and the smell of dried river-mud. This was a great day, without fear or lies.

Thwaite held his mother's hand and hoped she would never die; when he thought of her dying he had a lump in his throat. The ex-officer from the farther bank has come to tea; his pale-blue eyes do not work together, but are independent, one at the floor and the other, if it likes, at the ceiling. He advised Thwaite to play cricket and not to row when he went to school. Thwaite's mother smiled, because this was all so far away.

At sixteen Thwaite went into the wood on Good Friday (after the Hour's Agony) with a tall woman older than he, and under a tree he knew, had a little joy. His mother wrote angrily in her diary that They went off all afternoon and were not seen! But this was Thwaite's own conquest made privately in the woman's bedroom, and she was not to blame as Thwaite's mother blamed her.

8

Mr Thwaite has forgotten Allsop and blames a tall woman older than his son, he cannot talk to the servant who knows much that Mr T. would like to know. They went down into the kitchen garden and Mr Thwaite cracked his head on the lintel of the greenhouse door because he was preoccupied; this was serious because of the hole in his head from the Great War, and he went to lie down.

They came up to him from Llanpumpsaint with complaints and documents to sign, but his head ached and the former estate map was a grid on which his eyes hung. Mr Thwaite was a J.P.; he had no money and his son cost two hundred pounds a year at school. The farmers who are richer than he and have more land, call him Sir. Mr Thwaite sits on committees to regulate the farmers' affairs and their taxes, and the farmers produce food from the land and grow rich and call him Sir.

Mr Thwaite has no money and thirty acres of land; he had a stable without horses, and an estate-carpenter's shop without a carpenter, a former-estate map without an estate; a cupboard-full of guns with which he shot over his former estate by the charity of the farmers, and they call him Sir.

All the oak has been cut, and five hundred acres of the former estate are a desert as if shells had dropped there: sheep feed in the shambles and rabbits, and the villagers pick chips for firewood. Mr Thwaite was in Burke's Landed Gentry, and he had thirty acres: the farmers had money in the Bank and called him Sir.

9

The ladies of the Women's Institute were never thought of except as clothed. Not William Etty himself would have dared visualize Mrs Bound unclothed. Except dead on the dissecting table it is not to be thought. Only medicals have seen the Women's Institute unclothed, and they removed veins from them and nervous systems.

Father Owen is concerned with clothing; the Non-Conformist Minister of Llanpumpsaint has come and has not been persuaded to meet Father Owen. It is an extraordinary situation. Who *brought* Father Owen?

Thwaite was walking round the tin shed to go in and take tea. The horse-coper's daughter had gone, with the crushed plants picked at the turning of the moon. Perhaps Father Owen came in a trunk with the tea.

There are groups now in the hall: Thwaite shook hands with each and was asked about Darmstadt and the broad wide road; he was thanked by Mrs Vaughan-Thomas in a very short speech.

The horse-coper's daughter passed the young men under the clock, though they whistled and called, they did not leave the safe Memorial to attack her.

Farmers' wives ask Thwaite and hope that he will fall in line: "What will you be doing, young Mr Thwaite?" and that hypocrite answers "Yes," though he has no idea. Some people do not consider that he takes after his father.

The young men under the clock have a story about the horse-coper's daughter, but there are no village-dances for a month... the young men guffaw. No Welsh is spoken at the Institute, all is sing-song English except the gentry, and Thwaite, and Father Owen, who have other accents. The two priests, Roman and Dissenter, are no magicians; their masks are smooth, not carved and painted; nor has Mrs Bound stood in the moonlight with a crushed herb on her chest.

The horse-coper's daughter was back in the cottage and boiled all the herbs together in a pot; this is a northern village where some magic is practised still. Mrs Vaughan-Thomas wished to go home and stop mixing the classes, but Father Owen thought smooth thoughts, smooth like his face.

Suddenly the Non-Conformist Minister came up to Father Owen and then walked by him, turning his shoulder as he passed. A group applauded: was not this part of the One and Only Scarlet Woman? There is no purple like pride, no scarlet like Rome.

Mrs Golos-Williams carried away Father Owen, who had noticed nothing: (it was *she* that brought him). The Methodist is a hero; Mrs Bound says, Now this is Undenominational, strictly, but she too has enjoyed the scene. Thwaite says a litany of the line... Settle down, Nothing like a Steady, Their own Fault.

Nobody has quarrelled, nobody has shouted.

Eve of Something Will Be Done in a Week

Breakfast is at nine, at ten it is finished; by eleven the lunch is ordered, by half-past two it is eaten. Brainwork needs less nourishment than farming. Brainwork in the country is not understood by farmers. If you live in a house in the country you need never see the farmers nor anyone else. This is Ty Drwg, Llangummy, and here lives Elizabeth Cramp-Sturgeon, spinster, writing a novel about wickedness.

She ate her breakfast and looked out of the window: woods blocked the sight of the fields around. Parks, the servant, came in with more hot water. Cramp, though she had waited five years to ask him if he were a gypsy, (he had a gypsy name and a gypsy face), grabbed him instead by the hem of his coat and drew him to her with her arm around him.

"Not here," said Parks, "Not now. The windows." But he stroked her hair.

"Let us go into the wood," said Cramp, "This afternoon, after lunch. After you have washed up."

"No," Parks said.

"But we haven't for a week, I want you! You must come."

"Is that an order?" Parks asked, and left the room.

Cramp rose and walked through the wooden halls of her house to the table where her papers were. She sat at the table and drew her novel to her; *And at evening,* she wrote, *when the sun went down in a glaze of aureole incumbency, Raskolnikov-Jones crept among the oaks outside the female SERVANT'S quarters, and gazed through the yellow lighted windows.*

This was the ninetieth day of her novel! And at the rate of five lines a day it progressed. When she had written this sentence she took up the daily paper and referred to the astrology section: with her own ephemeris she verified it, and disagreed. At three p.m. Mars was in trine to Venus, that could not be watch out for storms with relatives.

And through the yellow windows, Cramp wrote, *Raskolnikov-Jones saw the clad figure of Ella Williams dreaming of lust*; this she crossed out and wrote, *Thinking of her man. There was a portion of lust in his eyes and a large lust in his heart. For anyone with breasts and rounded hips there was lust.*

She had closed her eyes, for this was perhaps her whole work for the day.

Raskolnikov-Jones will now creep to the yellow window and tap: he has been days getting there. With his forty fathers and a pedigree from Adam, Raskolnikov-Jones the wicked Welsh Squire, with the purple stocks and the yellow-checked waistcoats, should now arise at the window and make the old sign. This was her creation in the county of Cariad.

But Raskolnikov-Jones did not approach the rounded form of Ella Williams; Cramp made to bring him to that brick window, but he would not. Instead Raskolnikov-Jones stood in the room with her and blew his nose.

"Where there is no more control, there is no more life," he said, "There is death. That is my personal view; but I am not the angel of death come to take you."

Cramp's eyes were still closed as she tried to force him to that yellow window.

"It is that creature I am sick of," said Raskolnikov-Jones. "Too long contemplation is the slayer of lust, and I am a dead man in that respect."

"Man," said Cramp, and she opened her eyes.

When there is a squire alone in the room with you, your heart changes: a woman in the countryside is like a tree in a wood with others near but not touching. Cramp noted this thought among her memorandum, and turned to Raskolnikov-Jones.

"That girl's your mark," she said, "Go after her."

He blew his nose again. "I told you. She's a common little thing," he said.

"Many are the pleasures of coarse mouths and hairy legs," said Cramp.

"Then I have my pleasure," he said, and advanced on her, leering. Cramp took up her pen, and Raskolnikov-Jones raised a hand to the yellow window.

"It's not my will," he said, "I doubt if you have the right."

With his free hand he stroked the softer hairs above the collar of her jumper.

"You could use that hand for better things," Cramp said, and already he is opening the window of Ella Williams' room.

With his free hand Raskolnikov-Jones took up Cramp's other pen. *Elizabeth Cramp-Sturgeon stretched herself lasciviously upon an embroidered couch.*

"It is not true," said Cramp, covering herself with an embroidered rug: "Is not the Welsh Squire noted in every novel for his lechery? Is he not known as The Stallion in the villages of Wales?"

"What maid is safe from me?" asked Raskolnikov-Jones, "With my gold watch-chain and my violet stock, with my thousand acres and my fare to London?"

"The philosophy should be implicit in action," said Cramp, "Not clumsily expressed in words: for so my key to novels tells me."

And Elizabeth, wrote Raskolnikov-Jones, *Turned on her curved side with a liquid glance of her green eyes and her lips were parted as if the south-wind-of-love blew in or out of them.*

It was Ella Williams, Cramp wrote, *Who drew the Squire to her in tempestuous embrace.*

There was silence in the room, Cramp fanned herself with her unfinished novel, and the sweat of her desire was as steam, 'The trees lean together but do not touch,' stood written among her memoranda,

"For such," cried Cramp aloud, "Is the life of a gentlewoman"; and she looked at the portrait of her grandfather with the coat of arms in the corner, and was glad.

For the honour of her family she made this note, 'Control the characters in my novels, or ring for Parks,' for only so would her straight body be preserved for secret sin, and the scandal avoided. There are miniatures, near the fire, of her great-uncles in the Army and Navy, and she was glad she had done this for them. When one has sixty-four ancestors in the fourth degree, it seems a little thing to do for them.

Parks came in with coal for her fire, and she clutched him:

"Parks," she said, "Sin there is in Wales; attracted to each other are sinful bodies."

She talked the raw rich dialect of her novel so that Parks should know her simplicity and warm to her.

"You are a long time over that book," he said, "I must go now; there's the bell."

When he had shut the door, and Cramp had looked after him: "It is true. Shall I ever finish? Shall I never see my name in the *Sunday Times*? Shall I never meet Mr Charles Morgan and Mr Richard Hughes?" And she determined to do a great day's work, for it is by effort and hard work that masterpieces are made, and write ten lines.

In their sticky embrace were the Squire and the maid. Oh! how her frame warmed to him, Oh! How her body's rapture would serve him in a minute-and-a-half.

"I will not be party to this seduction," said Raskolnikov-Jones. "With her mother living at my drive gate. A great compensation and a great scandal would be mine."

"You cannot argue," said Cramp. "The destiny of the body is urgent and will not be denied."

"Don't quote from your own work," said Raskolnikov-Jones, "I should know it."

And Elizabeth Cramp-Sturgeon, he wrote, (for now both his hands were free), *gave up her novel for a life of uninterrupted sin.*

"I have had enough girls," he said, "In the first hundred pages to know my way about."

And when she was practised in sin, he wrote, *She had no more wish to write.*

Cramp is firmly seated on her two haunches, her two feet squarely grip the ground. With a practised hand she writes, *Raskolnikov-Jones threw Ella Williams to the bed, but the peasant's muscles thrilled to the occasion, and she threw him to the floor. His stock torn, his waistcoat burst, his left hip severely bruised, purple in the face from approaching apoplexy, Raskolnikov-Jones raised his head to the bed's level.*

"A truce," he muttered, and wrote: *In a first novel of exceptional promise, this competent novelist draws her characters competently with a pleasing competence, there is nothing here to offend the most susceptible, and in the sweet simplicity of her story there is something to tickle the most jaded palate.*

Cramp turned and seized him by the torn stock, "Fame! Fame!" she cried.

Elizabeth, wrote Raskolnikov-Jones quickly, *had surrendered to him completely; desperately her hard hands tore at his garments.*

"In seduction, as in everything, psychology is better than violence," he said.

Cramp tore away from him, and ran through the sounding halls of her house; and the boards sprang under her feet, and little fragments of plaster fell from the walls and ceiling.

And in the kitchen Parks said to the domestic, "There's the old stick running in the house again."

She ran in her heavy shoes through the wooden halls of her house until the gong sounded, calling her panting and sweating to her lunch.

"Parks," she said, "At once afterwards. Don't worry about the washing-up."

Parks considered the inconvenience, "Why don't you get a man?" he asked, "One of your own sort?"

"Show me a man!" cried Cramp: "Show me a man! Effete are men, degenerate; women are virile, men do not want us. I need you…"

"For my strong fresh blood," said Parks.

"Parks, are you a gypsy?"

"Me a gypsy? My father was from Wolverhampton."

"But now, Parks, at once, under the trees."

"Finish your lunch," he said, "And I'll be along."

Cramp bolted down her food and fled under the trees.

Trees are apart, leaning together but not touching. They grow slower than men. Man is peace and quiet for women. To this lonely woman, Man is her will-o'-the wisp.

Raskolnikov-Jones stood behind her in a clean stock and another waistcoat: "Quits here," he said, "No pen, no paper."

Cramp looked at her creation and blushed for the lechery of his eyes, for the lust of his mouth, for his whoring ramping life, for his guile at the Quarter Sessions, for his trickery on the County Council.

"Aha," he said, "Aha. There is space between the trees; if couples are here we shall see them. Passionate couples we shall see."

Cramp turned from him and settled on her broad feet; she took a sharp stone from the ground and scratched on the bark of a tree. But she could not write.

Under the trees Parks came with Ella Williams.

"Aha," said Raskolnikov-Jones, "A passionate couple. A man and a young girl."

"Do you know her?" Cramp asked in a voice of bitterness.

"I do," said Raskolnikov-Jones, "No compensation will I pay now. I will have no peasant embraces but a gentlewoman."

"Never!" said Cramp, but her guard was low and her mind was preoccupied. "There goes my strong man. Where shall I find a man now?"

"We will go over to them," said Raskolnikov-Jones, and took her by the hand.

"Parks," she said, "What are you doing here now?"

Raskolnikov-Jones grinned at Ella as if he knew her forever.

"You gave me the day off," Parks said, and put his arm round the girl.

"What if I discharge you?" Cramp asked.

"I shall go."

And he took his girl deeper into the wood, without speaking a word to her or her to him.

"And now..." Cramp said.

"And now," Raskolnikov-Jones said, "You will come with me? What is your fortune now? We are old enough to be practical, not young things to fly into the wood."

"We must count the cost," Cramp said.

"We must be sharp and wary," he said. "Come now, how much is it?"

And she told him the rough amount, concealing some details. "It is not bad," he said, "I have my fare to London, too."

So speaking of farms, and the interest on property, they went into the house, and when he had closed the doors and was out of sight of the windows, Raskolnikov-Jones took her in his practised embrace. This design of Nature being done, they sat speaking of their families, he of how the Raskolnikovs went to the attic and the Jones to Adam, she of the Sturgeons who went to the sea.

"There are the miniatures of my great-uncles," she said, "in the Army and Navy."

"Honour to them," he said, "And here," (slapping his head), "Are the trees and the pedigrees of my body, honour to them, too."

"And for your honour," he went on, "And for mine there shall be no literature in the family; no ignominious pursuits shall shame those sixty-four ancestors in the fourth degree, for though every man has just that number, few are they who can show no talent in their line. Wipe this," (and he waved the unfinished novel like a banner), "Unworthy evidence from your bland escutcheon. It is a little thing to do," he said, "For my honour and for yours."

Her mouth sore from his kisses, her bones aching from his lust, Elizabeth Cramp-Sturgeon took up her sinful novel and committed it to the flames. And in the black smoke that arose, Raskolnikov-Jones himself went up until he reached the ceiling and disappeared as smoke disappears.

And Elizabeth Cramp-Sturgeon was left alone, and from the wood that blocked the sight of the fields around, went up an exceedingly bitter cry as Parks was robbed of the body he was possessing.

Then Elizabeth Cramp-Sturgeon began to run through the sounding halls of her house, and she ran until in the evening she fell from exhaustion and lay sobbing and sweating on the boards of the sounding halls of her house.

Flaming Tortoises

The Master, pink upon a green lawn, was to be presented with a presentation for services to the hunters. They, going on booted feet towards a buffet and port and cherry-brandy, congratulated those who had made this fine spring day. Plas Parrott has no lawn big enough for a lawn meet, but to-day it must do; and the horses of the Mochyn Hunt are held in bunches under the neat Aracarian pine or monkey-puzzler, exactly before the yellow-brick facade of this neo-gentleman's house of *circa* 1890. Meantime the Master was not meeting upon the lawn but inside with the hunters and the drink, and the horses champed, jingled and stamped.

Through the balmy air of Cariad County the spring sun was to shine on the fineries of the Mochyn Hunt, and the natives, sons-of-bitches all, and other landworkers who had come to see sport, gently leaned their bikes against the railings which divided Plas Parrott from the king of England's highway in Wales: all too near for a gentleman's house, but Plas Parrott is dating from 1890 when land was dearer than before. While those with bikes watch the yellow frontage and the glimpses of the hunters at its pointed windows edged with purple brick, gay cars of ex-squires and rectors' daughters drive up, their mudguards fidgeting, their side-curtains flapping like inspired hens; and the eager red faces of those inside are seen for a moment through their leering wind-screens before they run inside to the company.

Not all are here: Cam-Vaughan, descendant of Welsh kings, hunts the Caucasian pheasant by permission of the English syndicate that owns his shoot, and not the Welsh fox; Raskolnikov-Jones is on the Board; Yr Arglwydd Jones is in New York signing a treaty so he thinks; the Earl of Mum is in Mum Castle. For all these absences many gentry are present, and those in riding outfits are gentry too, for is not to hunt to be a gentleman? And the near-squires of Cariad have spared no boot, hat, not startling pin: sleeker and plumper also are their horses' flanks than some lean nags tottering in the paddocks of more ancient families.

The tootling of the small hunting-horn shows that the spread inside the yellow house has had its effect. Those inside begin to come out, and first of them is the man with the purple face and a check waistcoat — Mr Daniel Puke, five days a week at his desk in Liverpool, but a jolly purple-faced squire on the sixth, and tootling a horn too. Puke's face is hidden from those on the road by the spikes of the Aracarian pine, but they can see his gorgeous lilac breeches blending nicely with the yellow front of Plas Parrott. Comments are made on the scene and more feet are seen under the branches. In the country there is always entertainment free; and when it is not the fun of Duffy's Fair and Moving Menagerie, it is a lawn meet on the grass in front of what would be quite a gentleman's residence if only it were further from the road.

At present there is a rearing and commotion among the horses, because only one groom has stayed from the free beer at the back, and the six horses of the field have been disturbed by Mr Puke's tootling, and by the rattling and backfiring of cars arriving; and are even more alarmed by the fierce shouts and commands of the hunters who rush towards them to calm the disturbance of the horses with oaths and loud curses. The groom is pulled in six directions, bridles snap, martingales are strained; the horses snort, eyes roll, legs quiver, front hooves do not touch the ground, the bit of lawn is destroyed under their hind hooves. The hunters seize the bridles and drag the alarming animals to that piece of ground known as the drive before the yellow house.

Mrs de Morgan stood in her habit on the step. She saw the struggle, added her hoarse cries to those which were to calm the horses; and now she marched, though habited, to the little man who held her bony beast, and gave him sixpence. This was wrong, since he was the owner of the house, her host, a member of the Mochyn Hunt, a near-squire with a yellow *plas*, his name being O. McCraw. It was hard that his face should be so unknown in front of his own yellow house, but it is certain that Mrs de Morgan needed that sixpence more than he. Taking his muttering for thanks, she went on in her thick apron, leaving him to take the coin or give it to the horse: she swept the gravel with her habit, to stand by Major Wattle, M.F.H. during the presentation for his services.

The hounds were loosed in a cataract about the horses' feet, snarling, growling, biting scratching and lifting their legs: and Tom Bound the Whip, came round from the back wiping his mouth. All the hunters, except Major Wattle who had not yet appeared, cracked their whips and cried aloud to prevent disorder: horses reared and kicked, hounds yelled, and boys leaped the railings to hold horses' heads for sixpence and leave the hunters free hands for their business.

Soon most of the hounds were busy at their fleas, but three couple started a cat at the stucco wall by the greenhouse, and are away after it full cry. Whips cannot crack, nor throats curse, loud enough; nor can anything draw the crowd's gaze to Major Wattle M.F.H., who made this late entrance alone through the stained-glass front door, to be cheered for his services to the hunt, and even to walk towards the monkey-puzzler under an arch of crops. At the moment he appeared, Mr Puke was indeed tootling his horn, but not for him, and by mistake he has tootled the "gone away" and several more couple are over the wall, knocking down the small boys who were hanging on the sterns of the first three couple to balance them on the wall. Full of resource and beer, Tom Bound leaps on the nearest horse and clears the stucco wall, discovering, as he is unseated, that it was Mrs de Morgan's side-saddle he was sitting on. Thus Tom Bound is sitting on his seat among some cabbages, Mrs de Morgan's horse is cantering across O. McCraw's kitchen garden, and the hounds have treed the cat in a weeping-willow tree.

The Presentation speeches to Major Wattle began, and those old hounds who were deaf and did not hear Mr Puke's "gone away," or were busy with their fleas, or did not care, were marshalled in a correct manner about the M.F.H.'s boots. At last those hands were clapped which should have rewarded the M.F.H. when he appeared at the stained-glass front door. For fear of the hounds Mr Puke did not again tootle his horn; instead, he harmlessly smiled his purple smile. Mrs de Morgan is to introduce the M.F.H. to those who know him well, but she is cursing a groom and sending him to get her horse out of O. McCraw's kitchen garden; and all the hunters laughing and talking on the small lawn, does not top Tom Bound's hallooing and the cracks of his whip, as he whips the hounds off the cat in the weeping-willow.

Mrs de Morgan, whose apron had gone crooked and showed her stout knees, went back to Major Wattle's side and gets a smile back on her weathered face. Poor little McCraw had gone the back way into his yellow house to have a quiet nip; but his daughter, Daisy, stood in splendid hunting rig-out near Mr Puke's spotted son, and his wife had had the Liverpool limousine wheeled on to the narrow gravel so that she could preside at the presentation, only Mrs de Morgan was making a speech and the listeners had their backs to the Liverpool limousine. They would see it when they turned round. Though her face and Daisy's are known to some, poor O. McCraw's is not, since he is absent nearly all the time in Liverpool, making money for his wife and daughter to live in a yellow house in Wales.

"The old Mochyn Hunt..." said Mrs de Morgan, and here the relatives of ancient families in the crowd turned each to each to titter about the Mochyn, because of its history before, as a trencher-fed ragtag-and-screwtail lot of scrawny dogs, that raided the poor butchers all summer, and spent winter on the mountain followed by a riff-raff of small holders and other Welshmen, with sticks and guns and no horse among them. This was fifteen years before the present celebration, since when Wally Wattle, though careful with his money since Old Stink-o'Brass his grandfather brought it from Liverpool to be a Welsh squire with it from 1851, and bought out the Mostyn Morgans, which was how Moggy de Morgan's old father-in-law came to tack on a 'de' though he practised as a solicitor in Trallwm: Wally Wattle with the careful money from Liverpool, had done something towards turning the Mochyn Farmers Saturday Outing, into a pack for Gentry. Hence the pink coat on Wally Wattle, Puke's check waistcoat, and Tom Bound the paid Whip; also horns to tootle and the throwouts from the Llangibby and the Ystymcolwyn alongside the national screwtail all-purpose hounds. None of this was said by Mrs de Morgan, but by the hearers.

These, with the eccentric hats, looked at the smart near-squires and their polished horses, while these happy newcomers of thirty years back, and their sons and daughters, looked haughtily at the calm morning air. This is the legacy of cotton-booms, to breed near-squires in Wales, and build them yellow houses and check waistcoats.

Moggy de Morgan hoarsely finished her speech, hitches her apron to the front where it covers what it should cover, pushes back the bowler from her sweating weathered face. There is applause. It is Mr Puke's turn to speak. There is applause. "This is fine old sport," said Mr Puke, "Has been carried on here by a fine old Master." There is applause. Major Wattle has smiled ever since coming out through the stained-glass front door, and there he stands, a picturesque old-world figure in pink with all-purpose hounds scratching and growling round his boots, thus carrying out the wishes of his grandfather who settled in Cariad in 1851.

"And the greatest of these," said Mr Puke "Is Fox-hunting. It gives hay to the horses, fox to the hounds, sport to all, and a sporting chance to the fox"; there is applause. Mr Puke said, "The farmers..." all clapped here, "know better than any of us, though I am at present farming 250 acres and our good friend Mr McCraw 190 acres..." Here many asked who Mr McCraw was, since those present of old family with eccentric hats have nothing to farm but their kitchen gardens, and live on shares manipulated by the other half on bourses in Liverpool and elsewhere.

Mr Puke said, "Major Wattle has helped us to show what men are made of; and not like some M.F.H.'s I will not mention in the next county, we are proud to say we have never yet bagged a fox." A raucous kind of cheer rose at this from the rabble over the railings: "Never bagged a fox," Mr Puke repeated with his fine purple grin.

Wally Wattle who had not stopped smiling, nodded his head to say, "Yes, never."

"We never bagged a fox," said Mr Puke, "And so long as men are horses, and horses are horses, and farmers are foxes, I mean, the good old Mochyn hounds..." one of the riff-raff began a cheer for Wattle, or else some remark passed among them which raised a laughing cheer, for Major Wattle was one of that good breed, even though no older than 1851, which holds Wales together by owning her acres, hunting her foxes, and fraternizing with her farmers in the field. There was therefore a cheer for these good things, and Tom Bound whipped the last hound back over the stucco wall, and Mrs de Morgan's horse was led round from the back munching a cabbage.

Thwaite appeared along the road riding a camel. This, then, was what the locals with their better view of the road had cheered, for the buff beast was last seen in Duffy's Moving Menagerie on Thursday night, where it helped take the tickets in the big tent, and was afterwards banging a drum with its hind foot. Why is Thwaite riding a camel to hounds? Or does he mistake this presentation to the M.F.H. for a sort of gala? The gate is open, so the beast sways up the ten-yard avenue towards the yellow residence. The riff-raff are all cheering, but the horses smell the beast, dilate their nostrils, roll their eyes, set back their ears and rearing horribly, dangle the small boys from their bridles. The well-born owners of eccentric hats peer to see who is on the camel's back before they make up their minds. They see that it is Thwaite who was so drunk at the County Ball. Mr Puke is shouting, and Major Wattle has ceased to grin.

Some of the riff-raff believe that the camel is to be presented to Major Wattle for his services to hunting, but they cannot imagine why. Mr Puke, faced with something rather worse than a stampede after a cat, is about to use bad language like a real hunter: but while he composes a sentence that will shake but not outrage, Mrs de Morgan's bony nag, swallowing O. McCraw's cabbage whole, steps backward on his foot; so that he cannot swear but only cry "Oh! Oh!"

"What are you doing to my horse?" shouted Mrs de Morgan.

"Oh! Oh!"

Tom Bound is yelling at the hounds who run to escape the rearing horses' hooves, the small boys scream as they dangle, and in the narrow space under the Aracarian pine, the crowd backed as they roared at the camel and the frightened horses. Two hunters who had been rash enough to mount, were swept from the saddle and their faces scarified by the ugly tree; horses sat back on Mrs O. McCraw and her limousine and dented the body, but her daughter had gone into the shrubbery in spite of Thwaite who blew her a kiss as he came off the road.

Thwaite beat at the camel with a stick and the animal walked backwards with a sneering curling look. Major Wattle, bawling at last, his smile forgotten, bawls: "This is no flaming circus, Sir!"

"I can't get her to kneel," Thwaite called.

"This is no flaming circus."

"No flaming tortoise?"

And as the Major shouted "No!" the swirling hounds crashed against the back of his knees and he went down under all his old favourites. Thwaite beat at the camel's neck but still the beast went backwards: O. McCraw looking through his own window, saw the brute back into his greenhouse, and heard the horrid crash as the animal half sat on the broken glass and wrecked cinerarias and geraniums, then quickly it rose and kneeling almost unseated Thwaite.

A good rider, he remained seated on the hump, but Mr Puke, helping Major Wattle from under the hounds, shouts that it is an outrage. All give advice: some tell Thwaite to get down, some tell the camel to get up, some shout. Tom Bound is cracking his whip and some fool is blowing a horn. But the camel mistook a tub of hydrangeas for a big drum, and getting to his feet, banged at it with his front foot. Thwaite tried to stop this but the tub was inevitably split.

The horses were trying to get into the shrubbery away from the camel, but there Daisy McCraw was hiding her pretty face. Thwaite looked for her, and "Daisy about?" he asked O. McCraw as he ran out of the front door.

"I say, look at my plants."

"My god," said Thwaite looking aft, "I've cut my camel."

"Never mind your camel, look at my hydrangeas."

Filling a garden syringe with tarred spray, O. McCraw squirts it at the camel's rump: Camels cannot stand being tar-sprayed when they have been cut by glass, so the beast sneered and went down the avenue. Mr Puke shouted "Take that flaming circus out of here," as the camel reached the road.

"He said I said flaming tortoises," Major Wattle said, "Why the devil should I say anything so rum?" Puke did not hear.

Mrs de Morgan cried, "Blast it! Won't anyone give me a leg-up?"

The horses relaxed. Mrs de Morgan, mounted, pranced by the wrecked greenhouse: "Soon patch it up," she said, "Some glass, some nails, some wood."

"Some greenhouse," said poor O. McCraw.

"Mrs de Morgan," Puke called, "The presentation": and the ones on the lawn chattered cheerfully about the camel appearing at a lawn meet on such a small lawn. "Who does the house belong to?" they asked, looking at the yellow facade and the broken greenhouse, as if Mrs McCraw was not there in her dented limousine, and they regurgitating her poor husband's cherry-brandy.

The gauche rabble ran off down the road after the camel, rather than wait for the presentation they had come to see; but Mr Puke pushed Major Wattle into a centre place by the monkey-puzzler, and Major Wattle seeing this, began to smile again.

While the ancient cars raced their engines and the persons in them hiccupped gently cherry-brandy in little girks, Mr Puke made the presentation, saying: "And so in the name of all of you to whom the name of the old Mochyn Hunt is a name which stands for a sport which never grows old, so will we hope to see Major Wattle with us for a long time to come, and are going to present him in token with this fine inlaid leather saddle-bag, so that while he is with us he may never be without a bag while he is…" Tom Bound seeing that the speech was ending, urged the hounds to the road with shouts that even deaf hounds could hear.

"Mrs de Morgan," called Puke, "Where is the saddle-bag?"

"It's a quarter to twelve," she said hoarsely, and trotted after Tom Bound who was taking the hounds through the few farmers on stout cobs who had kept on the road outside the premises of the gentry.

It seemed that Puke and Major Wattle would be left alone. Puke shook the Major's hand: "Well, congratulations," he said, and pushed the Major towards his horse. As Puke hoisted himself, Daisy McCraw came out of the shrubbery: "All clear," Puke said with rather a cold nod, and it seemed that Mrs McCraw had had her limousine drive on and was following the field. Mr Puke trotted to the road with his heels and elbows stuck jovially out, and Major Wattle followed rather slower, because this was the last day he was to ride as Master, and a sad day for one who had done so much for hunting. Someone had mounted Daisy's horse, because it was not there. Maybe it was Knock, the groom. She hoisted her boots over the railing and clattered along the road towards the hunt. Her mother called out of the limousine, "Where's your 'orse, Daisy?"

"I don't know, Mums."

"Well get in 'ere," said Mrs McCraw holding open the door, "You don't want people to see you clattering along the road in that rig-out."

At a hound jog, the field is moving off; but Mrs McCraw's limousine cannot get through the bikes on the road. Ahead of the bikes, strode several persons in tweeds and heavy boots, and beyond these again can be seen the rumps of the field, some shaggy as a bull's tail, and belonging clearly to locals, but others, like the Pukes and Major Wattle's, as shining as a groom's arm can make them.

"Several people got their faces cut by that monkey-puzzle," said Mrs McCraw, "I must tell Oswald to cut it down; to 'ave it cut down."

"It was that awful camel," said her daughter.

"I never 'eard of people turning up to the 'ounds on a camel."

There is a hold-up on the road; "What's 'appened?" asked Mrs McCraw in the limousine, but Tom Bound is casting the hounds into the covert on the far side. The field is, of course, halted on a steep slope, for on the ground covered by the Mochyn Hunt, a run is the hunter running and dragging his horse up a steep slope, and sliding with him on his rump, down the other side. The hunters cannot sit comfortably on this hillside lane, since the forepart of their horse is higher than the rear: but they endure it. Major Wattle wishes to be at the front where the Master should be, and he attacked the rumps of the field calling, "Thank you! Thank you!" and "Thank you master!"; his voice was thus heard for the first time since he was about to make a speech of thanks for but was interrupted by Thwaite coming on a camel, and said 'flaming tortoises,' or 'circuses' instead. Mr Puke is behind him, shouting "thank you Master" even louder, since he is the secretary and must be by the M.F.H.'s side. Mrs McCraw in the limousine, said to her daughter, "Mr Puke says thank you master, because Major Wattle's the master."

"I know," said Daisy, and looking out of the window, "Where the hell's Knock with my horse?"

"Don't use strong expressions," said her mother, "He's somewhere, bound to be."

The people in tweeds and honourable hats said "SSSh!" because of the fox.

"There," said Mrs McCraw, "See what you've done?"

The covert must have a fox in it, since it is the nearest covert to the meet, and because it is wasting the time of hunters who have to be in Liverpool on a Monday to hang about all day Saturday waiting for a fox; and because it is for the foxhunter to help the farmer by riding over his land to keep the fox down. Therefore it would not be fair to the farmers to leave a fox in this covert, which for some reason is called Cloddia-llwch.

The fox is not yet in it though; Tom Bound is having trouble with a man, he waves his arms and signals to a man who hurries along under the hedge to the far end of the covert with a wagging jumping bag on his back. Many of the hounds were already in, nosing after rabbits, and their noble sterns waved above the briars, others, including the Llangibby and the Ystymcolwyn throwouts, lifted their legs and bit their fleas. The otter hounds are seemingly out for a day's sport too, since many of the pack have that villainous shaggy look known as a Welsh hound, and will hunt anything from sheep to field-mice, aniseed or otters. The hounds know well enough how many foxes there are in this place, and this racket is kept up with tooting of horns and hunting cries, to keep the field their right side away from the work: but the hounds flatter the bawling man on a horse, by giving small squeaks when a briar tears their tattered ear, and the ancients outside, snarl and lift their legs to show their keenness.

Tom Bound's tic-tac caused the man with the bag to break into a trot. But he is not only half an hour late, he is too late. Two of the ancient battered hounds lift their scarred muzzles; they give tongue: they start their old joints across the field at the man with the bag, and Bound's whip and cursing only sends the others faster. Younger hounds leave their rabbiting and break cover into the field. Bound saw some object swaying along over the hedge behind the man. It was Thwaite's head under its bowler hat. Every hound was in full cry. Making the best of it Tom Bound blew the 'gone away,' and down the wet lane towards the field in the lane behind the covert, slides Thwaite on the infernal camel. Horses rear back on the gentry in their tweeds, the gentry beat at horses with their sticks, but are knocked aside into the bank. A loud shriek comes through the covert in a higher key than Bound or hound. "It bit the hand that bagged it!" Thwaite cried in his joy, and in a fury Mr Puke and Major Wattle shouted "Gone away!"

It was now true, since all the horses were going helter-skelter away from the camel, and in the field the man with the bag has loosed the fox a bare ten yards before he would have been like a Welsh Actaeon torn for smelling like a fox, instead of having his hand bitten by the fox. He holds his hand and curses. Fox and hounds are through the hedge and down the sharp side of the dingle, and Bound's horse has broken the first fence of the day, and the field are galloping down the lane in another direction away from the camel.

For a moment at a loss, Thwaite raised his hat to Mrs McCraw in the limousine: "Once bitten, twice shy," he said.

"We can't turn the limousine," said Mrs McCraw, "Because of your camel."

"He won't back," Thwaite said.

"O, do go on Mums," Daisy called, wishing to find her horse.

"Is that Daisy?" Thwaite asked, raising his hat and not able to see, "I thought you were ahead, or is it astern, with the others."

"She's lost 'er 'orse," said Mrs McCraw, "Or rather, Knock has it."

Daisy could see the camel sneering down at the limousine's bonnet, Thwaite she could see up as far as his waist. He was not correctly dressed for the hunting field, since he had on loosely baggy trousers and Turkish slippers: his black skirted coat was better, and she was sure he had on a bowler hat; but he was riding on a camel.

"It isn't quite usual to come 'unting on camel?" Mrs McCraw said, "Shall you come in to tea after?"

"Sorry," said Thwaite, "But I have to get this thing back to Duffy by five."

The camel did not like the limousine, but it passed it in a rush and went off swaying down the lane. The music of the hounds was stationary as if they had treed the fox. "Drive on!" said Mrs McCraw to the chauffeur through the speaking-tube.

"Oh, Mums!" cried Daisy.

"The 'ounds," said her mother, "'Ave gone the opposite way from the 'unt."

Mrs de Morgan called hoarsely, "Forward here!" as she bounced on her bony horse ahead of the M.F.H. and spattered his head with mud, as he spattered those behind him. This part of the run was halted by a tarred gate, and the field slid and bumped till they halted in a tight crowd. "Thank you!" cried Major Wattle, but nobody could move. A man with his arm in some kind of an improvised sling, came out of the hedge and opened the gate with his good hand, there being fresh blood on the other. "Put some iodine on that," Mrs de Morgan shouted, since she is President of the Trallwm Red Cross, and galloped on with the M.F.H. close after her calling "Thank you!" The man got no iodine, but mud on his bitten hand as the field splashed through the gate. "There's gratitude," he said, and left it open.

The stationary music of the hounds in the dingle lured on the hunters. Drawing abreast of Mrs de Morgan, the M.F.H. cried, "Damned thundering flaming..."

"Are you speaking to me?"

"Camel!" he cried, and several farmers on shaggy beasts careered past him and cleared the hedge down into the dingle in fine style. "Pretty steep this," said Mr Puke slowing down his horse at the top of the field towards the fence.

"Saving the mare's wind," said his spotted son.

The M.F.H. and Mrs de Morgan are at a walk; others, on polished horses come slowly up behind. The M.F.H. thought, then took out his horn and blew a toot.

"Where'll we take it, Dad?" asked Puke's spotted son.

"I'd take a bit off there," said Puke, and brightly the lad leaped off his horse to pull the fence into position for passage.

"Take it down, don't break it down," said the M.F.H. and Mrs de Morgan, looking after those farmers said, "It's their own fences if they want to gallivant over them."

With a pull or so, young Puke had a good gap pulled in the hedge : "After you Master," said Puke, and the M.F.H.'s well-trained old-stager bore down steadily with his off and near fore till all was good and flat in the gap and anyone could walk through. "Damned thrusters," said the Major looking after the farmers when he was thus over the fence. "Will I put it back?" young Puke asked, wishing to do what was correct.

"No," said Mr Puke, "We might be coming back that way."

The better-mounted part of the field were now at the top of the sharp side of the dingle, but the pack had divided into those ancient hounds making music round a tree at the bottom, and the others who were not there. "Bound!" shouted the M.F.H. wishing to know how his hounds were being hunted but Bound was not within hail, and the wretched farmers were calling "Loo after her!" and jeering up at the tree as they went up the far side. It seemed some of the old ones would rather hunt a cat than anything. Leaping forward on his horse, young Puke would have cut a figure sliding down the sharp slope of the dingle, but his father dismounted: "Better take it easy on her forelegs," he said, and all followed his lead in leading their horses down into the dingle, except the M.F.H. and Mrs de Morgan who slid on ahead.

Now there was a new view-hallooing from the ridge, and against the sky they saw figures in hats and waving sticks, hounds, Tom Bound, and another horseman, who might have been Knock, on poor Daisy's mount. "View-halloo!" called the parties in hats, and "Gone away!"

"What the devil are they view-hallooing?" cried the Major, whose horse floundered in the stream at the bottom of the dingle, sunk in the dead leaves and slithered on rotting branches, "I can view nothing."

He was at the tree, and there was that damned cat, come, no one knew why, from Plas Parrott to the dingle. "Cats!" snorted the Major, and thrashed the old hounds with his whip till they yelled. The younger hounds and the otter hounds were on the skyline after the fox.

Somehow Mrs de Morgan and the farmers had made headway up the dingle. The M.F.H.'s horse slipped at every step, branches banged him on the head. "Better take it easy on her wind," Mr Puke advised, and the well-mounted ones having led their horses down one side of the dingle, now began to pull them up the other side. The Major's spurs sunk in rabbit holes, his horse trod on his heels: he goes one side of a tree and his horse goes the other, he is too old for this.

Up on the skyline there is no more view-hallooing. Panting, their flanks heaving, the hunters drag their horses out of the dingle on to the ridge. Everywhere around it is silent, except for the usual crowing and lowing of the countryside. But away on a distant hill, figures wave their arms. "Must be those wretched foot-followers," said

Mr Puke, "And if they'd have kept quiet..." then all see the hounds going up the side of another hill with Tom Bound's pink coat after them. "Nice going," said the M.F.H. and young Puke said, "Good Gad makes you feel good eh?"

The field cantered down a steep bank towards a level bog below, where they hoped to enjoy a real ventre-a-terre gallop after hounds half-a-mile or so ahead; but at the bottom was a fence so they had to turn aside until they found a lucky lane where they could gallop as quick as a gent out hunting. The M.F.H. had all the old hounds round him who treed the cat, and when he blew his horn the little cavalcade had that fine old appearance which is the backbone of rural life. As he blew his horn Major Wattle looked forward to galloping along lanes with his new silver inlaid bag, and Mr Puke smiled his purple smile.

The lane was not long level and started to go steeply up. The field jogged to save the horses, and hounds were far ahead still. The lane wound and bent by windy barns and sunk deep between its banks.

There is Mrs McCraw's limousine stationary in the lane between the high banks. "Thank you!" shouted the M.F.H. but there was argument inside it. Daisy was half out through the door and then her mother pulled her back. Daisy said, "Mum I'm damned well going to hunt properly. I want my horse." And her mother answered, "I won't 'ave you clattering across the mud in your good boots. Anyone'd think you was a foot-follower. And I won't 'ave you use strong expressions." "Oh Mum!" Daisy exclaimed, for many of the persons in eccentric hats were of the oldest Welsh family and eligible for anything. "Well," said her mother, "I mean, you wait. Because Knock's bound to be somewhere, and then you can 'ave a ride," she shook her daughter's arm, "And of course a lot of very nice peoples follows the 'ounds on foot, even if they 'ave got funny hats." Behind her head was a loud report, and Major Wattle was whipping the back of the limousine.

"Thank you!" he shouted.

"Drive on!" cried Mrs McCraw through her speaking-tube. "We're stuck," said the chauffeur. The wheels spun in the mud but the car stood still. Major Wattle heartily thrashed the hood. Daisy made for the door.

"Daisy!" cried Mrs McCraw, "Come back or I'll... he'll whip you!"

"I want my horse," she said, and jumped out. Then the limousine managed to move, while the horses were squeezing past it. "Keep it still!" Mr Puke shouted: and thinking the shouts were curses, Mrs McCraw held her hands to her ears till all were past. Ahead, Daisy slid and floundered in the mud. "Serve her right," said Mrs McCraw, "And 'oo is 'e to whip the back of our limousine when we could buy 'im up... well, no, perhaps we couldn't buy the Wattles"; and she plugged in the plug of her tube lest the chauffeur hear her.

One of the many small patches of gorse and briar which Welsh farmers cultivate so well, has caused a check. This helps all to catch up, but the M.F.H. and his party are separated by a fence from the hounds. Jumping is out of the question since the hedge is too well-set to break down. They canter through a gate, but ahead is a ditch where the farmer is growing his reeds and rushes for winter feed. "Steady," says Mr Puke and back they go to the lane. It is intolerable that the M.F.H. is separated from his hounds by hedges and ditches.

They cantered towards a farm: "Gate! Gate!" cries Mr Puke, and terrified children leaped the hedge to get out of the way; "Gate! Gate!" and his heavy horse slides into the gate. It falls down, and there in the farmyard is Thwaite's camel and the farmer's wife giving it a feed of hay. The horses press on because they cannot stop, though the riders pull hard on curb and snaffle.

The camel raised its head from the hay and gave a sneer. Young Puke's horse leaped sideways into a muck-heap, and only by horsemanship did young Puke hang on under its neck. "Don't let go!" shouted his father whose horse was backing into a hen-run, and against their will, the rest of the field were carried through a duck-pond when their horses bolted and off towards the check, wet but full of zest. Back across the pond, Major Wattle shouted, "Didn't I tell you this was no flaming circus, Sir?"

"I thought you said flaming tortoises," Thwaite answered.

Children yelled behind young Puke's horse, and away it went, leaving the poor lad on the muck.

"Look at my hen-house!" cried the farmer's wife, and beat at old Mr Puke with a broom.

"He shall pay, my good woman!" Puke shouted, and tried to point at Thwaite.

"Dam' hunters!" called the woman, "Would be all nice and quiet without you and your tam' trespass over our places!" Hens flew, dogs barked, geese cackled.

"If you don't mind my saying," said young Puke, getting up off the muck-heap, "It's not quite playing the game, that camel." But Mr Puke, bellowing above the hens, and his horse sliding on mangels and farm-tools, bawled, "He shall pay!"

"I'm sorry," Thwaite said, "But I've no change."

Away out of the covert crept the clever fox, but the parties in hats and the local rabble who had caught them up, saw, and voiced their view-halloos. They were all after him down the hedge where he ran, and clearing the bottom like antelopes they fell down into the next dingle where he went. Next came the active hounds distinguishing the scent among the many feet, which luckily was breast-high and so escaped the fee: then came Tom Bound on whom all depended, with the poor old hounds. The cunning fox ran down the stream, scenting only the water with his feet, but this did not deceive several old parties who had hunted the otters all summer, and who saw through the ruse. Now also came the turn of those otter hounds who ran with the pack masquerading as fox hounds, and happily they splashed downstream to show what they could do. Those who could see through the wood and the trees, saw the fox break from the brook, and lope like a small sinister dog up the green slope beyond. Once again they view-hallooed.

The otter hounds howled, the ancients pricked their old ears: Tom Bound blew his horn, and down on them, lathered and mucked, descended the famous farmers on their hairy beasts. "Boyoboyo!" they said, "Round the whole country, mun!" as if they had hunted another fox on their own. "Fox!" they cried, "Pluddy hare, mun!" Since the Mochyn pack has harriers and near-beagles in it, this had certainly happened.

Like chamois, the old squires' and parsons' daughters in their heirloom hats, leaped up the dingle side. Bellowing as if for blood, they topped the ridge and disappeared. Tom Bound and the farmers, racing neck-and-neck are out on the green slope beyond, and surely Knock is with them on Daisy's horse?

Along his own hedgerow, John Jerman, stout churchman, went with his lurcher Lady and a gun under his arm. Beyond the hedge is John Jones the Gwyllt's land, and it is there Lady is trained to run and turn the game back. Lady cocks her ears: something is running towards them in the lee of John Jones' hedge. There is of course, a sound of hounds in the parish, but John Jerman would never have thought to see a fox in front of the Mochyn. What runs towards him now is a fox. John Jerman tightened the loop of string which held stock to barrel. He fired. The fox fell. Lady and John Jerman leap the fence; they are on John Jones' land, but they snatch up the body.

"Why tam," said John Jerman, "What are those pluddy dogs doing?"

It looks as if the hounds will get the fox. John Jerman runs with it towards the lane. The hounds are in full cry. They are on him. They seize the brush, they trip John Jerman up and knock him down. And on his back the Mochyn Hunt killed, or rather ate in the open. Another few steps and they would have torn and eaten him too.

Tom Bound and the farmers came neck-and-neck across the field, Bound shouting "Worry! Worry! Worry!" while under the heaving pack John Jerman fought and cursed, but Lady ran away. Bound leaped from his horse into the kill. "Break him up!" he yelled, "Tear him up!" but there he found John Jerman.

"Tam' pluddy dogs," said Jerman, as Bound got him up.

The farmers roared, "What you at underneath, Johnny? What you on Jones the Gwyllt's with a gun, Johnny?" and John Jerman shook his fist.

"Worry, worry!" Bound cried, and grabbed a bit of the fox to show. The foot-followers are coming up, among them well-born daughters yelling for blood, but it is nearly all swallowed by the hounds. The M.F.H. and the Pukes came along the lane. "Killed eh?" said Wattle, "Worry, worry, worry, boys!"

"Broken him all up, Sir," said Bound.

"First rate run, Major," Puke said.

"Coming over, Sir?" Bound asked.

"Can't jump it, I suppose?" the M.F.H. said, with a little laugh. Mr Puke supposed not, so they got off and crawled through the thorny hedge.

To those around Puke said, "It gives great pleasure that on the Presentation Meet, the Old Mochyn Hunt…" here some old parties sneered, "Have done what we haven't often the luck to do, that is kill our fox, that is kill our fox in the open." Here John Jerman shouted "Hey!" but the farmers did not allow him to interfere, and many thought he called out, "Hear, hear!"

"It's my pluddy skin!" he said to the fellows.

"What's left of it," they jeered.

"So while men are hunting and hunting is foxes," said Mr Puke, "May we ever gallop behind someone like Major Wattle: though I hope we don't think there is anyone like him! in the fine tradition of this fine sport, which will be carried on next Saturday please note at our Hunt Ball at the Mochyn Memorial Hall, which is only half-a-crown to show this is a democratic hunt in keeping with our times and government." Here some applauded and some whistled.

A grinding and a sliding sound showed those who wished that Mrs McCraw was coming in her limousine to be in at the kill. "There," she said to Daisy who was in with her, "I told you we'd be up with the 'ounds when they killed."

"There's Knock," said Daisy, "Blast him," and leaped out of the car as her mother said, "Strong expressions," and put her hand up to her mouth as if she had hiccupped.

Daisy came through the hedge, and having mud all over her, including her face where the lipstick showed red in the mud, she must have followed the hard way, on foot in hunting-kit, till her mother caught her up. Knock had dismounted off the lathered horse: "Just warming her up for you Miss," he was going to say, but as she came at him, Mr Puck caught her: "Here's a little lady," he said, "A gallant little lady who flies all her fences," and he beamed his purple beaming grin above his bright waistcoat and the lilac breeches like a jovial highly-coloured squire; and Major Wattle grinned a red grin, and Puke's spotted son smiled, all of them at Daisy's round, muddy face and the lipstick in the middle of it. "Blood is right," Daisy said looking at Knock, but Puke held her, the M.F.H. began, "I only wanted to say," but Mr Puke had not done. "The gallant little lady has come to be blooded!" he cried, and snatching a piece of fox from Tom Bound he daubed it on her muddy cheeks. Mrs de Morgan shouted "Yoo-oy!" disturbing the daughters of squires and clergy as they licked their lips; and as she shouted she startled her horse into clearing the hedge from John Jerman's land, and she landed among them still in the saddle. "That was a near miss," she said, "I got caught in some damned wire: fellow should be shot," and really her habit was astonishingly torn.

"She must have sat on it," said the local rabble when someone helped her down.

Several local ladies ran to her, crying, "O, Moggy sit down!" offering tweed coats to hide her drawers.

The M.F.H. began to say what he wanted to say, and in the limousine Mrs McCraw said through the speaking-tube: "Sparks, you will be taking Miss Daisy to the County Ball in nine months time in the limousine, because young Mr Thwaite 'as kindly invited 'er. 'E's a very nice young man when 'e came down off 'is camel. So you'll drive Miss Daisy to the dinner-party at Thwaite Hall next December the 28th, I think; don't forget."

"Yes, Mum."

"I 'ad thought of not letting 'er go to the Mochyn 'Unt Dance as I 'ear it's only 'alf-a-crown, and in a Village 'All, isn't it, Sparks?"

"Mixed Mum. Farmers and so on."

"Are you going Sparks?"

"Not at 'alf-a-crown, Mum."

The M.F.H. went on and thanked all, even the farmers and other locals, but people began shouting and pointing and there on that high earthwork, Castell Twmp, Thwaite was seen running on foot after his camel. It was clear that he had been thrown by the beast and was chasing it over the prehistorical fortress. The camel was running towards a stampeding lot of cattle, which was galloping away from it.

Major Wattle said, "Serve the young beggar right." John Jerman grinned and nudged his neighbours, since they were Jones the Gwyllt's cattle and would probably break their legs in rabbits' holes now.

Mr Puke said, "If that fellow comes to the Mochyn Hunt Dance, I shall personally see he does not get in."

"Like a damned circus," said the M.F.H.

"And I'll advise Mrs McCraw not to let him take her daughter either."

"Wonder how he'll catch that beast," said Mrs de Morgan, now done up behind in coats, "If he hasn't a lassoo." All laughed: and joking in their various ways, though united by the sport, all moved to the lane; the rabble laughing at the camel, the hunters at Thwaite, the farmers at the 'kill' in the open, the ladies at Mrs de Morgan behind, and the Major and Puke laughingly pushing through the hedge to their horses. "Congratulations Master," said Puke, and they both laughed.

"You can wash it off at 'ome," said Mrs McCraw to Daisy, meaning what was on her face, "I'm sure that young fellow's too busy to notice now." Mrs McCraw gave the order through the tube to put the limousine in gear, and the Mochyn Hunt moved home after a fine day's kill and sport in the open air.

Generous Patrons

A monstrous fête, an effort of the Reco-ordination Council, which those who are always ready to stand by while others labour for charity, said might well be its death-rattle; or at best a case of *mus parturiunt montes*, was to be held on several acres of Lord Jones' Stud Farm. To help the fête, the Stud Farm was put up for auction during the preceding weeks to get it out of the way, and everything disposed of and the men given their notice. To those critics who said the Lord Jones Stud had only come into operation two years ago with a fanfare of almost Reco-ordination size about the public services its owner would be doing improving the county's cattle, and that to sell it was a rich man's whim and was throwing men out of work, it was pointed out how the men would be absorbed by the gangs of levellers with steam-shovels and other modern equipment, at present levelling the hillocks of the ex-Stud Farm, and building concrete public lavatories and concrete rostrums for speeches to be made from. *The Mid-Wales Advertiser* took two columns telling its readers they would not have to walk uphill at the fête owing to Lord Jones' magnanimity in having the little hills removed.

Meantime other Reco-ordination activities came to something of a halt, while every one braced themselves for the fête. Even those ignorant persons who do not hear what their public men are telling them, knew that there had already that year been an unusual amount of Charity. That is, in addition to a record number of Whist Drives, Dry and Wet Dances, Bowling Tournaments, White Elephant and Rummage Sales, there had been the not-unnoticed Weeks of Hope,

Baby Weeks, Mothers' Union Weeks, Rabbit Weeks, and also Reco-ordination Weeks. It would be too much to claim that a long word like "Reco-ordination" was on everybody's lips, though it was in all the papers every week; but sums of money came in from all these functions, and after the usual deductions, were forwarded in English and Welsh and sometimes in postage stamps, to the Secretary at Lord Jones' seat, Plas Mangel, Llanmangel.

This being Wales and not quite England, culture was not neglected. All were agog for the Massed Festivals (Reco-ordination) to be held at Llanmangel. The high spot was the performance by the massed brass and silver bands of the whole county accompanying massed choirs from every village, specially augmented by five hundred Boy Scouts, of Mendelssohn's Elijah. As a *bonne bouche* the North Wales Philharmonic was to play a few items, specially conducted by Sir Mark Bending.

Great men are there to be stared at and Rhys had made up his mind to watch the rehearsal at Llanmangel, even though his mother could not imagine why any one wanted to hear the same piece played through several times, possibly incorrectly. At the last minute his father refused to let him drive the car, so he had the choice of crawling in the ignominious train to Llanmangel or being driven by Pella. This sprang from rumours of Rhys being drunk at a dance some time ago, and shaving the gatepost coming home. So they bowled along with Pella at the wheel, Rhys not saying a word because of the unpleasant scene he had had with his father on the doorstep. He sat fuming and burning, and thinking how unpleasant Pella looked in the daylight; but as his parents owned the car, what could he do?

He remarked that the conductor was Sir Mark Bending. Pella agreed, and the talk lapsed. For the fiftieth time he decided, looking at her out of the corner of his eye, that her nose was too big, and that under her tweeds she appeared to have no breasts at all. She simply did not do. Also her expression was serious, and agreed with fathers who will not let their sons drive their cars.

Without any excuse whatever she asked:

"When are you going to find something to do?"

Rhys jumped and clutched the seat. At least he had expected to be left alone on this subject by Pella.

He said, "It's not my fault. You needn't think I like being stuck here."

Pella said, "You'd like it less being stuck in an office. I only meant you'll find it dull doing nothing."

Rhys saw how impossible it would be to explain to this woman how his father drove him frantic over the car, and that his mother was an extremely aggravating woman, since they had probably put Pella up to this. As usual when cornered he had to name some profession.

"Rather thought of being... secretary to a film company," he said, not having thought of it till that moment.

"Bud knows some people in that line," Pella said.

Thinking of Bud's gold watch and suede shoes, Rhys asks what Bud did. "Nothing at the moment," Pella said rather stiffly.

Thinking it better not to keep sarcastic silence in case the talk came back to him, Rhys asked:

"And Abe?"

"Well," said Pella, "Abe was in the Birmingham Police."

It seemed better not to ask why he wasn't there now.

"But of course his people are rolling in money," Pella said. "It was rather funny about Abe and Grizel, wasn't it?" she went on after a pause. Rhys had noticed nothing funny except that Grizel was fat and had a loud voice.

"You remember," Pella said with a soft smile. "The night we played sardines?" Rhys remembered being jammed up against Bud Harness, who smelt of sweat and eau-de-Cologne. "Well, Grizel and Abe were behind you and Bud in the trunk cupboard." She paused, still smiling. Rhys waited. "Abe said afterwards he barely escaped with his pants."

"Who?" Rhys asked.

Pella looked a little cross. "Grizel, you fool!" she said; then smiling again. "Abe said when he went, 'After all, why should one write to the week-end girl?'"

Rhys asked, "What did Grizel say?"

"He didn't say it to her, you fool!" Then Pella began to smile again.

Rhys wondered what they all did in the trunk cupboard. He felt a sour dislike for all of them. And he should have remembered to give a loud sophisticated laugh at the end of the anecdote. What a fool he was ever to have thought of kissing that bony sophisticated face, or holding one of those sinewy hands. He wanted to burst out against his father, but for whom he would be holding that steering-wheel, but now he felt equally irritated with his mother, who had obviously told Pella to pry into what he was going to do. Therefore, if like a fool on the night of the play he'd tried to kiss her, he'd have been in a nice foolish mess by now. He could just hear his mother's remarks about it. And Pella was certainly not good-looking; she was too old.

If he didn't keep talking the next thing she would ask was why he wasn't kinder to his damned aggravating mother. So searching his brain, he brought out, "Jupiter Symphony, isn't it?" Meaning what was to be rehearsed. And of course Pella had to say, "I prefer the G minor." G minor what? Whose G minor? Rhys found he had forgotten the name of the composer of the Jupiter. However, Pella was well launched and if he listened he might hear it.

"The minuet's very delicate," she said, "and of course the finale… though my cup of tea is some of the horn passages in the second movement." Whose horns? What minuet? Whose second movement of what? "Mozart," she said, "always handles his horns so well." And Mozart was the missing name; he hung on to it. "You know the Horn Concerto, of course?"

"Yes," Rhys lied, wondering if it was not a G minor concerto or the second movement of a Horn Symphony, and if she was still on Mozart. "I like his Symphonies better than his Concertos," Rhys said, not sure whose symphonies, but hanging on to the Mozart straw.

Pella put on a face of acute pain. "Ogh!" she groaned. "Think of the A major; what about the Coronation? The B flat major piano?"

Rhys had never heard of a B flat major piano, so he said, "I'm sorry they're not doing Stravinsky's Petrouchka," taking care not to say Petrouchka's Stravinsky.

"Rather dated," Pella said, but Rhys was glad to have got the name right even if it was dated.

Then Pella began firing off names which for all he knew might be conductors, symphonies, or oil paintings. "Take Appollon Musagetes," she told him, and went on that his Pergolesi period had charm, but that his Bach period was dull. Rhys was now wandering among rose gardens of classical statues and pergolas. "Though in the Sonata," she went on, and this was equally Petrouchka's sonata; or Apollo's or the Pergola's, however the Pergola came in, "he had a very interesting way of making Bach ornaments into phrases..."

Rhys sank low in his seat and his eye searched the landscape through the windscreen for an answer, but saw there only sheep and fields; and now Bach had written the Pergola Sonata for Horns. "And Jeu des Cartes," she said, "has far more of the *timbre* of Mozart." Why on earth had she dragged in Mozart again? She was saying that something reminded her of Hindemith's treatment when Rhys thanked God they arrived at Llanmangel. "Pity we haven't got a score of the Jupiter," Pella said as they stopped by the aeroplane hangar where the rehearsal was. "I didn't know you were musical."

The hangar had been brought back by Evan Jones from some war, to be the nucleus of the abortive Evan Jones North Wales Air Scheme. Various things then showed the great man his scheme was twenty years too soon, and the hangar at Llanmangel became therefore a useful Memorial to his progressive idea. It had been renamed the Evan Jones Memorial Hangar and given a coat of tar. In what had been the green fields of the Lord Jones Stud they saw a mechanised corps at work preparing the soil for the fête and laying concrete foundation for various things.

They went into the hangar and across two acres of benches saw the North Wales Philharmonic, a decent body of amateurs, but looking like a cluster of little flies in the corner of the stage which owing to the construction of the hangar was 150 feet wide, but only 20 feet high. Although amateurs, the orchestra was making a fine volume of sound, and the man in shirt-sleeves waving his arms in front of them was clearly the great conductor.

They sat down on a bench, and Pella's trained sense helped her point out that the race between strings, brass and woodwind then going on marked the end of the first movement. Rhys hovered between movements by Bach, Mozart, and Petrouchka, but a damned yell from the conductor which topped everything, brought the North Wales up to a ragged halt. A flute finished last.

There was not that silence they had expected, broken only by the conductor's technical comments. While the flute was finishing, a loud parliamentary voice, which Rhys well recognised, reverberated round the hangar, and about thirty yards away there was Lord Jones dictating to a white-haired young man at his side. The dictation must have been going on obligato, all through the movement.

The conductor made some comment, but well above his voice came, "In the cause of international something, I have spared no something nor have I ever flagged in my something. Every thinking something is aware that the present day something is..." the resonance of his voice made some of the words indistinct, and it seemed the secretary put in a word, because Lord Jones called out, "I don't care if I've said it *thirty* times! I'll say it a hundred if necessary!" And the secretary bowed his head and scribbled.

Pella nudged Rhys. "The horns are playing cards," she said. She seemed unable to keep off the subject of horns.

"Second movement!" the conductor called, trying to raise his voice above Lord Jones' dictation.

"Hey! Hey! Hey!"

The conductor's back showed he did not wish to hear. "Hey, you, sir!" Some of the violins grinned, also the woodwind. The conductor raised his tired arms at the players, but Evan Jones called out:

"Ought to be slower and more resonant, I think!"

Very slowly the conductor turned his head, and said over his shoulder: "We are coming to the slow movement now," and would have got on with it, but Jones, having got the idea into his head, could only get it out again by crying, "Too fast! Too fast!" at every second bar, as if there was no one in the hangar but the conductor and himself.

Pretending not to hear, Sir Mark stopped them and turned again, holding his hand to his ear. "What is too fast, Lord Jones?" And the woodwind, seeing a joke in the making, began to grin.

"Oratorio should be taken at walking pace," said Evan Jones, "for sacred reverence."

"What Oratorio?"

The whole orchestra held their breath for as loud a laugh against Lord Jones as they could afford.

"Elisha, man!" Jones cried.

"Elisha?" Sir Mark nodded at the leader to include him in the joke, and came down to the edge of the rostrum. "Would you go so good as to *sing* us some of Elisha, Lord Jones?" This was so audacious that many people expected a catastrophic typhoon of rage, but Evan Jones clambered over several benches and shouted:

"My good sir, our taste here may not be the taste of the circles you move in, but the sacred oratorio of Elisha beats very near and dear to the hearts of Welshmen throughout the Empire." And standing on a bench he began to wave his arms and bawl: "Go—up—thou— BALDHEAD! That's music, sir, whatever they may think up in London!"

Putting out a hand for support and resting it on the head of the first violin, Sir Mark gasped out:

"There is no such oratorio... my good sir... there is no such... We are rehearsing the Symphony No. 41 in C major by Wolfgang Amadeus Mozart."

Here the audience imagined the intermezzo would end; and the first violin, too respectful to show that it was his head and not a knob under Sir Mark's twitching hand, hoped to be released. Lord Jones called out:

"Will you kindly let me know when you've finished practising, and are ready to begin 'Elisha'. It's a boyhood memory of mine." He smiled at the secretary, who smiled back.

"Mendelssohn's Eli*jah* will be undertaken this afternoon by several brass bands, augmented, so I am informed, by five hundred Boy Scouts."

"Very well, sir, that's what I asked you. Don't waste your time and ours."

As Sir Mark pivoted himself on the first violin, muttering "Baldhead," Jones threw after him in a parliamentary *basso buffo*, "Two of your fellows are playing cards, and I don't blame them."

Sir Mark made no comment. "Second movement!" he snarled. "*Cantabile! Forte piano!*" and bellowed up at the horns, who were stuffing the cards into them, "And you, *tenuto*, damn it!"

The movement began, but there was a hitch because some of the strings had forgotten their mutes. And when they had them on, Jones called out:

"What are those, sir? Singing mice?" The secretary laughed quite loudly, but Sir Mark took no notice.

Through the calm opening of the muted movement Jones was saying or dictating, "We stand on our own feet, we take off our hats to no one," meaning his hat, as he strode up and down a bench and his secretary followed as if uncertain what to do. Pella, who did not understand the local *mœurs*, asked, "Does that man own the conductor as well as the orchestra?"

"Only the orchestra," Rhys said. "At least he's its Patron." Pella, suddenly remembering "Reco-ordination," began to giggle. A number of people kept coming in to speak to Lord Jones, and throughout the slow movement could be heard, "Absolute rubbish—ferro-concrete or nothing—international justice—damned Bolsheviks—telegram to the Prime Minister——" — And, "Tell the Bishop I'll be there if I can!" showing how many and important were Jones' interests. "Bow! Bow!" he shouted, and as the conductor made a half-turn, "Not you, sir! Bow!" And Major Bow, the agent, came limping in an exhausted manner towards him. "Don't go, Bow," said Jones to Bow,

who was coming. "You'll have to go to Llanfihangel about cement...
wait a minute!"

Sir Mark laid down his baton and, turning, said: "It occurs to me,
sir, that there might be——"

But Jones interrupted with, "It occurs to me, sir, that we should
include a Welsh Symphony in the programme."

"What Welsh Symphony?"

"Any one. In my opinion this is a Welsh Festival of Music, and it
should have a Welsh Symphony."

"I am not aware that there is a—— of course there's time, you've
got all morning," Sir Mark simpered sarcastically.

"What's that little piece you're at now?"

"I have already explained that we are trying to rehearse a Symphony
by Mozart. Unfortunately not a Welshman but a German."

Lord Jones nearly knocked down his secretary and Major Bow.

"Good heavens, sir, are you out of your senses? There's no good
German but a dead German!"

"Mozart is dead," Sir Mark said. "He died 150 years ago." And
with a look that none of the orchestra dared face, raised his baton.
In spite of all interruptions they were at a passage near the end of the
movement where the horns scrape together in consecutive octaves.
No scraping was heard. "Horns!" called Sir Mark, and after his echo
died away the E flat clarinet said, "They went for their lunch, sir."

"Lunch!"

"Quite right," Jones said. "Must get mine too!" He waved at his
bystanders and they hurried away to get it.

"They missed their breakfast," said the E flat clarinet in a small
voice.

"In my opinion," Jones called out, "you are overworking the golden
goose; you've kept my lads here two hours."

"Perhaps you'd care to conduct your lads yourself?"

"Certainly. Any time. And if I were you, I should apologise to those
horns. Shake them by the hand." And as Sir Mark staggered to an
exit, Jones called after him, "A stitch in time saves nine don't forget!"

And to the orchestra, "Well, lads, what'll it be? Ta-ra-boomdeay or *Swspan fach*?"

There was a roar of joy at their patron's joke. "Or lunch," said Lord Jones, and as the orchestra threw down their instruments and rose happily to their feet, he saw Rhys and called, "Young Rhys, eh! Can't play the horn, can you? My regards to your good father. Have some lunch?"

"May I introduce—?" Rhys said, but moving at high speed Evan Jones went after Major Bow shouting some memorandum about cement.

The happy orchestra, whose salaries were assured by several noble patrons' names on their notepaper, ran like cheerful boys to lunch, beating each other, tripping up the slow and telling musical jokes. Everything possible was being done for them and their art: there was free soup, free cut off the joint, free veg in Lord Jones' servants' hall. No beer was provided, since Evan Jones was life-patron of the Royal Welsh Abstainers (Total), but there were jugs of chemical lemonade and fizz.

Although two footmen were stationed at the front door of Plas Mangel to see that the orchestra went round to the back door, Rhys and Pella should not have been pushed rather roughly down the steps by the men crying, "Band at the rear!" To Rhys' protest that he was an invited guest, the footmen replied that they did not care if he was a bass-drum. It was Pella who suggested that they should hide in the laurels till the footmen went in, which they did.

In some part of the building a series of hoots and yells showed that Lord Jones was inside, and as they warily went up to the front door, bells rang, feet sounded, orders were ordered and counter-ordered. "I thought we were going to have lunch?" Pella said.

"So we are," Rhys said. "My father's on the committee." He pressed the electric bell and received a severe electric shock which threw him on the ground. Pella laughed so much that she had to clutch the creeper. Rhys writhed on the ground and cursed. A young butler, who from his appearance was a failed B.D. from some Welsh theological college, opened the door, took in the scene, and slammed it shut again. Like a rolling greenhouse a limousine hissed down the drive, with Evan Jones gesticulating, and probably dictating, in the back.

Rhys, picking himself up, said, "You've got a dreadful laugh. If it wasn't for you, we'd have been let in." But Pella couldn't stop laughing, and was now pointing through a window.

"We can't get in," she said; "but he can't get out." And through the window Rhys saw Sir Mark Bending clawing at a door by which he was clearly locked in. It seemed that of the two great men, Evan Jones was the stronger.

Gothic Halls

In the gothic halls of Rhiwsaeson there was a blast from the ancestral trumpets, and the shields shook on the walls and the suits of armour clashed together, for John Belial was to be elected, was to go up to London to sit in the Parliament for the county of Cariad.

Like ferns in their pots his supporters sat about the room of John Belial mopping like ferns at the dew which fell from his decanters. The shields are plaster, bearing the arms of all the families in Wales with which John Belial is unconnected, and they are all the families of Wales; but the armour is good and was bought in Liverpool. Like ferns in their pots his supporters flourish in the halls of this proper Welsh landlord, and the Hon. Mrs Belial... for John has married among the nobility... pours out the decanters for them and the hearts of these Welshmen are glad.

With a bushel of true-blue-tory-ribbon in his button-hole, Cam-Vaughan, the rich and unambitious, descendant of Welsh kings and chairman of the English Conservative Association in Wales, caught up the threads of discourse, the backbone of argument! "Shall the county be given over to reform?" And from the potted princelings around came shouts of "No!"

"Social reform is for hotheads," said Cam-Vaughan.

Thwaite, who has been driving a car for the Blue Cause and giving lifts to Socialists in secret, took a large glassful from the decanter. It warmed him, it would improve his driving.

Relays of car-owning Conservatives came beaming into the room; others go out to take up the same work.

"Forty people I took to the Poll and beat off the Socialists with a boxspanner! Sixteen miles from the Poll, and they cannot vote now!"

"Ha! ha!" from the assembly.

And in Thwaite's view the bottles which surrounded these landed and landless squires were filled with roses, which sprouting twined in the hair and moustaches of the gentry, and when they spoke their mouths were filled with thorns.

"Distilled from the Roses," Thwaite read aloud from the label of a bottle near. "That grow along the banks of the River of Tongues where languages and speeches are invented among the stones that rumble under the flowing of the stream, and all are washed down to the sea."

"Mark my speech well," Cam-Vaughan was saying, "And do not interrupt me in Welsh"; the thorns caught among his teeth, "The agony of the great," he was saying, "We are the great and our agony is greatness."

But other squireens stood up by Cam-Vaughan and they were greater or had more or less money, or longer or shorter family-trees. They stretched up together and when one stretched an inch beyond another, the rest strained up above him until they were thin and drawn-out like dough.

Thwaite watered their feet with whiskey and tied them together with bunches of true-blue-tory-ribbon, exclaiming:

"Grow, squireens, grow up to hell."

And he went out, skating down the encaustic tiles of the passages like a fly on the water.

Cutting their knots and tearing away the clinging roses, the more normal squires embarked in their cars, emblazoned with the blue banners and blue slogans of BELIAL FOR CARIAD, BELIAL'S BETTER WAY TO WISDOM. Thwaite watched them as they hurtled in strange convoy, through a hole in the hedge:

"What is wisdom?" he said to the air, and the echo came back, "What is Belial?"

Belial is in the town of Trallwm which the Lord forgets on election-day, seated in a special room in the hall, a fine post-Victorian baroque, while the sons-of-bitches rave below for a result. The fair-haired girls sat at a green table and the votes rained down on them from cornucopias in the gilded roof: their hands were rough with the toil of counting and the shouting of the porters at the locked doors who bet on the result. And the poets in the streets were shouting their ballads in the ears of the sons-of-bitches: scurrilous lampoons on Belial and others.

The votes are thrown into baskets as they pour down... Belial's basket and one for the Socialist. In the lanes the squires were dashing in madness in their cars to the town of Trallwm; it seemed that they would kill anything in the road but they did not, for the law rests on squires. And the smoke rising from the sons-of-bitches, stained the facade of the hall and suffocated the sparrows that lodge under the eaves. This is the scene.

Flushed with pride and port, Belial strutted the passages like a bull, but there was Cam-Vaughan with thorns in his teeth and blood running from his mouth to his collar.

"The man of agony!" said Belial as a joke, and Cam-Vaughan's face twisted in a smile half-crucified on the wall.

"Think of your arse, man!" cried Belial, clapping him on the shoulder, "Of the power and the glory, etc. Smile!"

But Cam-Vaughan had his mouth full of thorns and Belial was menaced by the ticking of the clocks on the wall.

"Ticking," said Cam-Vaughan.

"They want oil," Belial said, and passed on. He cannot enter the room where the fair-haired girls are counting, etiquette forbids him to bet with the shouting porters at the door. He paced the passages in time with the ticking clocks.

We are in the main street awaiting the result. "By damn!" says one, "Old humbug!" another, "Off my foot, now! Will we raise a howl if the old bastard gets in!"

So is the will of the people milling in the main street, some of us drunk, all of us hot and excited. The last lie has been told on the platforms, the last canvassing jiggery-pokery done; now if the fair-haired girls at the green table are honest, there is no help till the result... and they are too tired to care.

And now a spark from a strictly-forbidden cigarette has fallen among the votes in Belial's basket, and the fire has run into the basket of John Evans, the Socialist, too. All the votes are burned. Dismayed the girls stamped on the flames lest the smell of the smoke reach the porter shouting outside; then they laughed, for this was the end of their labour.

According to the hallowed and time-honoured tradition no one can go into the room or come out of it, papers must be passed under the door. The girls giggled and made paper darts of the last votes falling through the cornucopias: in the grate they made a pile and called it Belial, they made another and called it John Evans and saw which burned the quickest.

They said, "Who shall we give it to?" and some said John Evans because he had a long moustache, others Belial because he is rich. But the moustache has it, and they write JOHN EVANS upon the sheet of Announcement; this is a pleasant end to all their labour and the girls dance and sing "Tipperary" when the sheet has gone under the door.

The porter takes the sheet to the Mayor who signs it, to the clerk who stamps it, to the Commissioner who folds it, to the Seasoner who opens it, to the Mayor who cries aloud the result from the balcony. Belial is sweating in his room.

John Evans has it. Boyo! do we shout and run about on each others' feet! Some of us lean in the pub doorways and take in the scene.

And John Evans follows his moustache out on to the balcony above the cheering and tells us how glad he is that the will of the people coincides with his. The girls who did the Will slip away to put their feet in hot water before the dance.

John Belial was dragged out to say that it was a good clean fight and no hard feeling; but his supporters had thorns in their mouths and ears and drank blood, and we sons-of-bitches below, hooted. And the poets were cheering in the streets and giving away free the unsold copies of their scurrilous ballads which were bought for a penny before.

Like bees in a swarm the pricked squires are off in their cars, and Johnny Evans, the Socialist, gives beer to his picked supporters out of party funds.

The fire has spread from the piles of votes to the rest of the building and when the Mayor and his officers have run screaming into the air and fallen on the stretched canvasses of the Fire Brigade below, the flames roar to the sky and the people cheer to see the Town Hall burn.

Back in his grey stuccoed halls, John Belial and the Hon. Mrs drew up bills of sale. The squires had gone home to bleed by their own fires and there was no celebration at Rhiwsaeson that night; the decanters lay stoppered on the sideboard. In Rhiwsaeson (built A.D. 1850) there were no ghosts to wail his defeat, nothing but wealth and John Belial.

"Now perhaps we can leave this dreadful place," said the Hon. Mrs "And you'll get in somewhere else. Barbarous people of Cariad!" Such is a wife's comfort.

Such was the sale of Rhiwsaeson in 20 lots, 4 cottages and 15 farms, commodious mansion in the gothic style. Genuine sideboards from the Paris Exhibition, 1859, organ from the Crystal Palace, 1868, 5-ton chandeliers from dismantled Chateau du Bonsoir, France; real marble staircase from dismantled Palazzo della Figa, Italy; coats-of-arms of principal extinct families of Wales, selection of useful armour. Such were the treasures piled in a marquee on the Rhiwsaeson lawns.

And the squires had crept like ants among the throng, and we sons-of-bitches from the Town of Trallwm were there to stare and see if we dared jeer. And we said, "O John Belial will not be at the breaking-up of his home for sentimental reasons;" but he was in a closet at the back of the marquee noting down what it fetched and checking-up.

And the sideboards were shown, twenty feet high and adorned with leaping lions, with angels, and with family trumpets, and genuine beds were shown warranted slept in since 1852, and pillars of statuary in soap-stone and marble, and five-ton chandeliers. But the people muttered and fingered the half-crowns in their pockets. In vain the auctioneer pleaded and put his case, in vain he patted the sideboards, the sons-of-bitches muttered and made no bids.

Stacked piles of 1860 Spode were shown, 197 pieces to a service, and bedroom utensils, and useful cast-iron hat-stands; pictures of life and death and resurrection and defeat copied from the best masters.

A parson bought a dictionary but there were no other bids.

John Belial bit his nails at the back of the marquee. He bit his pencil through. The muttering wounded him. The lack of bids pierced his heart.

He came out on to the rostrum, and they were all silent while he made his personal appeal. They saw there, he said, the vestiges of his poor home, the wretched remains which cruel circumstances obliged him to put before them (for everything of value had long been taken to his new house in his new constituency); He knew, he said, That he had not been a success among them, (a tear fell from his eye), but he had done his best.

Here Mr Belial was so moved that he was obliged to stand down; there was scarcely a dry eye amongst the audience. Choking with emotion the auctioneer turned his dim eye from sideboard to public.

Some generous spirit offered him a half-a-crown.

It was Thwaite.

For half-a-crown he had a sideboard 20 feet high, he had leaping figures of lions, and angels, and family trumpets.

Cam-Vaughan, generous soul, descendant of Welsh kings and chairman of the English Conservative Association in Wales, bought a chandelier.

"And who will buy Rhiwsaeson Hall, that princely residence?" asked the auctioneer with a reviving voice. An old and bent woman in rough tweed and country boots answered, "I will."

She was John Belial's aunt. She would buy the house of her fathers' since 1851.

"I was sorry to lose the sideboard," said Miss Belial, "But I have the useful armour and the coat of arms." Cam-Vaughan, royal and generous soul, presented her with his five-ton chandelier.

Touched by these moving scenes, the squires crept to their cars and drove guiltily away. The sons-of-bitches melted away to Trallwm, for fresh scenes of riot, for girls, for dancing and for drink. Thwaite went apart and sat thinking of his sideboard; the auctioneer had said he could build a yacht out of it.

John Belial sat adding up his figures, and was Five pounds to the good. Such was the sale of Rhiwsaeson, commodious mansion in the gothic style.

Homecoming

Coming back after a long time overseas, everything is very small and falling to bits. Especially the front gates of big houses with the manorial balls leaning off the posts towards the ditch. My car, by contrast, was very large and well held together, being well-made in the US and about thirty feet long.

Down in the village nothing stirred because it was ten o'clock in the morning, but the big house was not in earshot of the village and never had been. Nor had there been anything to hear about the big house since Mr Robert was sold up and that was the last of all of them. That is to say, there was an auction at Llwyn-y-brain for the carved-ivory inlaid-chippendale occasionals and the dirty, dark Dutch pictures: and I believe all Mr Robert rescued was a print of a laughing girl, and the *Death of Admiral Lord Nelson*, on glass, in red and yellow.

The rooks stayed. They cawed round the house, built their nests, did a shillingsworth of damage and eighteenpennorth of good, as ever. And in the church they bought the parish magazine under Mr Robert's uncle's cross from Flanders, decorated with a button or two from his coat: and this was Mr Robert's great grand-uncle's marble Admiral RN. 1809.

These are the humped green hills of Wales of which the exiles in Ohio, and beyond, think. Sound your hooter and try the gate, I said to myself. But there is no one to open it, and that sort of gate has a joke that if you blow on it it falls on you. The house, too, though I hope not.

The grand thing, I remembered, about Mr Robert's disgrace, is that no one knows what it was. Maybe I could ask in the village. But how do I ask in the village? Try asking.

"D'you... of course you'd remember Mr Robert, I mean young Mr Robert?"

O yes, they remember both Mr Robert, and Mrs Robert. And I remember Mrs Robert, too. Or do I? Or is she the old woman with the swollen leg and the bandage dropping down: and half a petticoat hanging down, and the heels of her shoes worn down, and a torn old fur coat worn down to the skin, and a feathered hat? Yes, she is.

When I was a little boy I dreamed of lawns and balustrades, lead statues and peacocks like Lord Mum has. Had. Mum's dead? Dead. My old father used to say he threw coal out of the window to stop the peacocks screeching at four o'clock in the morning. I well remember the coal in the scuttles year after year, for no one ever had a fire in their bedroom so no one used the coal but the cat.

I have an idea old Mr Robert shot.

"Old Mr Robert now, a good man with the gun now?"

"O ah," they'll say, "With the gun," and we know who was good with the gun.

Did young Mr Robert take after old Mr Robert?

No, he sold up and went.

Where?

Ah.

Coming home after a long time abroad I didn't expect to find the same old faces, though there was Morgan Watkin went into the Bear after eighteen years in Thibet and elsewhere and they said "I haven't seen you lately." If young Mr Robert went to Thibet, he went some time ago, because it was about the time I went that it happened.

Mum's a great loss, they said: the loss of the head of the tail. And Lord Jones, too, another loss for Wales: another madman the less for poor old Wales. All will long remember the schemes of Lord Jones and the fortunes of time and energy poured out on them, all will recollect the fantastic fetes of Lord Jones and the crop of arteriosclerosis which followed them among the weak. Few will find monuments of lasting worth left after him, for it was for the mountains of paper and cubic yards of wind that Lord Jones was loved. I well remember him in my poor old father's time, sprawling his stomach across our dinner table at Sunday supper, and my poor father struggling with his breeding and his collar whenever Lloyd George's name came up, and Lord Jones looking up to heaven whenever he spoke of God's anointed of the Welsh Nonconformists.

Mum was a different sort of Lord from Jones, since he looked like one. His heir killed himself out of a red racing car, the chorus-girl was, as usual, unhurt, and the title is extinct.

It was Mum up there in the Castle entertaining the Prime Minister, and our (Wales' too) ambassador to Tokyo, that helped us all to look down on the doctors in Trallwm, even when they bought our farms off us out of death and illness: and down too, on the bank managers and their red-haired daughters, and down on the poor, lean-chapped solicitors and their lean wives. And owing to Mum, we never saw the secondary school teachers, nor did a dissenting minister ever fumble at our tables.

Old Mrs Robert's dead, too, and after all the lingering on and patching the roof and patching their legs when they fell to bits through the bandages. This gate doesn't need paint, it needs a new gate. My father said a house is all right till the roof goes, and he should have known.

There was a time we came to dinner here, through this gate, before Mrs Robert's leg fell to pieces. My poor father and I came over in the old black car, and my poor mother stayed at home with cold. And there we sat like gentlemen before a plate of tough mutton, like gentlemen, without our bellies and elbows sprawling on the table before us.

"Idris is he?" said old Mr Robert, meaning my name, and young Mr Robert would have sniggered at me if he had been at home, which he wasn't.

Then there was some joke about Taffy was a thief because Idris was a Welshman, and very loud laughter from my father and old Mr Robert.

Then I half stood up, half screeched that our name being Brain we should live at Llwyn-y-brain, not somebody called Mr Robert.

And all the laughter stopped.

On the way home, my poor old father told me how Mr Robert was the grandson of the heiress of a black-toothed little lawyer who won Llwyn-y-brain at cards from somebody called Devereux Brain in 1790.

"Then whose is the carved stone coat of arms over the door?" I asked.

"Ours," said my poor old father.

I dare say the people at the Mill might remember about young Mr Robert. I came across the sale bill when I was home from school, and the Mill stuck in my mind since it was held in fief. I had some ideas then about leet courts, and hommagers, and manorial dovecots.

Seated in the sunlight under the pine trees by this decayed gate, into my mind floated a picture of me standing by my nurse's side in the dark by some gate, while she warded off a man with her right hand.

At another time she joked with me that I would one day come and see her in a Rolls-Royce and she would give me tea.

"That is another person I must see if she is alive. Old Hannah."

I had several times meant to come home in a large car, and I was at the gate in a large car. But not my gate.

My home was down in a hole, faced north. And is it now further down in the hole and used as a cow-house?

I do not know.

Nor have I yet asked anyone. There was no one on the road coming up, but an old man I did not know.

Driving up from the boat, the country looked small enough all set about with hedges; but there people on the roads and pigs and sheep and hens. But here all objects were half-size, and there was no one at all but this old man, and he had gone round the corner.

There are two ways of visiting my old home: one way is to stumble about the mud which was my poor mother's garden and about the forage where was our drawing-room floor. The other way is not to visit it.

When I was a boy they told me the Kingdom of Heaven was at

hand, and I left home. There followed a time of being in the world and round the world and through the mill and up the tree. Now follows the car thirty feet long and the trip to the home county.

Cariad.

I am not young Morris Williams went to America and patented his screw cutter and lives in luxury among the film girls. Nor am I Dicky Pugh became Professor at McGill. Nor poor Gwalchmai the Tailor's son who made God knows what wheels go round in Sidney.

No.

When I was a lad, and leaning on my red leather I looked at the fields and the pleasant shimmer that hung on them this morning, and I thought a farmer was the best sort of man and I wanted to be a farmer. Did they give me a farm? No. They laughed. And they put the money into Buenos Aires Pacific and Malayan Jungles, Ltd. And the roof fell in. But not till I'd gone and so I never had to listen to Mother thanking God my poor old father hadn't lived to see it.

I saw my poor old father into his yellow box and under the ground, and I didn't cry for him until I got drunk and fell down the cellar in Salt Lake City, where poor old Father bought a watch when he went round the world in two years. And I remembered his silver watch and I sat down in that cellar and wept.

Now if I had the house I could farm all the thirty acres on the finest principles of science. One old horse in a field by himself was the farming I remembered old Mr Robert doing. I might take them for a drink tonight and find out about young Mr Robert. But no one knows anything, and into the pub I see myself going and good fellowship going up the chimney. Did you ever walk into the pub at home when you were a boy and order drinks?

No.

Hannah.

I'm by her and holding her skirt, and all down the dark lane she beats a man with her hand and giggles: beats him off and I crouch down against her leg and clutch.

Hannah.

I don't expect to see much except an old face without any teeth, and grey hairs streaming about on top.

Where are the Hannah and I who picked oak apples in the August sun?

I cried because when I was five last summer had gone.

Mother clutched the radiator in church and looked out of the window in the hymn, and only brightened for the General Confession. We had "done those things we ought not to have done." We never went inside a chapel, but Hell burned with its flames a few feet below the grass of the fields. And I was afraid to dig a hole in case I should fall down into Hell.

Who told us?

It was in the air and the ground, coming from many pulpits out of earshot. Our mild Mr Bach preached of his duty to our neighbour, and the messages of Christmas and New Year.

I read of the old fellows like the Lloyds who had a tame parson in the house: a humble sort in a spotted coat down the back of it. And a pied harper with a white face and black eyes. My poor old father used to tell me about the Tenants Dinner at the Canal House every year when they brought the rents, and how they toasted his old father and sang songs.

"Ah," said my father, "The Banks give them no dinners, now they've changed their landlords for the Banks."

And every evening when Old Batty Trow brought up the *London Times* from the station, my poor father read it all through.

The old boy was sorry we never sent a Conservative to Parliament but a Liberal. I remember the time some of them sounded me, Idris Brain, about that same Parliament. Mr Robert was the sort, the young one, they'd have liked, but he was sold up first.

If I came back, what sort of men would I get about the place? It takes twenty-five years to make an 'old retainer'. And if I settle here in the sun, how about the young heiress in the bedroom, and the grooms to muck the stables out, and a man in a yellow waistcoat to look at people through the door? What about the girls in the village?

Or is the whole country empty? Away on the deserted fields what stirs but the little haze?

We had a theory that the land was finished, and I could always get my poor old father talking about all the families that had sold up in his lifetime, and their heirs drunk their peaceful way about the Empire in its service. Also he knew who was the grandson of a Liverpool merchant and a Manchester merchant, and who was in the merchant's house before him. We were all descended from Brochwell Ysgythrog, with the exception of the Lloyds, who sprang from Cunedda Wledig.

Mother used to say young Mr Robert had every natural advantage, and on top of it he was in the Guards for a time. It was never clear why he left. Then, it seemed that the Roberts would be in Llwyn-y-brain for ever: though it will be I suppose, the wheel of fortune if I am, and old Devereux Brain will be said to rejoice in his grave, though he's very dead and very gone.

My poor old father used to cut the laurels and tidy up the trees in the autumn, and he had one or two days a week in the season shooting with Lord Mum. Old Mr Robert had a few decent coverts where nothing lived but fat pheasants, till he turned it over to a syndicate. Then there was the County Council and every other sort of Council, and the Vestry Meeting and the Cricket Club.

Mother found plenty to do, she was so interested in other people. A man, I often thought, might build himself a replica of Blenheim Palace in the prairies.

No one seems to live here at all. And the gentle haze hovered. No one in the fields moved about the fields. No dogs barked, nor hens crowed nor crows cawed. "Hoot your horn man and open the gate and have a look where the Roberts lived and look at Devereux Brain's coat of arms if that's all that's left of him."

With very modern methods I could farm these bits of pasture, but I'd be cramped. On Committees I could not sit for ever. Nor on the Benches, sending the poor away to prison and discriminating according to the unreformed Law. Nor indeed, remembering the stations of everyman according to his neighbours' opinion, or who is better than who.

My mother used to cry 'too too' like an owl after the dogs, and shouted after them in a very threatening way, and sat up with them all night when they were sick giving them teaspoonfuls of white of egg and brandy.

My eye travelled over the little rounded hills and the small sunny valley where the river flashed sudden silver patches, but my thoughts were on the evening of childhood with my face leaning out of the friendly window of home just before my supper, when the sky was an aquarium green and the rooks flew cawing home in the green sky, and the blackbirds called and chaffered in the darkness of the laurels, and the sky melted into the hills of the night. I sniffed away the tears that collected in my nose, and on my heart lay the ache of dear childhood lost, and on my heart also the images of girls smiling who'd have shared my life as they say, but dear, dead images of faces lost in the stream of past years.

Hannah.

I looked down through the haze, and in tangled recollection looked for traces of her cottage. There was a turnpike cottage with the falling chimney: that was in the middle of my eye when as a child I gazed up the valley towards the glorious future of my advancing life.

When I looked over the hills the whole gleaming, glittering world was beyond the hills for me to tread.

Hannah.

My mother said when she left us and married, she'd be broken up by the life, rearing chickens, running a smallholding, as poor Evan's wife. I saw her greying hair, my beautiful Hannah whom I kissed and hugged when she kissed me lovingly goodnight; I saw her gapped teeth and the tired skin falling about her bones.

What is she now?

Can I bear to see Hannah broken, and an old woman, like my mother said?

I have no one to bring back with me, as I'd pictured. That I'd re-enter my country with a glorious partner by my side. The years slip by very quickly, and people slip out of them, and you have no one. I come back to my country as I left it, alone, barring this long, rich car. How could I give away my heart to a woman, and throw it down before her, when it was buried here among the woods and damp pastures and the little rounded hills?

Or if I close my eyes and up the road she comes swinging and walking like she did, and holding her arms out to me.

But whose face?

Hannah's?

Mother's?

I opened my eyes and they opened on the same view of the same valley.

"Practically speaking," I began thinking, but no practical speaking was possible sitting here at this old gate. I ought to be looking instead at the old cow-house which they made our home into. I remember the stream that Mother swore ran under the house summer and winter.

I ought to be visiting Hannah, however old she is, and I ought to help her, not sit here with tears in my nose. It's a fact that I can get this place very cheaply from what I've been told, and what have I then? A house called Llwyn-y-brain and my name contained in it. And a bigger house than I lived in as a child. And no child of mine to bring up in it.

As I walked the distant cities I thought of other resting places. Rest, I wanted: to rest like I rested in loving arms where I could cry out my heart and bury my face in their loving arms.

Hannah.

My poor old father knew. "You'll never live here," he used to say sadly to me when I was a boy, "Everything's going." And I was very sad. But he was right; the roof fell in and I went away, and what little I left behind has vanished like grass. You carry a huge heritage about with you, as you think, and rich memories and visions, and smiling faces, and many people. And now when my eyes are shut I see it all, and when I open them I see only the empty beautiful valley, empty for me, beautiful for every one, through my wretched tears.

Young Mr Robert had enough sense never to come back. Or if he did, no one ever knew. I doubt if he ever came and sat at his own drive gate to sniff tears.

It isn't my drive gate.

Our gate fell off its hinges and rotted and an old bedstead probably blocks up the hole. In one of her last letters I remember my mother writing to me half across the world, and she said, "Why don't you write? I am so very lonely. I never see anyone. The gate fell off its hinges and there's no one I'm afraid to put it up."

I pressed the starter to start up the engine, thinking: If I go away what have I but the two pictures? The old ones I had with me all these years, and the new one of the beautiful empty valley, smiling no more for me than for any spectator.

"And I'm no spectator," I said, "if I inherited a country, and this valley with it. And my inheritance fastened to me like a chain, pulling me back across the world."

I looked down at the empty road, as the engine purred, and nobody walked on it.

"What is the future?" I thought, and thought how the future rushed on you like a river and left you suddenly old and lonely like an old stone standing unwanted in the land of your fathers.

Lords A-Leaping

When the Earl of Mum was in residence at Mum Castle, a flag with the Mum arms flew from the highest tower. In August Lord Mum was in residence; in August the County Agricultural Show took place in Trallwm.

At dinner the Prime Minister was civil to his host; (it is a great thing to be an earl and entertain Ministers civilly), Lord Mum had been civil and listened to the Prime Minister's opinions at dinner. Lady Mum left the table, with the wives of other notables.

"I imagine it will be fine," Lord Mum said.

"I hope so, indeed I hope so," said the Prime Minister.

"Show's no good if it rains," said Thrive, (Viscount, Mum's heir). The port went round: Sir John Spaniel, former Ambassador to Tokio, gulped his down, and Mum frowned; it is '68 port, not his best, but '68 port for the Prime Minister, and it should not be gulped. At the foot of the table sat Sand the Agent; when one gives a dinner-party one asks Sand, one's agent, and he sits at the foot of the table.

"In the course of my official existence," said Sir John, "There are occasions when frequently; fortunately I was never deceived, in this; I remember soon after the war."

"Personally," said General Sebastian to Sand, "If a man's a gentleman, he's a gentleman; put a man up in front of me and I'll tell you if he's a gentleman."

"There aren't enough gentlemen to go round," Sand said; but quickly and nervously because he was at the foot of Lord Mum's table.

"Exactly!" cried Sebastian. "The world's getting too big: Look at Ireland."

"Firbank," said Mum, "Didn't marry a Barbecue, or did he?"

The Prime Minister didn't know.

"His mother was a Roughty, though... Irish family, but quite decent... or was she?"

The Prime Minister didn't know.

"The Jap said something to me," said Sir John, "Couldn't understand though: I never learned Jap, of course; interpreter spoke French, but I never could follow French. I said something to the Jap though I don't remember what. Clear enough: nothing to discuss. We wanted to go in and out, they wanted us to go out and not in; didn't seem worth discussing, but the Jap wanted to discuss it, hot it was too, and I was due at the Club at five."

"It should be fine," Thrive said, "It was a clear sky at seven; when I was dressing I looked out and it was a clear sky; that's a sign."

"And his mother should have left it to the son by the first marriage," said Mum, "But she changed her mind, and it all came to young Firbank. Contrexeville hasn't a penny out of it... or has he?"

"He's one of my secretaries," said the Prime Minister.

"So he is! These young people grow up! How does he do?"

"He is a promising young man," said the Prime Minister, "I never see him."

"Some of those M.P.s," Sebastian told Sand, "Have no pretensions to being gentlemen. Think how they get in! Excuse me a minute I must speak to the Prime Minister."

Sand finished the dregs of his port since he would not get another glass and stretched his legs under the table.

"About my nephew," said the General, "Excellent young fellow!"

"I already have six secretaries," said the Prime Minister.

"Oh come!" exclaimed the General, "You'll never notice another; good family, too, mother's a Ragborough."

"A Ragborough?" the Prime Minister asked, "The Duke's daughter?"

"Of course!" cried the General, (didn't the man know anything?) "You never see them, you'll never notice a seventh."

"I'm running Pharaoh and Jiminy Rose to-morrow," said Mum, "D'you know *Sand* has horses in again?"

All of them looked at Sand who tucked his legs under his chair again and sat up.

"Horses, Sand?" they said. "Capital! capital! Hope you win something, very good putting horses in, etc."

"How does *Sand* manage to run horses?" said the General in an undertone.

"Not on what I pay him," Mum said. "The beggar must have an income."

"Oh-er-ah!" exclaimed the General.

"Tell young Ragborough to see Contrexeville," said the Prime Minister, "He'll put him down."

"Sebastian is the name!" cried the General. "Mother's a Ragborough."

"Oh well," said the Prime Minister, "Tell him to see Contrexeville."

"I should think," Thrive was saying, "That if it doesn't rain to-morrow, it will be fine."

As they left the dining-room to join Lady Mum and the wives of the notables, the General had a word with Mum. Sand is hardly a gentleman, but he keeps horses, not one but two; he has a brother in Ireland who breeds horses. Lord Mum's horses come from the shires, of the best blood, and Sand was in a good county regiment in the last war.

Sand excused himself and went out of the Castle: down the steps of the Castle among the shrubberies. When one is the last to be served the dishes at dinner, one has little dinner. Sand was prepared, and sitting in the shrubbery produced ham sandwiches from his coat and ate them.

Arrived at the little house where he lived at the bottom of Mum's park, he visited his loose-boxes and heard the warm champing of horses: in a shed nearby is the light vehicle on which jockeys sit in trotting-races. Mr Sand was a little man and his own jockey.

When the day reached ten o'clock the sun gleamed on the new wooden grandstand and the new wooden enclosure in Mum's park. Around the enclosure is bright-painted farm-machinery and the white tents of seed and manure merchants, tents of poultry exhibits and tents where beer is bought. With a Guard of Honour from the Territorials, plump men presenting arms, the Prime Minister and Lord Mum advanced to declare the show open.

According to Lord Mum, we must thank the Prime Minister, according to the Prime Minister it is agricultural shows and his government's policy which make England (though Trallwm and the County of Cariad are in Wales) what it is. The Show is open.

After examining some pigs and acknowledging salutes, Lord Mum and the Prime Minister went back to the Castle for a drink before lunch. The other guests had just breakfasted, but were ready for lunch.

Sand was busy; the servants were complaining because they had had to carry so many gallons of water for the Prime Minister's bath, (there is but one bath in the Castle, and Lady Mum uses that). The situation was more than the butler could deal with: some of the servants' had to be dismissed, some for insolence, others for incompetence. Sand was busy.

After lunch he (Sand) changed into his jockey's silks and went down to the field with a thick overcoat hiding them: the day was warm and Sand sweated.

Lord Mont was in the poultry-tent saying encouraging words, through the flap he saw Sand:

"There's Sand," said Lord Mum to the General, "In all his glad tags."

"Hot that coat must be," observed the General. "Fine leghorn you've got there" (to a farmer's wife).

"Mine's the brown, Sir," she said.

"Brown's fine, too!" exclaimed the General.

"I must go and see Mace," Mum said, "Damn Sand!"

As he passed the red and green elevators, the yellow and blue tractors, farmers touched their hats to his lordship; Sand they saluted too, and hated him, considering his soft job and thinking that he cheated them.

Mum avoided Sand, who, after all, had two good horses in the same race as his employer, and took his seat by Lady Mum in front of the grandstand with the Judges. Townsfolk from Trallwm, gentry, and other representatives of faction, leaned over and hoped that Lord Mum would be successful; it would be gratifying if Lord Mum were successful.

Lady Mum said in a low tone, "Sand's got horses in again."

"I know," said Mum.

A horn is blown: in pairs, and drawing the delicate cart on which the jockey perches, the high-stepping trotters parade past Lord Mum. His lips smile at Sand, his heart at Mace, his own jockey.

They line up: a gun is fired; the race is on! Sand streaks away at the start, leads all the way round, and wins by a good nine lengths. Mace is third.

Tongue-clicking and head-shaking from the gentry at the table who don't know what to say to Lord Mum; polite clapping from the gentry in the grandstand who are more interested in their daughters in the hunter-trials (next event); riotous cheering from the body of dismissed servants on the far side of the ring: booing from three drunken labourers in the beer-tent quickly silenced by the licensee.

"Very bad luck, Sir," said the Prime Minister.

"Ah well," said Mum, "Sand did very well," and the gentry at the table were relieved to see Mum take it like a sportsman.

Later on, when Sand came up for the silver cup, Mum shook him by the hand and his lips smiled at him.

"A nice pair of horses, Mr Sand," said the Prime Minister.

Lady Mum did not look too pleased.

All is now over; the hunter-trials are finished, the agricultural machines bought and sold, the farmer's wives encouraged: the drunken shouts from the beer-tent fade into the distance as the tent closes and the drunks make their way to the pubs in Trallwm.

In the Castle, Lord Mum's butler wrestled with the disorganisation of the household. Servants had been dismissed, nothing was in its place, the water was not hot in the pantry tap. Fresh relays of servants were carrying up water for the Prime Minister's evening bath and cursing the marrow of his bones. The silver is not clean, there are no clean napkins; the butler rages and drinks a tumbler of the port that must not be gulped, to steady his nerves. His heart beats with anxiety as he looks at the laid table and goes to bang the gong: he hears a distant crash... some unskilled servant has dropped the soup.

Host, hostess, and guests were seated.

"No soup, milady, there was an accident."

"What accident?"

Sand won his lordship's own race, not by accident, but by deliberate ill-will and ingratitude. The fish tastes more of fish than cooking.

"I can't tell you, Prime Minister, how greatly we appreciate your coming down and opening our little show."

"The Government, of course, has an agricultural policy; agriculture is very near the heart of every member of my government." The policy is further expounded, but consists, essentially, of these words.

Everyone is in agreement with the Prime Minister.

"Lovely day for the Show," said Thrive. "Everything at its best."

"Be quiet, dear," said Lady Mum, "When your father is speaking."

"Of course Sand is all right in his way," Lord Mum was saying, "A bit ostentatious, though; it didn't look well this afternoon."

"Quite right," said the General. "It didn't look well; he ought to race his horses elsewhere."

"No one to a man owning horses," said Sir John Spaniel, "In Tokio all my secretaries ran their ponies, but not against me. Not etiquette."

"No one objects at all," said Mum.

There is a long pause between courses: the sweet comes in looking dilapidated in a tarnished dish. The back-premises were in an uproar, the butler in despair. He had taken another tumbler of port and thought he was steady on his feet. Lord Mum saw that he was not.

"The strange thing is," says Mum, "Sand's mother was a Sacheverall. Sacheverall-Sand he calls himself; I call him Sand."

"Sacheverall?" said the General. "Would she be related to the..."

The Prime Minister didn't know.

"Our foreign policy with regard to Japan," said Sir John, "Is many years of patient endeavour; of course Williamson, who's there now..."

"We must see the thing through," said the Prime Minister, "Interests are at stake."

"It should be fine to-morrow," said Thrive, "I looked out of my window as I was dressing." And he fell silent. He is Mum's heir, and must preserve his energies for the responsibilities that one day will be his.

Mum beckoned to his butler and drew from his pocket a note already written and scaled into an envelope: "Send a man down with this to Mr Sand personally," he said. "There is no answer."

"Yeshmilor," the butler replied.

A footman walked happily from the chaos backstairs to the little house where Sand lived at the bottom of the park. He was admitted to the room where Sand sat reading the *Times*.

"Come in," said Sand.

"No answer," said the man.

"Come in," said Sand, and yanked the man in by the collar; though Sand was a little man, he was strong.

"Drink!" said Sand.

"No Sir, thank you Sir. No, I won't drink." (in a more insolent tone).

Sand caught him by the lapels and lifted him in the air; for a little man Sand is strong.

"Now drink that," said Sand, thrusting a glass of brandy at him.

The man is so scared he gulps it down.

Sand locked the door.

"Aren't you going to read your note, Sir?" said the frightened footman.

"I know what's in it!" Sand shouted at him, "I know!"

He tore it open and thrust it under the man's nose. It ran:

Dear Sand,

In view of certain reorganizations, I shall not be requiring your services after the end of the month.

Yours truly, Mum.

"I'm very sorry to hear that, Sir," said the footman.

"You're not, damn you," yelled Sand, "And drink this down." The scared man gulped down another large glass of brandy so that he had now about half-a-pint in him.

"Won't you, Sir, won't you drink anything at all, Sir?"

"I've had all I want," Sand cried, and seizing the man by the back hair, forced more brandy down his throat. The footman began to hiccough, and Sand thrust him from the house.

"Out of my house!" he cried, and the man reeled back to the Castle with a burning inside him. There he began a drunken quarrel with the butler, and increased the chaos backstairs.

Neighbours heard a commotion in Sand's little house, and his voice calling for a pot of paint.

In the morning Sand was gone, and his horses were being put in a horse-box. On the walls of Lord Mum's lodge and on the entrance walls flanking all the gates of Lord Mum's castle was daubed in black paint:

SACHEVERALL-SAND.

Milk of Human Kindness

Morgan Morgan bellowed into the air.

"It seems," he bellowed, for he was deaf.

He adjusted his electrical apparatus for hearing and waited, but there was no echo.

"Seems?" the hearty Mrs Morgan Morgan shouted, "Plug in your plug, man! How can you hear if you don't plug in your plug?"

"Do you shout to deafen me?" asked Morgan Morgan in a whisper.

"It is a scandalous thing," said his hearty wife.

"I was going to say it is a scandalous thing," Morgan Morgan shouted in a severe manner.

"There is no need to shout," his wife said.

There is no need to shout the disgrace of Thwaite: he has been found lacking in the milk of human kindness. He has shown himself without the milk of human kindness by his recent behaviour. He has not behaved according to the traditions of his class, he has not acted with *esprit de corps*; he has behaved contrary to other people, he has behaved contrary to the principals on which good breeding, on which Kindness or the dealing in a magnanimous way with inferiors is based. Thwaite does not acknowledge his inferiors: and he has no reverence! He has none of the milk of human kindness possessed by the inhabitants of the county of Cariad, who conform.

"Scandalous is the word!" muttered Morgan Morgan, "I'm meeting Wallnut: if I meet Wallnut we can see what can be done."

"If you meet Wallnut," said Mrs Morgan Morgan, "See that you plug in your plug; what's the good of meeting Wallnut if you don't plug in your plug?"

"Reminds me of a limerick," said Morgan Morgan, "Very funny limerick:—

Was a young man with a plug
plugged in his mug in a rug
but the plug and the rug
and the bug and the mug..."

"Anyway," said Mrs Morgan Morgan, "Something will be done in a week."

"Why?"

"Why! It's flag-day! Something bound to be done. Fifty-seventh anniversary of the Queen's Concatenation..."

"Ah, of course," said Morgan Morgan, "I must see Wallnut."

"Where?"

"Where! At the cross-roads! Where else should I see him?"

"Don't shout," said his wife, and he was gone.

He went with his plugs and his deafness to the cross-roads. Wallnut was there.

"We are now on the last forty bricks of the lower passage in the pyramid of Cheops," said Wallnut, "Each of those bricks represents forty years; obviously, or there wouldn't be forty more. That makes 1,600 years: last our time, but we must stamp out vice. About Thwaite. And you can't say anything against that because it's in the Bible; forty days and forty nights clearly refers to the forty bricks; the forty thieves, too, that's not in the Bible."

"Can't say anything against the Bible!" Morgan Morgan shouted in a hearty manner.

"About Thwaite."

Mr Wallnut said, "Thwaite is a disgrace and a good family too."

Morgan Morgan said, "My wife says something will be done in a week."

"Why?"

"Because it's flag-day. Must respect the Queen's Concatenation."

"There's nothing about flag-days in the pyramid," Wallnut said. "Nor in the Bible. Obviously there will be no flag-day."

"We must show young Thwaite," said Morgan Morgan.

"Can't show him if he won't see, now *I* have a plan... Look out!" Morgan Morgan cried, "Damn it!"

In the scrawny wood by the cross-roads is the Rev. Codger. There are pheasants in the wood, these are Morgan Morgan's pheasants. Rev. Codger has a gun and a dog, a long-legged lurcher. The two squires stand stiff as the signpost at the cross-roads; Morgan Morgan points to Trallwm. Wallnut to Llanpumpsaint.

The dog puts up a pheasant, it screws back over Rev. Codger, he brings it down. "Good shot!" Morgan Morgan cried. "I mean— no bird sir!"

Rev. Codger saw the two squires, picked up the bird and fled into the scrawny wood.

"After him!" they yelled.

The old men galloped across in the turf and crashed into the scrawny wood. Ahead among the scrub and the young oaks, ran Rev. Codger blazing a trail of broken branches, cartridges, fragments of clerical cloth and beer bottles. They all ran, and Wallnut outstripped Morgan Morgan, and Rev. Codger outstripped them both.

Torn and heated they came out into the open but there was John Jerman, stout Churchman, in the field. He saw Rev. Codger, Calvinistic Methodist rushing towards him, he heard the cries of the charging squires, he saw the dog and the gun. John Jerman, stout Churchman, wrapped his strong arms round Rev. Codger and held him. Rev. Codger fought and bit, but the squires were upon him. He bit John Jerman in the ear and John Jerman swore. "No respect for my cloth!" cried Rev. Codger.

But they held him and drew pheasants from his right pockets, bottles of beer from his left. The squires drank the beer, and Rev. Codger's dog bit Wallnut.

"That's two summonses," said Wallnut.

They brought Rev. Codger before Sir Gam Vychan, magistrate. On the table, as exhibits, were the gun, the beer bottles, the pheasants. Sir Gam's moustache danced like a little black fly above his angry words.

"In India!" he cried, "You would be shot. In the Malay you would be flogged! In Africa you would be chained up!"

"They had no respect for my cloth," said Rev. Codger, "They chased me, they bit me, they struggled with me."

"Shame!" said a man in the Court, "To drag up a minister for a little bit of poaching; and he a Calvinistic Methodist. Shame!"

"Silence!" cried Sir Gam, "How do you explain these?" pointing to the beer bottles.

"They are bottles," Rev. Codger said, "Which formerly contained beer; I put them in my pocket with the intention of drinking beer and thereby refreshing myself."

"Good," said Sir Gam, "Good. So you admit that you put bottles of beer in your pocket with the intention of drinking the beer. Do you know that you are a very depraved parson, I mean person?"

"Shame!" cried a man in the Court, "To browbeat a Minister; and him Calvinistic Methodist."

"Silence!" cried Sir Gam.

There was a commotion at the back of the hall. Mr Cambyses was coming in.

"Ah, Sir Gam!" said Mr Cambyses, striding with flapping clothes and high-pitched voice towards the Bench.

"Mr Gambyses, behave with proper decorum," Sir Gam said.

"I wish to give evidence," Mr Cambyses said, "I wish to bear witness to this man's integrity, to show that he cannot possibly have been in the place mentioned at the time mentioned."

"Mr Cambyses, you will stand down and be seated, Mr Morgan Morgan is in the Box."

"And so," said Morgan Morgan, "He fired a shot, we saw him: a good shot. I said 'Good shot!' He turned: he fled: we ran."

"You ran?"

Morgan Morgan put the microphone by Sir Gam, "In there," he whispered.

"You ran?"

"Of course I ran!" Morgan Morgan bellowed, and all the people jumped.

"You saw this man run, and you ran?"

"Rams? There were no rams! John Jerman rammed him! Ha ha! Very funny."

"Rams!" Mr Cambyses cried from the public gallery.

Sir Gam looked at Mr Cambyses and made a note.

"We met at the cross-roads," Wallnut said. "To discuss. To discuss something of general concern."

"What?" asked Sir Gam.

"A question of morality."

"Oh, a question of morality."

Everyone leaned forward and licked their lips.

"Not equality!" Morgan Morgan said. "No such theory! Keep off the Bible, Wallnut."

"I will mention no names, but there is one among us who lacks the milk of human kindness."

"Extraordinary!" cried Sir Gam, "Who is it?"

"No names, but we all know," Wallnut said.

"Bring him before me," said Sir Gam, "And I'll give him fourteen days; fellow can have no morals... or is he a woman?"

A man oppressed with justice, Rev. Codger stood up, "I was not in the wood at the time mentioned, I was not poaching, I do not possess a gun or a dog. I was in Mr Cambyses' summer-house reading with him Elias Jones on Moses. Ask Mr Cambyses."

"You cannot tell a lie," said Mr Cambyses, "He was in my sawmill at the time stated. Smelling the smell of wood."

"That was later," Rev. Codger said.

"No, earlier," said Mr Cambyses.

"Later!"

"Earlier!"

"This," said Sir Gam, "is a serious case. In sentencing you I take into account your belonging to the wrong denomination of the Church, your not being a gentleman, and your having poached my friend Mr Morgan Morgan's pheasants; which I hope to be invited to shoot next week; eh, Mr Morgan Morgan," (into the microphone).

"Yes, yes, hoot away by all means," said Morgan Morgan.

"Seven days or two pounds," Sir Gam said.

"Shame!" cried a man in the Court, "To fine a minister, and it comes out of Chapel Funds."

"I pay the fine!" Mr Cambyses called out, and led away Rev. Codger.

As Sir Gam left the Court for lunch, the police-sergeant gave him a note: —

"Mr Cambyses regrets to inform Sir Gam Vychan that his prize RAM, Owen's Pride, is no longer available for Sir Vychan."

"Blast!" cried Sir Gam and ran into the Bear Hotel.

He telephoned Mr Justice Darrel on vacation at his Welsh seat, Rhosllanerchrugog.

"Barrel!" he cried, "Cambyses is withholding his ram."

"Ah," said Barrel, "Why?"

"I fined his preacher, Codger. Man's a poacher."

"You fined him, and Cambyses is withholding his ram?"

"I said that."

"I want to have the facts clearly marshalled: I should have to hear evidence of both sides. However we need not to worry ourselves unduly with Mr Cambyses' evidence."

"I should think not. He said Codger was in his sawmill when Codger was poaching Morgan Morgan's pheasants under Morgan Morgan's nose."

"No one," said Justice Barrel, "With as many books in his house as Cambyses could possibly give trustworthy evidence."

"Well," Sir Gam said, "There's a library at Plas Vychan, you don't hold that against me, I hope, ha ha!"

"Inherited," Barrel said, "Quite different: and of course you don't read them."

"I should think not!" Sir Gam said.

"Cambyses both buys and reads books," said Barrel.

"But the ram! How can I have prize lambs without the ram?"

"It would be difficult."

"And the insult! A bookworm has rams and will not let them out. He refuses me his ram!"

"On the *prima facie* evidence," said Barrel, "He seems to show lack of *esprit de corps*. I shall speak to my nephew."

He rang off.

Sir Gam Vychan had lunch, thinking of his flocks.

Mr Justice Barrel had lunch.

"Denis," he said to his nephew, "We must persuade Mr Cambyses."

"The bookworm?" asked Denis, who was a gentleman.

"There is no one better tempered than I," Barrel began, "God damn the dog!" (Kicking one). "No one better tempered than I, but Cambyses' action is a breach of *esprit de corps*."

"Thwaite broke it too."

"Thwaite is younger. It is not too late to ostracize young Thwaite. Cambyses is a magistrate, a pillar of his peculiar church. Where we cannot force, we must persuade."

"Good," said Denis, "Can I have the car?"

"Far better for you to go on a bicycle," Barrel said, "It's only twenty-five miles, and saves petrol."

Five miles from Mr Cambyses' house Denis' chain came off. It was a hot day. Denis sat down in the shade and waited to put on his chain. In a small car, Fred Owen, general dealer and prominent citizen of Trallwm, Fred Owen, with his red girl's mouth and paunch, drew up by Denis. He did not know Denis.

"I can't take a lift, thanks, I've got the bike."

Fred Owen got out of the car. "There's a pied hill-cock's nest in the wood," he said; Denis jumped up: "I heard her calling when I went past to-day."

"D'you think it's the bag-eyed variety?"

"We'll go and see," Fred Owen said, and took Denis' arm in his fat white hand to guide him into the wood.

Once under cover of the tree Fred showed Denis no pied hillcock's nest, but laid his hand on him lewdly. Denis punched Fred Owen in the paunch and ran out of the wood. He leaped on his bicycle, and using it like the early velocipede that had no pedals, shot off down the hill.

Arrived in Cambyses' grounds, he forgot Fred Owen and felt for his gear. He had paraffin, a box of ants, old eggs, string, a brick, matches, a box of beetles, dung, writing material, a notebook.

Cambyses' house has large vulnerable windows. It has a library extending through many rooms in the house. Mr Cambyses adds to his library, reads what he adds, and remembers what he reads.

Denis lit a fire by the front door so that the smoke blew into the hall, he threw dung into the dining-room, the ants into the library, the beetles into a bedroom, the eggs into the drawing-room: he put paraffin into the drains and lit it, causing an explosion, he threw a brick with RAM written on it through the largest window. Then he went in search of the RAM.

Such arguments convince any reasonable man of his error and he comes out and hands over his ram. But Mr Cambyses fired at Denis with a shot-gun and Denis fled pursued by a posse of gardeners with pitchforks. He cycled away in the dusk to Mr Justice Barrel of Rhosllanerchrugog, his uncle.

"Offence against Judge's nephew," said the Press in a few days:

"Alderman and Magistrate in Court. Grave charges against Alderman."

Arglwydd Jones in his series of stone shooting-boxes strung together to enlarge the original stone shooting-box to the size of a gentleman's house, read the papers and sent for his secretary. Seated among stuffed lions' and bisons' heads the great man dictated a letter.

"During all this trouble," his lordship said, "We must not forget Thwaite, the author of it. Thwaite's misdemeanours, though outside the present range of the law, are the cause, the *Er Spring*, to use a German phrase," (Lord Jones is educated).

"I am proud of my proletarian ancestry," he went on, (for this was a public letter to the Press).

"Libel, my Lord," said the secretary.

"Substitute Milk of Human Kindness for Thwaite," said Yr Arglwydd.

The letter remained unfinished; Lord Jones had another idea.

Dragging a hunting-horn from his breast-pocket he charged upstairs, blowing upon it, to play with his children. As usual the children were paralyzed with fear and could not play.

The secretary panted upstairs after him; "Take down memorandum for new Hospital Scheme," cried Yr Arglwydd: "Sanatoria on all the highest mountains of Wales with lifts and funiculars. Make the lifts and funiculars a separate company! My monogram in Welsh basalt on the facade: letters twenty-five feet high. Telescopes permanently trained on the monogram! Have them erected in all towns within sight. Charge them sixpence for a peep and pay it into party funds," he added.

Lord Jones settled down with a book on the organization of International Equality, he had an idea. For five minutes he was quiet. His children crept out from under the chairs where they had hidden when he came trumpeting up the stairs.

But he leaped up with a yell that sent them scurrying back.

"It's a case of International Justice," he shouted. "Owen and Cambyses are a test-case! Start a newspaper!" he screamed down the stairs to his secretary, "Get all the facts about them and put them on the front-page! Never mind the facts! Put them on the front page! Start it now! Call it the Defence of Decency!"

And Yr Arglwydd ran off to the hot-houses to spray peaches.

The next day the people of the county of Cariad under whose doors free copies of Defence of Decency, Editor, Lord Jones, No. 1, had appeared in the night, learned the true facts of the Owen-Cambyses case.

Fred Owen, they read, was the victim of an attack by the rich landlords on the small shopkeepers. Did they wish to see the small man, the honest trader, crushed out of existence by a reactionary and feudal clique?

Cambyses, they read, was a respected landlord most unjustly accused by a rabble of small shopkeepers, and other Bolshevist rifraff. Were they going to allow their cherished traditions, that great heritage which had made Wales what it is, to be blasphemously threatened by Moscow-paid upstarts?

The people of Cariad read, and Lo! they had opinions for the case. Men who had been battering their brains for some ideas slept soundly with the Defence of Decency at their bedside, and Mrs Olympia, that defender of decency, made her way to Cambyses' house. If she could do good, she would do good.

She passed in at the front door and the gardener was clearing away the ashes of Denis' fire with a pitchfork: in the drawing-room where she waited, the butler was picking up eggs with a shovel.

"Aha!" said Mr Cambyses, "You see? You see? You wouldn't believe it... what I could show you in the dining-room."

"Mr Cambyses," said Mrs Olympia, "We all make our mistakes. How you came to be associated with Fred Owen in this, I won't enquire. I came to tell you that whatever the world may say, I forgive you all. When you have turned from your sin you still have one friend, Mr Cambyses, that you can rely on."

"Ha!" Cambyses said, "And my ram? You heard about my ram?"

"Was it good, was it kind to withhold your ram from Sir Gam? After his distinguished career in India, in Malay, in Africa; after all he's done in the county, sitting on Benches, Committees. I see a tear in your eye, Mr Cambyses, do not be afraid to weep before me."

"It's sweat. You remind me of my mother."

"Your dear mother! Never off your lips! Her room..."

"Fudge!" cried Cambyses, his voice rose two tones in the octave. "On my lips! The old woman's branded on me! Forty-five years of my dear old mother! I'll never forget her if I live to be a hundred and ninety!"

"But her room! Kept as it was in her...!"

"A museum of suffering! I look in there for penance, penance, Mrs Olympia."

"Yes, we do penances in my group. But about your ram; if you were to allow Sir Gam, I'm sure..."

Cambyses sprang to a shelf of books and grabbed the first: it was a Latin Grammar: —

"Jam veniet tacito," (he read) "Curva senecta pede
senex promissa barba, horribile visu
non quivis homini quibus adire Corinthum
masculine are mons and frons
calyps hydrops gryps and pons..."

But the spell worked; Mrs Olympia vanished in her little car to Trallwm where Flag-Day was in progress.

In the irregular main street the town band was blowing down its silver-plated instruments and counter-marching with the citizens. They carried banners: —

Mr Cambyses for Justice, Alderman Owen for Decency. Defend our Antient Rights. Down with Feudal Tyranny.

They were singing the song composed and distributed that morning by Lord Jones' secretary: —

"Up with Decency, Down with Crime,
Cambyses and Owen every time,
for Arglwydd Jones looks after us well
and may all his enemies go to hell."

Then a prose-passage which many sang, not realizing that it was a foot-note. "In the cause of International Justice no effort is too great, no cause too small. One and all, old and young, supporting the Right, marching on with Decency even with their backs to the wall... Justice... Right... Truth... Freedom... Arglwydd Jones... Arglwydd Jones."

"Buy a flag!" ugly girls screamed at street corners, "Support the Queen's Concatenation! Fifty-seventh Great Anniversary!"

The Trallwm Express was afraid of Competition from Yr Arglwydd: it had a leader on supporting Decency and Right, Arglwydd Jones, and buying a Flag.

Mrs Olympia bought two Flags and watched the scandalous demonstration... the extraordinary demonstration, a great many respectable people seemed to be taking part.

Mr Wallnut was in the second row bearing a placard; he broke ranks and came to Mrs Olympia.

"A direct Fulfilment!" he cried, "*The Trumpet shall sound! it is sounding, And the dead shall be raised.* The dead obviously refers to Owen and Cambyses; they were unjustly accused and dishonour is worse than death."

The citizens marched before the town hall with the band which was now augmented by hundreds of mouth-organs and flageolets. They yelled for the Mayor and he came quickly out of the Bear Hotel by the side-door and into the Town Hall by the back door. Supported by his Corporation he appeared on the balcony. Enormous enthusiasm. The band played *Land of My Fathers*: there was scarcely a dry eye.

"Realizing that there has been a grave mistake," the Mayor said, when he could be heard, "And like a wise man, it appeared, Mr Justice Barrel has bowed to the will of the people, and is withdrawing on behalf of his nephew, all these charges."

The people were pleased. Cambyses and Owen were pleased, and best of all Yr Arglwydd Jones was pleased.

"But we haven't solved the problem!" Morgan Morgan bellowed to his hearty wife.

"No!" she said, "These are side-issues."

"These are side-issues," Morgan Morgan said. "How can I hear if you don't speak into the thing?"

It took the Pugh-Parallaxes to attempt the impossible. They gave a dry dance with lemonade in the drawing-room and a bottle of whiskey in the kitchen. The Pugh-Parallaxes' house is by the river: in it are moufflon heads, thunderous horns and assegais; you put your umbrella in an elephant's foot and hang your hat on a rhinoceros' horn. The sons are seldom at home together, to mild Mrs Pugh-Parallaxes' relief as they do not see eye to eye. Now three of them are here for the dance and it is already unfortunate.

Percy Pugh-Parallax, the naval officer, came out of the kitchen with a shining face.

"There's that damned planter!" he exclaimed, pointing to his own brother, James.

James said to Percy's fiancée, "Bloody fool's been jammed for promotion ten years!"

Lieutenant William P-P came back from the kitchen; he and Percy agreed for a minute while they abused James, then they quarrelled with each other for abusing him. Thwaite is in the kitchen by himself drinking whiskey.

In the drawing-room a gramophone was playing, the couples were dancing... the old and the young... the men with suppressed passion. Some of the men got a girl to come into the garden.

Mrs Pugh-Parallax ran distracted through her rooms: now she stopped her sons quarrelling, now she dragged ugly young women towards young men who ran away as she approached.

And her sons would not dance with anybody; they went away to the kitchen and they came back and quarrelled, and James had seized Percy's fiancée and taken her to another room. Guests kept disappearing and one girl came in muddy and dishevelled from the garden by herself. Where is young Thwaite whom everybody talks about?

The guests stride briskly to the corners of the room in time to the gramophone, the men forward, the girls backward; at the corners they make a brisk half-turn continue. And Mrs Pugh-Parallax's terrible sons are now all in one room furiously arguing. They discuss who played better football at school at the tops of their voices. Percy says he was a fine three-quarter and the others howl him down.

Percy's fiancée has gone into the conservatory to cry, and nobody has found her. In the drawing-room the Pugh-Parallax sisters hold grimly to their partners and will not let them go. Some of the guests are vigorously amusing themselves, but few have found the kitchen, and Thwaite is getting drunk. The boom of the voices of the terrible Pugh-Parallax sons can be heard in the drawing-room as they quarrel. Percy's fiancée stops crying for a moment to listen, and then continues.

With ever-increasing speed Mrs Pugh-Parallax rushes through her house to hold her guests together. But the whiskey was finished and Thwaite came out of the kitchen.

With shining face he leaned against the door-jamb, blocking the doorway, and when Mrs Pugh-Parallax approached, Thwaite smiled and began to talk. He cannot stop talking; if he stops talking he must move to let Mrs Pugh-Parallax pass, if he moves he will fall down. Thwaite talked, Mrs Pugh-Parallax dodged in front of him trying to get by, and Thwaite swayed and blocked her path. There is a commotion in the drawing-room, a crash from the kitchen where someone has found the empty whiskey-bottle and broken it; the gramophone is jammed, another girl has been insulted in the garden and come in with her dress torn, closely followed by a panting beast of a man. All this Mrs Pugh-Parallax saw below Thwaite's left arm-pit, and high above it sounded her sons quarrelling.

Five times Mrs Pugh-Parallax has asked Thwaite to let her pass but the monologue goes on uninterrupted. Thwaite is thinking I must not fall down.

Now there was a fresh commotion. Old Mr Morgan Morgan went out for a breath of air, tripped over some wire-netting and fell into river. He has been pulled out half-throttled by his electrical apparatus for hearing and they are reviving him on the drawing-room floor.

Thwaite's loud voice is heard, "Ha ha! Mrs Pugh-Parallax, Old Boy's drunk! Ha ha!"

This struck Morgan Morgan into action; he leaped to his feet, scattering his rescuers. He tried to speak but for a moment only a jet of water shot from his mouth. From another room came loud shouts and the thud of blows, as the Pugh Parallax sons set to at last.

Thwaite turns to face Morgan Morgan, but away from the door-jamb he cannot stand and he falls heavily to the floor; Mrs Pugh-Parallax rushes past him to her sons.

Words follow water from Morgan Morgan's mouth... "Look!" he cries. "At last!"

The house rocks. One of those earthquakes which sweep North Wales from time to time has seized the county of Cariad. The lights go out. Men grab girls and embrace them. Thwaite crawls on all fours into the garden and sits listening to the roar of the river, the howls of the men and the women embracing, the cries of Mrs Pugh-Parallax's fighting sons, the screams of their mother, the gargling of Messrs. Wallnut and Morgan Morgan who have become jointly entangled in the electrical apparatus for hearing.

"It is not true," Thwaite said sadly, "I cannot believe it. So much culture! Such breeding! So many admirable people in one house, and they are disturbed by an earthquake."

He sighed, and his good heart bled for the gentry of the County of Cariad.

Rich Relations

Coming from the station at sunset, driven by Bosseyein the glass-fronted fly, there are a few curves in the lane, a few cottages. They were lighting the lamps at the house.

His mother came out into the front hall and kissed him with dry lips.

"How long your hair is. You're getting fat."

His coat was too short and his bottom looked fat.

Bosseye brought up the small suitcase.

"Foreign labels," she said, "You've been abroad again."

"Not again. I should have told you."

"Told me? Would you, though?"

"I write often enough."

"Not so often. Once a fortnight isn't often, and you tell me nothing at all very often."

Here in the front hall, he thought, I've been two minutes in the house. With his hand in his pocket, he rammed the nails into the palm.

"Did you pay Stevens?"

"No." He had twopence left.

"You should have. Call him back."

"He's gone."

"Well, you're in your own room. We'll have dinner directly."

He looked for the small suitcase, but the maid had taken it.

"Hang your coat up before you go."

He went up the stairs, looked out of the window on the half-landing. Over the stable roof, a pale blue patch in the sky; the yard was dark; rooks cawing and flying back to the woods around. He listened to the rooks and breathed the good air smelling of leaves and grasses: he breathed after the city. Then he went on upstairs lest his mother should see him and speak.

The maid was unpacking his clean shirt, his pyjamas, his shoes: he asked her about her brother, her mother, the village, and she said yes, and she said no.

"You brought no evening clothes, Sir?"

"No, Alice."

She left him with a jug of hot water and he washed and came down. His mother sat under a lamp in the drawing-room, embroidering.

"So nice to have you back," she said, then looking up, "Oh, not dressed? Where are your evening clothes?"

They were pawned long ago.

"I didn't bring them," he said, "Not for a short visit."

"A short visit? You're not going away again?"

"In a few days. I'm rather busy now."

"Well, I'm glad you can spare me a few days if you're so busy."

"My work..."

"Yes, tell me about your work, I hope you're not still seeing that dirty person."

"Who?" Knowing who she meant from a chance meeting of hers. He could not say who this dirty person was.

"You know quite well who I mean: Mr Banner or something."

"Oh Vanna. I do see him sometimes. He's very brilliant."

"He may be brilliant. It always pays to know decent people; you'll be sorry when you're older: I have tried my best."

"Vanna's taught me a great deal, he's a famous man."

"Famous? I've never met anyone who's ever heard of him."

They went into dinner: soup, fish, entree, sweet, etc., silver on the table, linen napkins, two servants waiting. He ate a great deal, hungrily; while he ate he thought of what he had to do here, then of brightly-lit places where he spent evenings in the city.

He thought of his rooms and his girl. She'd be out to-night. She couldn't stay in alone. "He's gone down home," she'd say, "To get some money."

The maid gave him beer, his mother didn't get up wine for him. When the old man died she locked up the wine-cellar.

"We'll keep what we've got," she said.

He wondered what she kept it for and she an old woman.

"Tell me about what you do in the city," she said, when the maids had gone.

Now, he thought, what if I said I work sometimes, but not office hours, sometimes I get drunk, some afternoons I waste time; I often waste time, then I do some work?

One cannot say that here any more than one can drive a car through that door.

"I've been working rather hard," he said.

"Do you make any money?"

"A little now and then. Living's expensive though."

"That depends on how you live. When I was your age I never took a cab: no one could have done what I have on what I have; no one could run this house on what I do. I don't like to see you sitting down to dinner in that old coat."

"It's a slow business," he said.

"You're thirty-four," his mother said, "Your name's in the newspapers. Why don't you live decently?"

What she means is, Why have I not a salaried post, a fine English wife: why do I not figure at dinner-parties and bring distinguished men here for visits? Why am I not wearing a dinner-jacket?

"But always remember," she said, "Always remember this, whenever you're in a scrape, no matter what it is, come to me. Don't let there be any barrier between us."

This seemed a good moment, but he couldn't get the words out.

She was smiling at him: "Give me your band—just a little loving squeeze." I am thirty-four, he thought, And I must give a little loving squeeze.

"There's no barrier between us, is there? Sometimes I feel that you don't tell me everything. Why don't you tell me? I always know when you're unhappy; I'd always understand."

This seemed a good moment, still he couldn't get the words out so he sat holding the hard old hand.

"Come and give your old mother a kiss." She drew him with her hand, he kissed her cheek with dry lips.

"Things are very difficult," she said, "All alone in this house; I'm so lonely. And the servants are so difficult. Six of them for me to manage. And the car laid up, I know they cheat me at the garage."

He looked over her head to the still life, game hanging in a cellar by a Chinese pot... fruits and vegetables stacked below the game; at rich carpeted floors, shining magnificent polished boards, Adam mantlepieces, the leather-bound unread works of literature. The dozen empty rooms furnished with costly furniture, the servants chattering beyond the walls.

His mother talked; troubles, griefs of neighbours that one must share... How sad! What a pity!

"And I had to," she said, "Give five pounds for their whist-drive; people expect it of one."

I am not bad, he thought, If I do not work so much, some of my work is good; my work will last after me. My work is good, this work beyond solicitors practices, and diplomatic careers; beyond window's fortunes and country-houses.

"So many calls on me," she said.

For what, he thought, Five friends left at this advanced age, no contacts, no knowledge.

They went into the drawing-room; his mother stood up and arranged flowers on the mantlepiece.

I must say it now without thinking, or it will not come out.

"I am rather hard up," he said; his mother's hands stayed still on the flowers; her back was still, her head still, listening.

"Rather short, I wondered if you would help me. I don't like to ask you," he said, "I am rather in debt, I owe some money." (It was £50). "I wouldn't ask you, but certain things have fallen through and the money is not coming in. I wondered if you could let me have..." (He dared not state the amount) . . . "some to be going on with."

He stopped; his mother stood still with her back to him, she said nothing.

He was nervous.

"Well?"

She turned quickly, dramatically, as she loved to do.

"Well! Money! Debt! What do you expect? If you lived a steady life at a decent job; you have had every possible chance. You cast me down lower than I thought possible." She was growing angry. "After all I've done for you, how *dare* you come asking for money? In debt? *Debt*! And I was never in debt in my life. Slaving for you. What have you to show for it? Your work! Rot, I call it! I don't care if it *is* well known; what do decent people think of you? What's the use of it?"

He leaned back on the sofa with closed eyes: money changed her face, the poor lonely old woman who wanted a little loving squeeze at dinner, now snarled round her goods.

"Mine!" she cried, "Mine to do what I like with. How dare you assume that you have any claim on me?"

Now there is no barrier, he thought. Come to mother whenever you are in trouble; why am I not wearing a dinner-jacket.

After the luxury of abuse, (one cannot abuse the servants like one's own son), comes the luxury of giving. The son has crawled in; he has the fame and the brains, but I have the money.

She left the room wearing the face of a martyr, and went to her desk. She wrote him a cheque for £2 10s., then she reached for the bag with the six servants' wages in it; for one must run a house decently.

It will pay my fare back, he thought, and went up to bed in his old room. It was dark over the stables now, and the rooks had stopped their cawing.

Skirt in Long Strips

Old John-on-the-beach woke on the beach where he slept: put his books in the wheelbarrow: set off inland with the wheelbarrow. There was mud in the lanes by the upland farms by the sea: mud and stones. In the mud was the eternal indestructible water.

"I am on a journey," said John-on-the-beach to the rainy sky, and he came into the deserted uplands of Arwystli.

There was a woman in the lane, her bare feet in the black upland mud;

"You are not an Arwystli man?" she asked him.

"At my feet," he answered, "The everlasting soil of all nations"; and he passed on with the wheelbarrow.

But the woman followed him. "You are old John-on-the-beach!" she shouted after him, "Who sleeps on the beach with his books in a wheelbarrow! What are you doing away from the sea?"

He ploughed on through the mud and said nothing. But the woman followed him.

When he came back to Saeson Bank he whistled at the sky, and the rain fell around him; the woman came up to him.

"Here!" she said. But John took out a book and held it open and the rain fell on the pages and the ink ran all together over the pages.

Then the woman whistled at the sky but still the rain came down: she threw stones into the bog below Saeson Bank: at last she began to tear her clothes. Her skirt she tore in long strips: in her bodice she tore holes so that her breasts hung out. Her voice cracked and she sang hymns of glory and went down to the bog below Saeson Bank with her glorious ribbons about her: the body of a woman with strips and ribbons hung about it.

Saeson Bank is a ring-fort: of the Bronze Age. John-on-the-beach who lies there sees the sky and the rain coming down, he hears the woman's hymns and the chatter of the birds of the moor.

Venus Bank is another fort. There Miss Perigord had brought up her dolls. She is old; her hat is orange, her dress flame and green, her shoes are canvas. She cries to herself with her dolls because the rain falls on them and they are wet. She has her dolls and her dress of flame and green, but under her dress her body is withered.

There was a soldier on leave who wandered on the upland road searching for a woman with the bare feet; but he heard her hymning across the moor and could not find her. The soldier looked across the moor and walked among the bogs and the crags but he could not find her. He came to the Anchor Inn which stands on the top of the moor.

And old John-on-the-beach approached Venus Bank and heard Miss Perigord crying to herself, and he was afraid.

"It is my girl," he said, "She is crying fifty years."

He came closer, with caution: a doll's face looked at him from the edge of the fort.

"It is my girl," he said, "And the wind had preserved her fifty years."

And he drove his wheelbarrow up Venus Bank and burst upon Miss Perigord playing with her dolls.

The woman goes across the bog in her ribbons, treading on the tufts of grass without sinking. She comes to the Anchor Inn singing and dancing in the road.

The people come out of the inn to see her and they say, "She came out up out of the Bog!"

But the soldier came to the door, drunk and went and danced with the woman in the rain, and the mud splashed up the legs of his uniform as it splashed up the skin of her legs.

The people who saw them shook their heads and said, "She came up out of the bog!"

And as the minister came up the road, he shook his head at the dancing and went into the little chapel on the moor and rang the bell. But the people were watching the dancing, and no one went to the chapel.

Then the soldier fell down and lay in the mud, but the woman went away up the road in the rain, singing.

Old John-on-the-beach went up to Miss Perigord in her fort, and he said, "You are my girl for fifty years, I have left the beach."

She said, "Leave me to my children, now, leave me!" and gathered up her dolls together in a tight heap.

"You are crying fifty years," he said.

"Not crying—rain," she said, "Whistle at the sky and the rain comes."

"You are my pardon," said John-on-the-beach.

"What do you see?" Miss Perigord asked, "Leave me now!" She has her orange flaming green dress, canvas shoes—as it was.

He crawled towards her over the edge of the fort.

"Away!" she cried, "I have a root here: I suck up the rain with my feet—it's my food!"

"I have a root," said John-on-the-beach, and grinned. "Miss Perigord, your children are wax and paper."

"They suck up the rain," she said, "But they don't grow. What is there to do here?"

"When the spring rain comes down fresh in the spring, dance: and dance and love, feet in the mud and ribbons about you." Miss Perigord kneeled down and drew in the mud: "Here is the fort," she said, "And I mark Alpha where the fort is: there is the bog on the moor where you hear whispering all the twenty-four hours: and here is the Anchor Inn where the witch and the ogre and the giant and the duke live all together in one bed. What is it in your wheelbarrow below?"

"Books of truth," said John-on-the-beach. "Scientific and spiritual truth."

"This is truth," said Miss Perigord, "The giant loves, the ogre loves, the witch hates, the duke is indifferent."

"Symbols!" said John-on-the-beach and he crawled nearer to her.

"You think I am too old to run!" cried Miss Perigord, clutched up her dolls in an armful and ran across the bog in the rain, into the mist. John-on-the-beach picked up the shafts of his wheelbarrow and trudged along the path, for all paths lead to the Anchor Inn: and the rain ran off his hat into the wheelbarrow where his coat covered the books.

The path comes over the swelling hills of the moor, past the ruined farms, the felled and blasted firwoods, to a sickly clump of spruce where the Anchor Inn stands. He followed the track of Miss Perigord's canvas shoes and he came to the muddy space before the Anchor Inn.

The soldier lay drunk in the mud and asleep: round him, staring, stood the duke, but he was Hugh Pugh, not a duke; his wife, not a witch, but Pipette Pugh.

The giant and the ogre must be the same man; or the proprietor who comes screeching out of the door at his dogs, with a scarlet face and antique side-whiskers. Miss Perigord was not there.

"Pick him up!" cried the proprietor, "Bring him in!" He picked up the soldier and carried him into the bar.

"Pipette! Pipette! We're late!" said Pugh; but Pipette went in after the soldier.

"We're late!" cried Pugh waving his watch and showing his watch to the Inn door.

The proprietor stretched the soldier on a bench, and the rain dripped from his uniform to the floor. John-on-the-beach came in with his wheelbarrow, sat down and began reading. The duke and the witch stood watching him.

"We're late, Pipette!" cried the duke with his watch, but Pipette stood looking at John's feet near the pool of water which fell from the soldier.

"She's not here yet," said Pipette.

"A mouse!" yelled the proprietor and dived over the bar all among their feet.

"Got it!" he yelled. "Lost it!" and grabbed among their feet.

There was a loud roaring outside; through the open door they saw an old car lurching in bottom gear up the hill in the rain. Half in the ditch, half on the road, the car rushed at the open door of the Inn. Its engine stalled; it stopped dead.

Miss Belial got out in her skirt of sacking and her farm boots.

"Lucky it stopped," she said; "It's the rain in the petrol: my best friend."

"You've no business to drive," shouted the proprietor. "You're too old!"

"Call off your dogs!" cried Miss Belial, for they had crowded round her savoury skirt of sacking. "Call 'em off or I'll kill 'em."

"Eighty-nine if she's a day," said the proprietor and took his dogs inside.

"She's late," said Hugh Pugh, and put his watch in his pocket.

The duke and the witch got into the car with Miss Belial and it roared away in reverse. She found her course, changed into forward, and disappeared in the rain.

A woman came in the doorway with a flame and green dress on her body—canvas shoes on her feet.

"Ah! my pardon again," said John-on-the-beach.

"The soldier's drunk," said the proprietor, "He can't go out."

"Where is my pardon?" John asked her; she pointed out of the doorway; there was a pole standing in the rain, ribbons hanging from it, an orange hat on top. "Put a ring on the pole," said the woman.

"My pardon?" asked John.

"Marry it."

John came out and there was a brass ring on the pole and the woman put his arm through the brass ring.

"Where are the children?" she asked.

"The children are wax and paper," she cried, "Come here, proprietor."

He came and brought a book, and they married John-on-the-beach to the post, and they wound the ribbons round him until he was tied to the post.

And John laughed and the rain ran down from his hair into his mouth.

"The everlasting water," he cried, "The eternal soil of (all) nations at my feet!"

And the water filled his mouth and ran out down his side in a stream. He freed his right arm and waved it in the sky.

"Children of wax," he shouted, and his arm rent the mist that darkened the sky by the Inn.

He freed his left arm from the brass ring, and with his two arms wrote Omega in the mist by the Anchor Inn. Alpha on Venus Bank where the fort is: Omega before the Anchor Inn.

He heard the woman's voice, "You are old John-on-the-beach; why have you left the beach?" and the proprietor shouting from his red throat at his dogs.

And John freed his body and his legs and went into the Inn, but the proprietor barred his way, saying, "You are married to the post by the brass ring. Go back."

"I am on a journey," he said, "On the everlasting soil."

And he went into the Inn. By the soldier was the dress of green and flame and the canvas shoes. But the dress was stuffed with wax and paper and in the canvas shoes was mud and water.

The soldier turned on his face on the bench and out of the collar of his uniform came a torrent of mud and water. John-on-the-beach picked up the shafts of his wheelbarrow and went out, he shouted at the sky on the note of D; the dogs began barking, the sun burst through the clouds.

And a gust of wind came, and the post fell with the hat and the ribbons into the mud and water.

John-on-the-beach went along the stony lanes, in the black mud of the uplands of Arwystli. The soldier slept on the bench in the Anchor Inn.

The proprietor took up the dress of flame and green and put it on the fire with the wax and paper. But the pole and the ribbons, the orange hat, and the brass ring, he buried in the black mud of the uplands of Arwystli; and John-on-the-beach is on a journey on the everlasting soil.

The Anchor Inn stands on the swelling hills of the moor, by the ring-forts of Saeson and Venus. Smoke from its fires goes up into the rain in the sky; rain falls among the torrents of the swelling hills, is carried away in the soil, sucked up in the sky.

John is on his journey—where is the woman? The children are wax. The soldier sleeps and the proprietor looks out of the door of his Inn. From the door is a thin line, track of John's wheelbarrow in the deserted lanes.

The Lay Reader

The lay reader hurt his foot so we got another lay reader. I met him at the Station. "Don't look out for any mysticism from us," I said, "We're Welsh." We drove up through the village and he looked out at everyone we passed, though I thought none the worse of him for that at the time. "Ordinary people," I said, "with jobs." "Where I come from..." he said, "Davies the Lane," I said, "John Davies the Lane, that is; not his brother, his lad went to Cardiff. It's a long way."

"You don't say much for yourself," I thought, "And that won't do either." So I asked him how long and you're from South Wales; "It's a long way," I said. "Takes longer than to go to London," he said. "Oh so you've been to London," I said to myself, "And what did you do there, I'd like to know." "And some of the lads go to London," I said aloud. The lay reader was looking out at the people all the time, and there weren't so many of them, I thought "If you look out at them like that, you'll know them all right."

I put him down at Mrs Williams the Shop and went off to tell them. "He's been to London," I told them. And the next day was Sunday and we went out feeling clean and different from the other days of the week. And I wanted to get up near the front so that I could see that new lay reader we'd got, and what he looked like when he said our prayers for us, but Davies the Lane and his family, and Evans Cwm-llan and his family and Jerman the Bryn, and his second wife (that was a Williams from Llanerfyl) who looked well on the way too, had got all the front benches. Twenty minutes before time they must have been, and Jerman that always comes in while the first hymn's going on. I didn't think they should have come so early as that.

"From South Wales," I'd told them, but I suppose they wanted to find out something more. "He won't find any mystics here," I'd told them, "We're ordinary people." "It takes Johnny Evans' boy to spot a mystic," they said, and we laughed like we laughed about Johnny Evans' boy's poem last year, though I must say to be fair, some of the judges at the local thought quite well of it. "It's a long way from South Wales," they said, and "How will Mrs Vaughan-Thomas like him I wonder," (Mrs V.-T. of Glanmiheli that is). We couldn't do anything without Mrs V.-T. even though she is eighty-seven and old enough not to mind you'd have thought. "She'll have him come and kiss her on both cheeks," one young chap said, but we shut him up. It doesn't do to say things like that about Mrs V.-T. and she so generous to all denominations too.

"So you're from South Wales," we were all thinking when he gave out the hymn, "Well let's hope you haven't got any queer ideas." I saw him looking at us while we sang the hymn, and I thought "You'll know us when you've done looking." He read us about the ten talents, and those that have and have not: when we say 'talants' up here it means 'hay-lofts', so it sounded funny though of course he wouldn't know that, coming from South Wales, but all the same I got to thinking about young Davies the Lane and whether he was piling up anything in Cardiff that would be nice for his old dad later. I thought I'd ask the lay reader if he knew anything about young Davies, as he came from down there, but there he was looking at us as if he'd like to know something himself.

Afterwards he came and talked to some of us that stayed behind, and we didn't get much chance to ask him anything as he talked all the time about Rhondda and places. He got quite worked up talking about tin shacks and unemployment, but we thought "Why ram other peoples' troubles down our throats? Things aren't so bloody comfortable here." And Old Evans Cwm-llan spoke up for us, "Do you know what they sold sheep for last year?" he said, "Do you know what they were giving for fat lambs?" And some others of us could remember when you could get men to work for you without any of this minimum wage nonsense and insurance: that's what puts a man off employing, all this nonsense. "And things aren't so bloody comfortable," Old Evans Cwm-llan said, "We've had to buy our own farms. No landlords to do repairs now." "They're your own countrymen," the lay reader said, "Seventeen-and-six a week, no compensation, one room; they're your own countrymen."

It's no good arguing with a man from South Wales, and him with his funny clipped speech; it isn't proper Welsh with all that English in it either. I saw him back to Mrs Williams the shop: "Better watch out Mrs Williams," I said, "Proper Revolutionary he is!" He didn't take that as well as he ought to have, especially after telling us all that stuff about compensation and one room. "Things aren't so good here either are they Mrs Williams?" I said, "No indeed they are not," she said, "And I don't know what we shall do indeed."

So we knew all about the lay reader then, and he'd been to London, and was a proper Revolutionary, although we were only joking when we said this latter, there being some things we wouldn't stand for, even though we are easy men and not as narrow as some. And Mrs Williams said he read a good deal and went out for walks, which does no harm to anyone if they look where they're walking.

What got our tempers up finally was Mrs Vaughan-Thomas' Companion, "That woman," we said, "ought to be shot." "And the man along with her," some added. And what could Mrs Vaughan-Thomas be thinking of, she so good to all denominations too?

That Companion was an ex-barmaid if you ask me (though I never said that before this all blew up): hair as yellow as you like and her the wrong side of fifty. She kept Mrs Vaughan-Thomas alive with her own medicine which was whisky, and Mrs Vaughan-Thomas was very partial to the treatment and kept her on.

It wasn't a romance and nobody killed anybody else for love, passion, or other macabre motives (indeed there hasn't been any killing here since Jackie bach and his boys threw Keeper into the river and he drowned all one night. But that was a great scandal). And we discussed a long time if she was an old love of the lay reader's and he'd come all the way up from South Wales to see her again. We didn't like that, mixing love and religion: it isn't religion to go chasing all over the country for a bit of a woman. Not that he seemed as partial to the whisky as her and Mrs Vaughan-Thomas, we couldn't say that against him, but the other was bad enough without that.

Mrs Williams the Shop's young niece caught them at it, the first we heard: at least she didn't rightly catch them but hid behind the hedge so as not to intrude on other people's affairs. And that gave us something to think about: but we couldn't ask him right out exactly on account of him not being one of us and from South Wales. And we didn't like to say too much and make a great scandal when there wasn't perhaps too much in it.

So Old Evans Cwm-llan went to him and said he had nothing personally against Mrs Vaughan-Thomas' Companion, and a great respect for Mrs Vaughan-Thomas, and she so generous to all denominations. And the lay reader got mad at him and told him to mind his own business, and swore horribly, so Old Evans said and he should know having a fair command himself. "How could we control the young people?" Old Evans Cwm-llan said, "When the old ones went gallivanting?" And our young people are ready enough to go off and get themselves into a bit of trouble without any help from the old ones.

And as we had no proof really, except that the lay reader had sworn at Old Evans Cwm-llan which cannot be counted as a great sin, many others having often wished to do likewise, we went to Chapel and sat on the front benches showing our disapproval on our faces, and singing with a disapproving air. And we didn't stay to talk to him afterwards, though not so much from displeasure as because the lay reader had little of interest to talk about except Rhondda and other parts of South Wales.

But it got too much even for us when he walked down the street with her on a Saturday afternoon, and he would have given her tea in his room but Mrs Williams the Shop put her foot down there, and they had words about that which led to the lay reader leaving the Shop and setting himself up in that Ty ddrwg place on Jenkins Cefn-y-pwll's land which no one had taken these last years on account of the damp and the wasps in summer. The lay reader told Mrs Williams the Shop he'd be his own master thank you, and had Crooked Betty come in and cook his dinner.

When we asked Jenkins Cefn-y-pwll what he was thinking about encouraging sin, he said one man's money was as good as another, and Jenkins' landlord being Mrs Vaughan-Thomas, she wasn't likely to help us, she being a lady that would sooner see her cottages taken than empty. But Jenkins was never a good chapel man, and Mrs Vaughan-Thomas a bit indiscriminate to all denominations.

Then one day I happened to be passing up by Ty ddrwg, and I saw the Companion coming out of it, so I stopped and said, "That's a nice comfortable place you've got there now." And she said, "Comfortable? Not on what you pay him. Go inside and look for yourself." "No thank you," I said, and went on.

So we wrote to the Congregational and said we were sorry for troubling them again, we thought the lay reader they had sent was not quite suitable after all, him being from South Wales and that so far away that perhaps he didn't quite understand our people. But they never answered us, and the next thing we heard the Companion had left Mrs Vaughan-Thomas, Doctor having found them both drunk one day and threatened to make a scandal if the Companion stayed and killed Mrs Vaughan-Thomas with the whisky as seemed likely. And the Companion had gone up to Ty ddrwg permanently it seemed as was only to be expected.

We're not mystics here, we're reasonable men I think, with some exceptions, and some of us do well when we get to town like young Davies the Lane's boy, and there are some things that are too much even though we are reasonable and easy to get on with compared to some. So we had prepared to shut Chapel doors on the lay reader should he dare to come down and take service after what happened.

But he never came, he knew when he'd gone far enough although he was a Revolutionary. They can do those things in London perhaps but not here. And though some of us walked up quite close to Ty ddrwg we never got a glimpse of them again, so they must have slipped off down to Station and off to London or South Wales or somewhere. I remember when Davies the Lane's boy went off to Cardiff, he caught some very early train.

We got a man in from Llanpumpsaint to read Service, and when the Congregational answered us, the lay reader's foot was all right and he was on the job again.

The Life and the Burial

You may ride straight, you may tell the truth. You may go to garden-parties, where guests start and spill cups, trample the flower-beds and avoid others; where guests become slightly intoxicated by sherry and guests hand tea to others. Thwaite accustomed to such sights by years of endurance, drawing Miss Menzies aside in shadow of the staircase, planned.

Miss Menzies thought as she should think; guests passing the foot of the stairs, saw them.

Thwaite said, "There is another place outside this shire, where the people are less thick-faced";

Miss Menzies argued that the people were thin-faced and they discussed that.

Mrs Golos-Williams speaking to a lame man trepanned from the war of '14, and thrice decorated, told him, "That girl" (Miss Menzies is thirty-five) "Extraordinary with her head like a dead person."

The lame man had not seen her, now he saw her and was angry.

Mrs Golos-Williams picked the petals from roses which grew where she stood, saying, "I can't think why she looks like that; look at the bones in her face."

"You can't think," said the lame man.

"I think when necessary," said Mrs Golos-Williams, and actually she thought, At least I haven't a hole in my head, no man is normal with a hole in his head.

Mrs Golos-Williams crushed the petals in her hot square hand, "I like these either indoors or outdoors," she said, "Not half-and-half: they leave the door open like a sort of frame for those two."

"It might rain," said the lame man, "Or it might not. Not for a frame Mrs Golos-Williams but for convenience."

A servant brought them yellow drinks in little glasses.

"I cannot," said the lame man.

"In my day," Mrs Golos-Williams remarked, "There was a band at garden-parties, dragoons or guards, men with long moustaches, and the dresses were different. We had frilly parasols."

The lame man yawned into his handkerchief, as the weariness started in his knees and his ankles and rose through his battered spine to his skull and the plate under the black velvet cap.

A parson was exclaiming. The hostess stood by a shaped tree in a pot. The guests together in fours, in fives, some few in pairs, thronged the lawns and the narrow glades in the laurels with their cups of tea, their drinks, and their umbrellas. Others, looking at the overcast sky went into the house, glancing at Thwaite and Miss Menzies as they passed the staircase.

"There is Mrs Golos-Williams," said Thwaite, "A thick-faced woman."

"But such lovely country," said Miss Menzies, "If you go for walks."

"I do nothing," said Thwaite.

"If I was at many parties," said Miss Menzies, "I should die."

"Parties are all right," Thwaite said, "It's who you meet there;" and he grinned and Miss Menzies grinned, thinking what she should think.

Thwaite slipped the skin from her and looked at her organs while they swelled and groaned with the burden of living: and he looked from her heart to her lungs, and from her lungs to her viscera, and her pear-shaped womb. And he thought, shall I plant there a seed and run off with this bone-faced woman, and away from her when she holds me? And Miss Menzies had him by the waist as if they were both in a mist. This operation was invisible to Mrs Golos-Williams and to the other guests, for the pair had withdrawn into the crook or angle of the stairs, in the shadow.

Deserted by her own shadow under the overcast sky, the hostess and Cam-Vaughan (who is her cousin) walked along the straight gravel path, and as the lame man, tired and wanting to rest in some padded chair, watched them, they spoke in low voices of the mortgage.

Cam-Vaughan said, "A family matter, but if it were a family matter only, I could allow it."

"But not only a family matter..." the hostess interrupted him and said, "Not so urgent, not so hurried."

Cam-Vaughan said, "A family matter: but if it was, you cannot let family feeling interfere with business: if I did I should be ruined."

"This won't ruin you," said the hostess.

"A few more like this would ruin me," said Cam-Vaughan, "So long unpaid."

"I can't pay," said the hostess, "I've got to bring Arriba out."

"I am not mean," Cam-Vaughan told her: "I do not want to be mean, nor to be grasping: I have done so much for you that you couldn't call me mean or grasping."

She did not know what Cam-Vaughan had ever done for her; she thought bitter thoughts. Soon Cam-Vaughan knew that he had done her great services.

"Seek your own sin," cried the parson who had exclaimed too near the lame man's battered skull, "In the *skins* of others!"

Cam-Vaughan started, and they turned round. The parson grinned and stared over their heads.

"My own sin?" Cam-Vaughan asked.

"In other skins is every excuse."

"Mr Bach is a clever man," said the hostess, "You will be a bishop, Mr Bach."

"When all searchings cease," he answered, "Fame travels too slowly in Wales."

"The Welsh," said Cam-Vaughan, "But you are not actually Welsh, Mr Bach? Actually Welsh-speaking?"

"Indeed?"

"There's nothing to it," said Cam-Vaughan, "It is rot."

"Indeed?"

"You should defend your language, Mr Bach," said the hostess.

"Indeed?"

"There is nothing to defend," Cam-Vaughan told them.

"There is sin," Mr Bach said, "all around. In one of your own cottages, Mr Cam-Vaughan, there lives an old woman very close to God: she can pray down a parson."

Thwaite and Miss Menzies are even touching each other's hands in the crook or angle of the stairs. They should have moved. How long they stand there! The hostess is busy with her bitter thoughts and the mortgage; she cannot be directed to this wrapped pair. Mrs Golos-Williams was not obliged to think of one thing as she discussed another, for the lame man had not escaped from her. He turned his ear from the noise of her speaking, and watched his only son, now moved out of the crook or angle of the stairs and again framed in the doorway, as with Miss Menzies, Mr Bach, Cam-Vaughan, and the other men and women, he began to revolve among the flower-beds and the green-flowered dresses, the wide hats and the refreshments.

"We could go for a little," said Miss Menzies, "But not together. We must start separately. And then together. Oh dear!" and she squeezed Thwaite's hand as it hung near hers with her thumb and forefinger.

"Oh dear!" said Thwaite, "I can't wait."

*   *   *

The lame man walked to his car, but the soil seized his feet, and he took minutes to reach it. As he opened the door of his car he performed his last action but one: the chauffeurs waiting, saw him. He sat back in the cushions of the seat and he sighed once and he died. And the chauffeurs told Thwaite that his father was ill, and Thwaite came near the car. And the people of the garden-party watched him for signs of grief, wondering if he would shed tears.

*   *   *

You shall ride straight at a funeral in the thin shining line of saloon-cars; truth comes in your mouth with the responses to the litany of the Church of Wales. At a winter funeral it rains on the good government cape of the blue bobby who sees to the line of cars. In the church the coffin stands in the narrow aisle, and by this fine piece of wood-work Thwaite breathes some of the brandy he has been drinking, into the air around his neighbours. Church contains Lord Lieutenant, Chief Constable, High Sheriff and Sheriff, the Archdeacon, a baronet, two knights, many gentlemen to bear coat armour, and their wives. The wet policeman at the corner and the Lord Lieutenant are come to see decency done; that no one swerves from the thin line in the road, that the gentlemen of the county are properly united in the Kings-representer. Soldiers are there who will do their *feu-de-joie* over the ex-soldier's grave. The lame man is in Church and is prayed for, he will make journeys on the shoulders of other men before he is committed to what Mr Bach will call 'rest' in the trench in the earth which will bring about the collapse of his wooden coffin and the decay and absorption of the flesh of his body.

Mr Bach is reading in English the office of the Church of Wales: the Archdeacon is helping him.

Mrs Golos-Williams turned convulsively to the late hostess by whom she was sitting, and clutched her hand: "Oh my poor dear!" she whispered, "And at your own party. How dreadful for you. No one realizes how dreadful for you."

Startled from her contemplation of Cam-Vaughan's head three rows before her, the late hostess' face assumed a sweet acceptance of sympathy, and in Mrs Golos-Williams' mind as she saw this, was an indefinite image of the punishment falling on a man in the crook or angle of the stairs, for his behaviour with Miss Menzies; and in this image she had obscure delight. Cam-Vaughan jotted figures on the fly-leaf of his prayer-book; 5 per cent on £4500 for seventeen years' compound interest; looking for logarithm tables he found only the calculation of the Golden Number.

"Let him," Mr Bach preached, "Who is without sin, cast the last stone: it is his turn."

The late hostess looked at the necks of the many gentlemen, and at the neck of the Lord Lieutenant himself, and there was no one to take up her mortgage. Though Mrs Golos-Williams clutched her hand, only warmth flowed between them, less precious than cash. Now and again this lady turned to gaze at her in the fulness of her sympathy, and the rich sheen of her gloves was tarnished by the pressure and moisture of her fingers. Cam-Vaughan filled one fly-leaf with figures and drew a face in the margin.

"And the empty man," preached Mr Bach, "shall ring against the empty man, with a hollow sound."

Thwaite's neighbours smelt the vapour of brandy, and they did not lean over and whisper to him. They whispered among themselves about his grief and the amount of his inheritance. Around him the pews were filled with cousins: at funerals and weddings, they were a united family.

A cousin had acquired a pretty wife and had brought her. Standing behind Thwaite, the girl smelt the brandy, and wondered if he would keep on his feet.

"Bear up," she whispered and smiled when he turned.

Thwaite smiled and Mrs Golos-Williams saw him. But she thought, someone has given him a hymn-book, and he is thanking them.

The organ sounded and the congregation sang

Fast falls the empty banner now
In caution and confusion.

Cam-Vaughan tore out the calculations and the faces from the prayer-book, lest the public should see them:

Who shall my fainting courage fry
or in or out of season?

he sang, and a lump came in his throat because of the coffin in the aisle and the beauty of the words he was singing. He sat down, and when Mr Bach began to preach, Cam-Vaughan deplored his Welsh accent. Mr Bach said, "And that which is empty shall remain empty. And that which is full shall be poured out over the emptiness of the land."

And he blessed the congregation who were still alive; who were living in peace and justice and charity by the coffin of the man who was to be buried in the ground.

From their proper places the bearers came forward in their Sunday black and their blue serge; with their strong arms they swung up the coffin beside their red cheeks, and the procession formed in the aisle behind them.

Thwaite heard the pretty cousin say. "You're doing fine!" and she stood beside him, smiling through her veil.

"If I had a veil on," Thwaite said, "I'd smile at you," and as the procession moved out of Church, her hand touched his.

Thwaite fixed his eye on the lid of the coffin above the red necks of the bearers, for by this means his feet kept on a straighter course. The wind lifted the hair of Mr Bach, and of the Archdeacon, it disturbed the Lord Lieutenant and rocked the ladies' hats. The rain soaked everybody, but also the priests in their surplices.

Mr Bach was speedy with the Committal Service, for already the rain was touching the skin of his shoulders. And some of the guests departed discreetly to their cars because of their rheumatism.

Pretending to throw flowers into the trench that had been dug to receive his father's body, Thwaite edged towards his pretty cousin, so that he could touch her hand. He hoped that he would not overbalance and fall into the grave; the soldiers waiting with reversed arms were as bastions to him, and he leaned gently against each one as he progressed. He touched a stone with his foot and it fell into the grave, ringing on the lid of the coffin with a hollow sound: it seemed to Thwaite that he had seen the phrase "An empty box," written on the label of one of the wreaths. He was almost at the side of his pretty cousin, another step and he could discreetly touch her gloved hand.

Under the raised arm of the tallest soldier, he saw his father limping through the crowd. The Lord Lieutenant saw him and went very white and said nothing. The lame man came to the edge of the grave and he threw in a wreath of grass bearing on the label: "An empty box," in his own handwriting. And many people saw him, and they went very white and said nothing.

As the wind lifted his hair erect, Mr Bach saw him, and he paused in the Committal service, and muttered, "Diawl!" then he continued and brought the service to an end, and the soldiers released their *feu-de-joie*, and the Last Post was sounded.

But the lame man went away up the hill and disappeared as the dead should.

The Soldier's Return

In the drawing-room the old woman sat talking to Elizabeth. They both sewed.

"Hal always admired your dark eyes," she said. "But you're not so young now; did he love you, I wonder?"

"I don't know," said Elizabeth, and in some other room young Owen combined the *Marseillaise* with the *Dead March of the Red Army*, skilfully and contrapuntally, one with each hand.

"He's too young," said the old woman, "Playing the piano and pictures of Russia all over the walls. Look at this!" She held up a folder... U.S.S.R.... Land of Peace and Plenty.

"Yes," said Elizabeth, "He'll grow out of it."

The house is expectant. Upstairs the maids throw sheets on beds and clash buckets and crockery together; they tread on their tired servants' feet, on carpeted passages to and fro. Mrs Vaughan-Thomas looked at Elizabeth under the edge of her eyebrows. No, she's not young now; Lines under her eyes and flat-breasted. Elizabeth sat sewing, carefully sewing Tyrolean flowers on a white blouse.

"Oh, that Owen!" the old woman exclaimed. He could play quite well, *quite well*, if he wouldn't thump the piano. And those dreadful revolutionary songs.

"He'll grow out of it," said Elizabeth, "Young men like revolutionary songs."

"Rhys didn't grow out of it," the old woman said, "Going off to fight in someone else's war. That had nothing to do with him: (What has Spain to do with us?) Every day for a week I've thanked God on my bended knees that he's back in England. Why he didn't come straight home I don't know; you'd think that after being away at a war all this time he'd want to come straight back to his old mother."

"I expect he wants to have a good time in London," said Elizabeth.

"You would!" the old woman said viciously.

Elizabeth asked what he was going to do when he got back home.

"He's going to stay here with his old mother to look after him," said Mrs Vaughan-Thomas, "If his old mother doesn't look after him, who will look after him?"

Elizabeth said he would probably find some girl, and marry her.

Mrs Vaughan-Thomas put down her sewing.

"Now Elizabeth, just because Hal..."

"Hal is dead," said Elizabeth.

"Yes," said the old woman.

A maid came in.

"Did you want the big sheets on the small bed? And the blue towels?"

"Yes," said Mrs Vaughan-Thomas.

"And we're so glad, mum," said the servant, clasping her red hands and looking down. "We're so glad that young Mr Rhys..."

"Yes, yes," said Mrs Vaughan-Thomas, "And see that there's soap and candles, too." The maid went out.

"They're all so devoted to him," said the old woman, "Ever since he was a small boy. Owen is different. The servants don't like his familiar manners. But he has his friends, too."

"When will he be here?" Elizabeth asked.

"You seem very anxious..."

"Of course I'm anxious to meet him... after, all Hal..." she stopped and looked down at her Tyrolean blouse.

"Hal was his brother," said the old woman, "And Hal is dead. Rhys is much younger, much younger. And not at all like Hal in any way."

"I never supposed he was," said Elizabeth, "From his photographs."

"The train," said the old woman, "Is just going down the valley now. Oh why doesn't Owen play something *decent*? All this thumping!"

She waved her hands in exasperated imitation... "Bim bam, bim bam, workers UNITE!" then poising herself in her chair once more she explained to Elizabeth, "I can't help getting some of those things in my head when I hear nothing else all day."

Elizabeth embroidered a green flower on her Tyrolean blouse. Overhead the servants banged buckets and crockery together and threw things about. A car came quickly up the drive. The two women stood up. Owen, not hearing, swung into new and violent music.

The front door was flung open before Mrs Vaughan-Thomas could leave the drawing-room. A pause. The music swelled louder. Then, "Stop that bloody row! Oh."

He saw his mother, and bent and kissed her, already Owen was running along the hall shouting his welcome.

"How thin you look and pale," the woman said.

Rhys said Hullo to Owen and turned his back on him. He was lame and looked at the floor when he walked.

Elizabeth was standing dark and supple in the drawing-room. Rhys saw her, then he looked at the floor again.

"You were a long time coming," she said smiling.

Owen and his mother looked anxiously. Rhys was not like he was before. Elizabeth smiled at him all the time.

"What did you want to stop over in London for?" his mother asked, "When I was waiting so anxiously here?"

Rhys raised his eyes from the carpet, "I was having my wooden leg fixed," he said.

They were horrified and stepped back from him.

"Yes!" he shouted, "My bloody wooden leg! Thirty pounds of real wood," and he slapped it so that they all looked in horror at his leg and the wooden sound that came out of it.

The old woman pulled herself together, (Owen still stood staring at the leg, and now Elizabeth looked at the floor) and led him to a chair.

"Sit down here, dear," she said.

His leg creaked as he sat down and he looked from one to another of them.

"Stare at the bloody thing! Go on, look!" he pulled up his trouser and showed an inch of it.

Owen looked away.

"Would you like some tea, dear?" his mother asked, "You must be tired now."

"I'd like a drink," he said, "Whiskey. Oh go on, get me a drink!"

The old woman went out of the room and came back with the decanter. She poured him out a finger holding the bottle and the glass high, like medicine.

"Go on, give it to me."

He poured himself out half a glass and drank it off neat. Elizabeth looked at the floor. Owen couldn't stop staring at him.

His mother began to talk quickly about the people she knew, local happenings; anything so long as it was talk, to fill in, to cover up. She told him who was dead and who had fallen downstairs; about the nursing-association and a concert in the village. Rhys didn't hear a word, no one expected him to.

The Word Burning

The old woman born 18— (as they say), she sits with her accounts and mis-adds the columns. She has all the figures in her room, Death in a corner under green baize, Virgin Mary as Mother's Union, blessed J.C. cut out of a coloured picture-book when young and preserved with beard and burnous. There is the Word.

The old woman took her hands with the rings to the cupboard and inspected the lines drawn round her boxes on the shelves, but nothing had been shifted by the servants when they pried. She has Thursday for funerals, Friday for marriages, but she is not asked to marriages and her next funeral will be her own. Her living descendants are sons of daughters of sons; she has been to her friends' funerals, she has no more friends.

She rose and took up her tame Death from the corner; at the piano his old fingers are too stiff, neither of them can play the music of Ahn, Todesleben's variations are too quick. There is the Word: coloured figures on an Aegean island compiling the Word. She expects a visit of the parson: religion is a great comfort. She dusts the Virgin Mary and cannot find any of the servants. They are drinking tea in the kitchen.

The music of a harp comes through the front door and a child wanders about the polished hall:

"How old you are!" says the child.

And, "You are in *my* house, you are walking on *my* polished floor," says the old woman, "You are walking on my polished floor with hob-nails."

The child undoes her shirt and takes out a fish. "It looks like tin when it's dead," she says, "Tin! and it falls to the floor with a wet thud."

"Let me touch your hair," the old woman wanted it round her fingers, soft round her fingers.

"Can't catch!" cries the child, "You've got lumps on your fingers like my father."

"Rheumatics," says the old woman, "Rheumatics, gout, and arthritis."

"Lovely words... flowers: Flowering Gout, Arthritis Blossom. There are fish and blossoms under the river. I go under the river in my dreams."

"*God* watches you in your dreams," said the old woman, "And the angels who play on golden harps."

"That's my father harping: he wants sixpence."

The old man sits in the open doorway playing songs of longing: he lifts his bowler hat when the old woman comes.

"*Prydydd hir*," he said, 'The Long Poet."

The old woman looks at him, and she looks beyond him at the laurels and the hills and the sky, but to her they are an old man and bushes and hills and an east wind.

"I must shut the door," she says, "Thank you."

Her servant is behind her with the book of the Word. "It is time," she says.

"Put it on the stove. We are old and nothing has happened."

"There are the young people."

"The young people never come here: put it on the stove. Put the Virgin Mary in the stove, put J.C. in the stove, put that Death in the stove."

The old woman takes from the cupboard some of the hundreds of bunches of letters, some of the ten thousand photographs, the bills, the dead visiting-cards.

"Put them in," she said, "Heat it hot."

And she had a box of cobwebs for bleeding. "Put this in. Heat it hot."

And there was a view of Wales from her window: she pulled down the blind and it was a wall.

"All my bottles of tears are in the cellar."

"They are all gone," said the servant.

"And my black crepe for mourning?"

"You have never taken it off," said the servant.

"Let us have a hymn," said the old woman, "And the Word after. A last hymn and a reading."

"What for? We are both old and nothing has happened."

"A last hymn," said the old woman, "We'll hear of the golden tombs and trampling Jordan, as we heard of it when the angels harped and God was in the sky in a burnous."

"Play," said the servant, "The light is going, play quickly."

She played and they sang in cracked voices:——

"Over Jordan's palmy tomb
are banners bright and golden,
fresh dreams of mammons usual doom
our poor faith do embolden."

A fresh jig was being played on the lawn: the Long Poet harped, his daughter skipped over the grass.

"Pull down the blinds," said the old woman: "Shut the doors and the windows. It is too late."

"What have you found in the Book?"

"Stories," said the servant, "Stories and Law."

"Ah, God's law!"

"God's law!" cried the servant. "We live for ever! I am a ruinous woman worth in gold seven days beyond my value. No orchard flirt for me; no out-of-door rape."

"I think it is forty years," said the old woman, "Where is your young hope now? Grey, grey, at six in the morning. The Book is our hope. I am expecting the Parson."

"He will not come."

"He will not come. They will not come with bread nor with milk. The blinds are drawn, the house crumbles. There are birds in the ivy on the roof; in the cellar there is water and nothing alive."

The child that skipped on the lawn, came tapping at windows: Tap! Tap! at one window... tap! tap! at the next. And the old woman and her servant sat still in the dark room and listened. The harper is walking through the garden singing and picking flowers which he scatters on the paths.

Night is coming down, the sky joins the hills, and the birds sleep in the laurels.

And the old woman and her servant sat still in the dark room and listened to the house crumbling tap! tap!... the fragments come down on the path.

The old woman took up all the figures of Life: life as love, life as action, life as happiness, and they burned them; and she took all the figures of death... as a dove, as a man, as a woman, as a reaping-machine, and they burned them.

"My accounts are correct," she said, "There is the money."

"There is no money," said the servant. "We have bought the Word."

"Get the harper in!" cried the old woman, "Light the lamps! Open the windows!"

It is too late, it is dark. The child is asleep. The harper is asleep.

And the wall of the room fell away, and the old women sat; looking through the gap into the darkness.

"Is the fire hot?"

"It is."

They got up and put the Word on the fire, and the Word burned.

And the child came up and looked through the hole in the wall at the Word burning, and the child laughed and ran away. And the servant put her hand in the fire till it was black and burned, and the old woman looked at her and hated her because she had burned her hand. She hated her servant and when she hated her she wished to kill her but she had no strength.

The old woman called for the harper and the Long Poet came through the hole in the wall.

"Kill this woman," she said, "She is burning the Word."

But the harper sang a song of longing, and his child came in quietly and warmed her hands by the fire where the Word was burning.

"Where are your angels?" asked the old woman, "Who keep watch? And your Christ? Your Death and your Life?"

The harper said nothing, but looked into the fire. The servant put in her other hand until it was black and burned; and she put in her head until it was black and burned, and the old woman hated her because her head was charred and she could not smile.

The Word burned and the old woman took up the green baize and put it over the servant.

"She is a better figure," she said, and she put her tame Death on the fire.

Where the Virgin Mary as Mother's Union had hung, she hanged up the harper's child; but the child was asleep and its head lolled as if it were crucified.

And the wind blew in from the night where there was darkness and no bushes, no hills and no sky; and the flames roared up from the fire into the darkness.

The harper looked steadily at the old woman and she knew what he meant. He did not touch his harp, he did not move his eyes from her. The old woman knew and she cleared her right hand of the air and lifted it to the coloured picture of Christ.

She looked at the Long Poet and he was weeping, and tears fell from his eyes hissing in the fire.

"Thirst!" she said.

And the Long Poet kicked the grate and the fire went out, and they were left in darkness.

LIBRARY OF WALES

The Library of Wales Series is committed to making classic English-language writing from Wales more widely and readily available. Launched in 2004 with the support of the Welsh Government, it published fifty titles under the editorship of Professor Dai Smith, encompassing fiction, poetry and memoir.

Now under a new editor, Professor Kirsti Bohata, it will continue to publish a Welsh literature that, emerging from a unique historical and linguistic situation, makes us, in all our complexity, a nation.

Kirsti Bohata is Professor of English Literature at Swansea University, where she is the co-Director of the Centre for Research into the English Literature and Language of Wales and the multi-disciplinary Richard Burton Centre for the Study of Modern Wales.

LIBRARY OF WALES
FUNDED BY

Noddir gan
Lywodraeth Cymru
Sponsored by
Welsh Government

PARTHIAN

CYNGOR LLYFRAU CYMRU
BOOKS COUNCIL of WALES

"No boundaries will limit the ambition of the Library of Wales to open up the borders that have denied some of our best writers a presence in a future Wales. The Library of Wales has been created with that Wales in mind: a young country not afraid to remember what it might yet become."
Dai Smith

"One of the best things we have supported as a government."
Rhodri Morgan

PARTHIAN

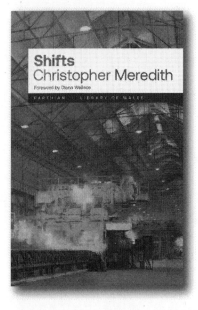

A new edition of this classic Welsh novel by Christopher Meredith with an introduction by Professor Diana Wallace.

"the prose is spare and poetic, at once plain and rich, musical in its rhythms of speech and clear descriptions."
The New York Times

Shifts is a novel of the decline of industry and the battle of a working-class community to remain true to itself in the valleys of south Wales during the 1980s. A funny, lyrical and poignant lament of the expectations and realities of life framed with love and driven with a desire for a better future.

PARTHIAN

In association with Planet Books, a new edition of this seminal book of Welsh literature by Charlotte Williams with an introduction by Professor Hazel V. Carby.

"It is Williams's Welshness that makes the examination of her mixed-race identity distinctive, but it is the humour, candour and facility of her style that make it exceptional... an engaging and perceptive voice describing an engrossing and particular personal story." Gary Younge, The Guardian

A mixed-race young woman, the daughter of a white Welsh-speaking mother and black father from Guyana, grows up in a small town on the coast of north Wales. From there she travels to Africa, the Caribbean and finally back to Wales. Sugar & Slate is a story of movement and dislocation in which there is a constant pull of to-ing and fro-ing, going away and coming back with always a sense of being 'half home'. This is both a personal memoir and a story that speaks to the wider experience of mixed-race Britons. It is a story of Welshness and a story of Wales and above all a story for those of us who look over our shoulder across the sea to some other place.